21

[Each story is followed by a letter received by the office of Ray Charles at various dates throughout 1999. Names have been obscured to protect privacy, but the letters are entirely authentic.]

Robert Goodin

THE TALL MAN

by CHLOE HOOPER

TRAVELING TO PALM ISLAND the pale green sea is so radiant and so fecund, and the plane flies so close to it, you see seals, and what might be dugongs and giant turtles. As the plane turns to land, the island unfolds. The mountains meet the palm-lined shore which meets the coral reef. But step from the plane into the hot, still day and you notice something is not right. The cinder-block air shelter is decorated with a collection of the local fourth-graders' projects on safe and unsafe behavior: *I feel safe when I'm not being hunted,* one project reads.

Palm Island lies between the Great Barrier Reef and the coast of Queensland in the far northeast of Australia. Queensland is a boom state: minerals, cattle, tourists, and retirees, like Florida and Texas rolled together. The World Heritage-classified reef with its luxury island resorts is, as the state's advertising slogan goes, "beautiful one day, perfect the next." But no one wants to holiday here. Palm Island (pop. 2,500) is home to one of the country's largest Aboriginal communities and, according to a random entry in the *Guinness Book of Records,* it is the most dangerous place on earth outside a combat zone.

Two black men in their early thirties are stumbling around, leaning on each other.

"They're brothers," a local tells me. "They're blind."

I assume she means blind drunk. One of the brothers then shakes out a white cane. "How did they go blind?" I ask.

"Nobody knows."

The men are connected with string: the man with the cane holds the string leading his brother through the dark by the wrist.

I am traveling with two criminal lawyers. Two months earlier a drunk Aboriginal man had been arrested for swearing at police. Less than an hour later he died with injuries like those of a road-trauma victim. The police claimed the man had tripped on a step. The community disagreed and a week later burned down the police station. Aborigines make up 2 percent of the Australian population, but are eleven times more likely to be jailed, and account for one-third of all deaths in custody. So far, no police officer has ever been charged. The lawyers are here for the state government's coronial inquest into the man's death; they're representing pro bono the Palm Island community.

The island's mayor, wearing a hat crocheted with the red, black, and yellow flag of Aboriginal Australia, collects us from the airstrip and drives us into town along an old road fringing the water. We pass a large boulder with TALL MAN spray-painted in purple across it.

In the township there is a jetty, a beer canteen, a hospital, a long-broken clock tower, and one store. Outside the store a child sits on an upended trash can while another child cools him with a fire hose.

Two white women—teachers, or nurses, or police—are

walking briskly in shorts and T-shirts. They look as awkward and out of place as I feel. "Who are they?" I ask the mayor.

"Strangers," she says.

One of the women smiles at me, curious perhaps, and briefly I'm not sure whether to reciprocate. I feel luminously white.

"Isn't it beautiful here?" says a lawyer, trying to make conversation.

It is very beautiful. In 1916, the island was, to the government official designated "Chief Protector of Aborigines," "the ideal place for a delightful holiday." The surrounding shark-infested waters also made it "suitable for use as a penitentiary" to confine "the individuals we desire to punish." From 1918 on, Australian Aborigines were sent to the Palm Island Mission in leg irons. They were deemed variously: "a troublesome character"; "a larrikin"; "a wanderer"; "a communist." Usually they had made the mistake of asking about their wages, or were caught practicing traditional ceremonies. In its isolation the mission became increasingly authoritarian—a kind of tropical gulag with all the arbitrary abuses of power that term implies.

Blacks were not allowed on Mango Avenue where white mission staff lived. Blacks were required to salute any white person they passed. Whites got choice cuts of meat; blacks got bones. At the cinema whites sat on chairs carried by black servants, blacks sat on blankets. Permits were needed to fish, permits were needed to swim. There were garden competitions and European dances, and those who did not participate were questioned by police. A brass band learned to play jazz and marching tunes, but failure to attend band practice could result in a jail sentence. White authority was absolute and unchallengeable: each superintendent "got the law in his own mouth." Even in the 1960s a man could be arrested for waving to his wife, or for laughing. A teenager whose cricket ball broke off a short length of branch could spend the night locked up. If anyone complained they were sent to nearby Eclipse Island with only bread and water. On Eclipse, prisoners tried to catch fish with their bare hands.

From the town jetty, you can see Eclipse and the other surrounding paradisiacal islands, formed—the traditional owners believe—when an ancestral spirit, the Big Snake, broke up and left behind fragments of its body. One of the fragments, six miles away, is Fantome Island. Until 1973 it operated as a leper colony, with a "lock hospital" for those with VD. At the colony, there was often no doctor, and patients took care of cooking, woodcutting, grounds and sanitary work, while Roman Catholic and Anglican missionaries fought over who would perform the funeral rights. Dying lepers were sometimes re-baptized several times as their overseers vied for souls.

In the 1970s, when it became legal for Australian Aborigines to drink alcohol, a canteen selling beer was opened on Palm Island. For people long used to intense subjugation, it was an opportunity to literally be "out of control." It also unleashed a violence that had always been under the surface. Despite evidence that the grouping together of different tribes could be disastrous, over forty different tribes with incompatible territorial, language, and kinship ties were sent to Palm Island. The community is now a study of dysfunction taken to its ultimate degree: there is 90-percent unemployment; more than half the men will die before the age of forty-five; sixteen young people have committed suicide in eight months; people are regularly killed in disputes over cigarettes and beer. But the police, who are almost exclusively white, far from being seen as saviors, are viewed with great suspicion and sometimes hatred.

The mayor drops the lawyers and me at the community "motel"—a series of spotless rooms with no apparent overseer. My room has barred windows, a steel-framed bed, a ceiling fan, and a nail on the wall with a coat hanger dangling from it.

Outside it is humid. Cicadas tune in and out of the heat. As it grows darker, I sit with the other "strangers" on the veranda, drinking contraband red wine. We should, in theory, be safe: the motel is next to the locked police compound. Through the high cyclone wire fence, I can see a group of police in a mess room playing pool with some of the nurses. Two officers drive up and park their van before heaving an old mattress over the windshield to protect it from the nightly barrage of stray rocks.

November 19, 2004, must have looked like another grindingly banal day. Shortly after ten a.m., Senior Sergeant Chris Hurley, thirty-three, the island's officer-in-charge, and Lloyd Bengaroo, the Aboriginal Police Liaison Officer, were escorting Gladys Nugent, a big gentle-looking woman, as she went to collect insulin from her de facto's fridge. She needed the escort because her de facto, Roy Bramwell, had just beaten her.

Hurley waited on Dee Street, where among the frangipani trees every second house has broken windows, graffiti, small children playing in the trash. This was Hurley's natural environment. He had spent most of his career working in a succession of Far North Queensland's Aboriginal communities: Thursday Island, Aurukun, Kowanyama, Bamaga, Cooktown, Laura, Pormpuraaw, Doomadgee, and Burketown. All hot, despairing, impoverished places with chronic alcoholism and violence.

Lloyd Bengaroo, in his late fifties, was overweight and overburdened. A police liaison officer is supposed to work with police, representing the interests of the community, but Bengaroo did not convince in the role. Instead he was seen as a police "watchdog" or "errand boy" and was not much liked or respected.

While the two men waited, Gladys's nephew Patrick—drunk and high from sniffing petrol—started calling them "fucking queenie cunts." Hurley arrested him. Bengaroo held the doors to the police van open.

Cameron Doomadgee walked past. "Bengaroo," he said to the police aide, "you black like me. Why can't you help— help the blacks?" To which Bengaroo replied, "Keep walking or you be arrested too." Doomadgee, thirty-six, a happy-go- lucky character who loved to hunt and fish, had been drink- ing cask wine and "goom"—methylated spirits mixed with water. For all he'd drunk he was "walking pretty good, stag- gering but not falling over." He retreated, but when he was twenty-five yards away, he turned and appeared to say some- thing. Bengaroo didn't hear anything. Others, closer than Bengaroo, reckoned he was singing. But Chris Hurley heard something disrespectful, and decided at 10:20 a.m. to arrest him for creating a public nuisance.

What happened at the police station no one can unravel: as Doomadgee was taken from the van, he was "going off, drunk, singing out and everything." Struggling, he hit the senior ser- geant on the jaw. Two witnesses say they then saw Hurley punch Doomadgee back. In the station's doorway, the men tripped on a step and landed side by side. Hurley then stood and pulled his prisoner into the hallway. He didn't, at the time, notice there was another Aboriginal man sitting, waiting to be questioned.

Roy Bramwell, twenty-nine, had been brought in to the police station to answer questions relating to the earlier assault of his de facto, Gladys, and her two sisters. The day before, he and the sisters had started drinking at eleven-thirty a.m., and Roy had drunk forty cans of beer before he went to bed around midnight. He got up early in the morning and had six more. Standing on the sisters' veranda, Roy—"plenty drunk"— became angry because Gladys wouldn't go home with him to take her medication. According to his police statement, they started to fight:

During this argument I punched her sister, this is Anna Nugent, and hit her in the face. I punched her with one punch and this knocked her out. This was in the front yard. I punched Anna because she was being smart with her mouth.

I then punched the other sister, this is Andrea Nugent. I punched Andrea for the same reason. I dropped her on her knees and then the smart mouth did not get back up.

I then got into Gladys. I punched her once to the face and knocked her out. This was in the front yard as well. Gladys dropped to the ground and was on her knees. I started kicking into her and kicked her about three times. I kicked her in the face. I did this cause I was angry with her cause she didn't want to come home with me.

After beating the three women, he returned home alone. He took a shower to cool off, then headed to the post office to pick up his welfare check. While waiting, the sisters' uncle found him and another "tongue bang," or argument, began. Another policeman came and brought Roy to the station.

Roy was sitting in the station when Chris Hurley dragged Cameron Doomadgee into the hallway. Roy heard Doomadgee say: "I am innocent, don't lock... Why should you lock me up?"

Chris dragged him in and he laid him down here and started kicking him. All I could see [was] the elbow gone down, up and down, like that.... "Do you want more Mister, Mister Doomadgee? Do you want more of these, eh, do you want more? You had enough?"

Roy's view was partially obscured by a filing cabinet, but he could see Doomadgee's legs sticking out. He claims he could see the fist coming down, then up, then down: "I see knuckle closed." Each time the fist descended he heard Doomadgee groan.

Cameron, he started kicking around and [called] "leave me go" like that now. "Leave me go—I'll get up and walk."

But Roy says Hurley did not stop:

> Well, he tall, he tall, he tall you know... just see the elbow
> going up and him down like that, you know, must have
> punched him pretty hard, didn't he? Well, he was a sober man
> and he was a drunken man.

Doomadgee was then dragged into the cells. Moments later, Chris Hurley came back and Roy saw him rubbing his chin. He had a button undone. Roy says Hurley asked him if he had seen anything. Roy said no, and Hurley told him to leave. Roy went to get his welfare check, along the way telling some friends: "Chris Hurley getting into Cameron." They told him, "Go tell someone, tell the Justice Group." But none of them did anything. They went on drinking.

The cell's surveillance tape shows Doomadgee writhing on a concrete floor, trying to find a comfortable position in which to die. He can be heard calling, "Help me!" Another man, paralytic with drink, feebly pats his head. Before he dies, Doomadgee rolls closer to him, perhaps for warmth or comfort. The camera is installed in a high corner, and, from this angle, when Hurley and another police officer walk in, they look enormous. The officer kicks at Doomadgee a few times— which later in court is referred to as "an arousal technique"— then leans over him, realizing he is dead. At 11:22 a.m. Senior Sergeant Hurley called an ambulance. Three minutes later the ambulance arrived and determined that Cameron Doomadgee had been dead for at least twenty minutes. The tape records Hurley sliding down the cell wall with his head in his hands. Doomadgee, it would turn out, had a black eye, four broken ribs, and a liver almost cleaved in two. His injuries were so severe that even with instant medical attention he was unlikely to have survived.

* * *

I visit Cameron's sister, Elizabeth Doomadgee, a handsome woman in her early forties. After her brother's death Elizabeth was given one of the island's newer houses, and she has dragged large rocks onto her block in order to landscape the garden. Frangipani branches stick out of the sun-blasted earth, as do other off-cuts she has planted: lychee, pepper, guava.

Two naked toddlers are playing under a tap. Elizabeth stands at the door. She has an almost stately quality. But during this first meeting she seems fierce, as if controlling, just, a steady rage. Awkwardly, I tell her I am a writer hoping to follow the inquest into her brother's death. She is circumspect, but later in court I hear her complain to the island's chairwoman that people are taking notes. She asks for everyone other than me to be banned from writing: "We got our writer here."

Elizabeth does not have a telephone and one evening before the inquest begins the two lawyers and I drop by unannounced. Elizabeth invites us for dinner. We sit down at a table on the veranda that she covers with a purple batik cloth, and upon it she lays the household's best food: a large economy packet of biscuits, two bowls full of fruit. Small children use this opportunity to sidle up and eat freely. Ten-year-old Sylvia, Elizabeth's youngest child, tells me a secret: there is a plug on Palm Island, and if there were ever a war the elders could remove it so that the island would disappear.

"What would happen to all the people?" I ask her.

"They'd swim," she says, as if I must be crazy.

The Doomadgees were sent to Palm Island in the mid-1950s after their father, Arthur—a man from the Gangalidda clan—punched a missionary at Old Doomadgee, in the Gulf country of northwestern Queensland. Doris, his wife, of the Waanyi people, had ten children, of whom, Cameron's sister Jane tells me, "only three are dead." Five of the surviving sisters live on the island and on the day Cameron was arrested, Carol, the eldest, went to the police station "to take feed for him." Although her brother had been dead for two hours, Hurley turned her away, telling her to come back at three p.m. Later, in the afternoon, a policeman from Townsville visited the family. "The detective had a red book with him," Carol recalled, "and he read it out to us telling us we lost Cameron." Two weeks later their mother died. Mothers, Elizabeth tells me, will always try to protect their sons: her mother was following Cameron to the afterlife so as to look after him.

When dinner is ready, two large bowls of stir-fried wild goat and rice are brought to the table. The goat, I later realize, had been hunted by Cameron. Elizabeth thanks God for the food on the table and prays for those who do not have as much as her family does. Inside the house I can see a room with no furniture. People sit on the floor watching *Shrek* on television. Elizabeth prays for Silvia's sore foot to heal, and for any children in the hospital: "May God with his great hands heal them." She thanks God for our being in her home: "Only you know what's in their hearts." She prays for the lawyers' mouths, so that at the inquest they are bold, and for my ears, so I don't miss any important details.

Three plates are laid on the table, and only the lawyers and I are served. It is humbling to enjoy a dead man's bounty. Only after we refuse second helpings does the rest of the family also eat. Later I step into the kitchen and there are at least ten others enjoying small portions. Among them is Eric, Cameron's fifteen-year-old son, a quiet, polite boy wearing an American basketball shirt. He lives down the road with his aunt Valmai, and twenty-two other people, at Elizabeth's old house. Some of the residents have drinking problems, and if Valmai has trouble she calls in Jane and Elizabeth.

"We go and straighten them out properly," Jane tells me.

"How?" I ask, laughing. They are both fairly slight women.

"Either with our fist or hit 'em with a stick."

Elizabeth talks about her concerns regarding the inquest. She wants Cameron to be referred to as *Moordinyi,* a term used in languages from the Gulf of Carpentaria instead of the deceased's name, to prevent the living calling back the dead. She is also worried that one of the sisters, Victoria, an epileptic, might throw a fit and frighten the coroner away. Jane, meanwhile, is worried her brain tumor will keep her from learning her police statement by heart. They also want the lawyers to find a hearing aid for Valmai, who is thirty-six and, for reasons they don't understand, partly deaf. Elizabeth is diabetic but won't take medication because she believes God is protecting her.

We ask Elizabeth how she will feel seeing the police give evidence.

"I'll forgive them what they done, because Jesus said *love thy enemy.*"

"If you say that then it doesn't matter what happens," one of the lawyers suggests.

"It doesn't matter," Elizabeth answers, "because it's in God's hands."

"I'm not that patient," the lawyer replies.

Elizabeth tells us that Aboriginal people have no choice but to be patient. "If I didn't have God in my life..." she says, then pauses. She has something else in her life: *blackfella* protocol. She could put a curse on Lloyd Bengaroo. She could take his clothes off the washing line, and send an item to her relatives in Australia's Northern Territory. They would make sure he'd grow sick and die. But she tries to love him and to be patient. In prayer meetings, she has been praying for justice. "We want justice for Cameron... that's to make his spirit free. We want the truth. We want to hear the truth."

I suppose no one knows their own capacity for vengeance until the worst takes place. Elizabeth is both Christian and blackfella, both Old Testament and New. She can afford to love

her enemy because she believes fiercely in divine retribution.
"I work for God, so he gotta work for me." Later, she tells me
she has been doing a course in firefighting. One day standing
close to the fire, she thought, "This is what hell must be like.
This is what whoever killed Cameron will feel. Where they'll
go. Just imagine how dry it will be. You'll want to drink and
drink and drink."

That night the lawyers and I walk to the jetty. It's eleven p.m.,
the Milky Way is close above, and people sit along the jetty's
edge holding their fingers, with baited string attached, above
the water. ("What are you fishing for?" one of the lawyers asks a
young man. "A fish, mate, any fish I can find.") Predominantly
they are women and children. One child lies in the center of the
jetty, asleep on a pillowcase; others are dozing in their strollers.
Perhaps it is safer to bring them out, away from the drinkers.
It's low tide. You wouldn't think there would be much to catch,
but children use a flashlight to spotlight the dark water.

A thin white-haired woman is sitting with three of her
daughters, one of whom is a hopeless alcoholic, a "drone." The
mother looks to be in her eighties, but is probably closer to
sixty. This was an island of stolen children. Like most older people I meet, this woman, a "half-caste," was taken by police from
her parents, from the "retarding influence of the old myalls,"
and sent to live in Palm Island's dormitory. In that dormitory,
girls were "belted out of bed at five a.m." and made to attend
church three times on Sunday. To leave the island, to marry, to
draw wages from a bank account, they had to seek permission
from the Protector, often a local policeman. Permission, as this
letter to a new bride attests, was not often granted:

> Dear Lucy,
>   Your letter gave me quite a shock, fancy you wanting to
> draw four pounds to buy a brooch, ring, bangle, work basket,

tea set, etc. etc. I am quite sure Mrs. Henry would expend the money carefully for you, but I must tell you that no Aborigine can draw 4/5 of their wages unless they are sick and in hospital and require the money to buy comforts... However, as it is Christmas I will let you have 1/5 out of your banking account to buy lollies with.

The old woman on the jetty says things were better in those days. Palm Island was spotless. Everyone had a job, even if no one was paid. All the gardens were beautiful. There were Christmas trees for the children. Dances. A football team. Drinking was banned and so there was far less violence.

On the jetty are three boys who look thirteen, but claim to be sixteen. A cigarette butt is tucked behind one boy's ear. He tries hard to light it. When finally he succeeds, the three share the tiny stub between them. "Miss, what song you like?" he asks. They like rap: Eminem, Usher, and Destiny's Child. Michael Jackson is "Sharpnose."

One boy stands to perform a dance routine. Another shows us some punches he's learned in boxing. The third boy makes a series of birdcalls with his hands.

We start to walk back to the motel and the boys follow.

Someone gives a two-dollar coin for each time a rock hits the old, long-burned clock face. Not one shot misses.

"What do you do for sport?" one of the lawyers asks.

"Throw rocks at coppers."

We ask the boys about the TALL MAN rock on the road from the airstrip. In all sincerity, they point to a nearby light post to show the Tall Man's height. "His feet as big as a giant's," one says. "You can see his red eyes when the lights turned out on the football field." Later, I ask other children about the Tall Man and they report he's covered in hair with shriveled skin: "He smells of stinkin' things." "He smells as bad as a bin." "A bin tipped over." The Tall Man lives in the hills but comes down and watches people while they are sleeping. For no reason he will slap you across the face.

Chris Hurley is a tall man: *He tall, he tall, he tall, you know.* In one witness statement, an old woman recalled: *The tall man, get out and arrest him. I saw the tall man grab him by the arm...*

Headlights warn a police van is approaching and the boys bolt. They're gone before we say good-bye.

On the morning the inquest is to begin, it rains lightly. "Blessing rain," Valmai tells me. Small planes full of lawyers and police and journalists fly to the island. After one arrival, an Aboriginal man stands waiting for the passengers to disembark before he boards. "The white people fly in and we get out," he says. There is a sense of the circus coming to town. A policeman in full regalia walks into the air shelter. "And here is the head clown," the man says.

"What do you think will happen?" I ask him.

"The same as usual: nothing."

Local witnesses will give their evidence on the island. The police—for security reasons, it is argued—will give theirs in Townsville, on the mainland of Australia across the Barrier Reef. Court now convenes in the gymnasium of the newly opened Police Club Youth Centre, the only community venue on the island. About a hundred locals attend but most sit at the back or stand close to the door where it must be impossible to hear. Only the five Doomadgee sisters sit in a line at the front, wearing their best clothes and holding dishcloths in case they need to dry their eyes. Seemingly from nowhere, their brother's dog arrives and sits beside them. (Later, Elizabeth tells me the dog bit a witness who gave bad evidence.)

It is distressing to watch the Aboriginal witnesses being examined and cross-examined. They are asked to read through and swear by their statements, which is impossible for the many who are illiterate. They are questioned in detail about the timing of events, but very few Palm Islanders wear watches. They are asked leading questions in complicated legalese and some of them, confused or intimidated, try to guess the correct answer.

There are seventeen lawyers lined up along the bar table, and all but Andrew Boe, the Burma-born lawyer working pro bono for the Palm Island Council, are white. The Doomadgee sisters rely largely on their lawyers' facial expressions to gauge what is happening. "Black man pretty hard to understand white man's language," one witness tells me. Likewise, often the lawyers can barely comprehend the Palm Islanders. One thin barefoot woman breaks down mid-testimony and sits with her head in her hands, distraught because no one understands her.

Patrick Nugent is the young man who shared a cell with the dying Cameron Doomadgee, or Moordinyi, as he is now referred to in court out of respect for Elizabeth's wishes. Nugent retracts his statement—in which he claimed he'd seen Hurley punch and kick Moordinyi—and then retracts his retraction. He admits he'd been drinking heavily and sniffing petrol the morning it happened, and it's clear he has at best a rudimentary understanding of what is going on. He is labeled a liar by the police lawyers. That evening he goes home and tries to set himself alight.

More dogs arrive to lie in the shade. Children collect the empty water bottles the lawyers leave lying around. As the day wears on, I can feel myself nodding off. Earlier, I had accompanied Elizabeth and a lawyer on a drive to encourage witnesses to stay sober. We'd stopped by a house shuddering with loud dance music. Teenagers, all of them wasted, started to crowd around the car. They were young, some no more than thirteen, and the closest things to zombies I've ever seen. One girl put her hand to the car window, staring in, and clearly saw no one. Beer cans lay all around; small children were underfoot. It was nine o'clock in the morning.

In the Youth Centre Roy Bramwell is now the star witness. He has been reading his police statement every day, trying to memorize it. "It's like a daily prayer for him," Elizabeth says. But Roy's examination begins badly. Although this is supposed to be an inquiry into the truth, not the worth of Roy's character, there's no forgetting that he was at the police station because he'd just bashed three women. If this ever went to trial would anyone believe him?

Roy says he saw Hurley punching Moordinyi and the police lawyers work hard to discredit his testimony. Roy gets aggressive because he feels the lawyers "put it all together and twist it." His frustration is palpable. Unbidden he stands up to *show* what he saw. Roy rests his knee on the ground, as he alleges Hurley did, and punches. For a moment everything is silent: it is clear that a big tall man's knee to the chest of someone pressed against a concrete floor would cause extreme injury. Quickly, the court is adjourned.

The next day is bogged down by legal argument about releasing Hurley's police records. It emerges that there are twenty to thirty official complaints against him. Later, the coroner stands aside when it is revealed he has presided over eight of these complaints and each time adjudicated in Hurley's favor.

Throughout the day, mothers watching the inquest approach me to tell their own stories about the senior sergeant's dealings with their sons. It is suggested he liked to fight. Two of the young men he is said to have attacked were schizophrenics. One boy, "on doctor" (on medication), was rude to Hurley, who he alleges then broke his ankle. The other boy was also rude to Hurley while having an episode. He alleges the senior sergeant punched him to the ground: "Come up here talking shit, you little black bastard." Another man alleges he was sitting talking to his grandson on the family trampoline when Hurley came up and arrested him for public drunkenness. In the cells, he alleges, Hurley throttled him until he urinated on the cell floor. Barbara Pilot, Moordinyi's cousin, shows me her foot; she says Senior Sergeant Hurley ran it over. It often aches, making it difficult to walk. She went to the police station to lodge a complaint and was told to piss off. She had tire marks on her leg afterward, and the bone stuck through the skin.

One Sunday Elizabeth took me to one of the four churches on the island. It was a plain wooden building with white pews, arrangements of plastic flowers, and broken windows. Twenty or so people swayed and sang hymns, accompanied by two white-haired men playing steel guitar. Children squirmed like church children anywhere. Babies were passed around the congregation and held as if they'd bestow some blessing. A man arrived with his German shepherd. He sat and the dog made small circles beside him until it found a shady spot under his pew. *All I had to offer Him was brokenness and strife,* we sang, *but he made something beautiful out of my life!* After the hymn, everyone clapped for what God had made out of their lives. Then we sang: *Stand up, Stand up for Jesus!* A little girl in white played chasey up and down the aisle, and around the pews.

Framed on the wall was a small needlework warning:

> Flee from the wrath to come.
> How shall we escape
> If we neglect so great salvation.

In the middle of the hymn, the black preacher arrived and immediately sang loudest in a high-pitched, strident voice. She was a big, stern woman with a long gray plait and reading glasses on the end of her nose. Her dress hung from her bust like a tent. "Tribulation times are coming!" she cried, "and they're going to be very hard, brothers and sisters!"

She gestured behind her, perhaps to the hills covered in boulders, and told us that come the Apocalypse rocks will rain down. "When He speaks, just at His voice even the rocks cry out and praise Him as they smash. Little pebbles crack like His word tell us." She'd been browsing the Web, and now saw the end of the world was nigh. "The returning Lord will come at an unexpected time, but a time with specific observable signs. There are signs all around us," the preacher claimed. "There are murders, there are rapes, there are all kinds of things going on." Disease, pestilence, famine, floods, and earthquakes: I assumed she was talking about Palm Island. But she continued, "We are fortunate in this community because nothing has happened to us yet."

In the previous month, a man had critically stabbed his brother in a dispute over a beer. One woman had bitten another woman's lip off. A man had poured petrol over his partner and set her alight.

We stood to sing: *Yes, Jesus loves me / Yes, Jesus loves me / Yes, Jesus loves me / The Bible tells me so...*

During the hymn, someone deposited in my arms a plump toddler with dark skin and uncannily bright blue eyes. She was the preacher's granddaughter and she lay in my lap, sucking on her bottle, her free fingers wrapped in mine. Around us, everyone sat, exhausted-looking, praying. I had the sense there were twenty people in this church trying to hold back the tide.

Earlier, on the jetty, I'd met a white policeman fishing. As soon as he caught anything, he admitted, the birds swooped down and took it. I asked him how he liked the island. He said he couldn't believe there were three thousand people and not even a barber's shop. It was strange also to be locked each night inside the police barracks. But he and the other officers did a lot of bush-walking during the day. While we were speaking, little children approached him, saying "Can I have a jig, sir?" He showed them how to use his jig, a line with small hooks and colored glass beads to attract the fish.

A mother was sitting on the other side of the jetty with her back to the water, staring at him. The policeman seemed oblivious, looking out to sea. But when the children turned to her, excited, she mouthed, "He a copper." She smiled as she did this. It was the perfect opportunity to teach a kind of don't-trust-white-strangers lesson. And who could blame her?

Up until the 1970s, the *bulliman* (police) came to take children from their parents who were believed to be unfit to raise them. On Palm Island, after Moordinyi's death when the community burned down the police station, the state government invoked emergency powers, flying in special squads trained in counter-terrorist tactics. The police came in their dozens, wearing balaclavas and riot gear, with garbage bins full of batons, and stun guns, and semiautomatic rifles. They went from house to house, sometimes in the middle of the night, arresting adults and teenagers, while their children lay face down on the ground, guns pointing at them.

The policeman sits, jiggling the line. The sun is setting—it's shockingly beautiful—but around him it is growing dark. He says that although the locals seem friendly, it frightens him that at any moment they could turn. He recommends I don't walk around at night alone. "They are a very violent people," he says quietly.

While the inquest is adjourned, Elizabeth takes me on a trip to find taro root. Halfway up one of Palm Island's mountains, the borrowed four-wheel drive can be coaxed no farther. We start walking through the mission's abandoned plantation. Enormous pine trees stretch above us, and Elizabeth says, "This remind me of *Blair Witch*."

As she leads me down a steep embankment covered in long grass, I sing softly hoping to ward off snakes. We pick our way through the rocks to where the taros—with tall green stalks and wide leaves—grow in a shallow creek bed. Elizabeth puts on her boots and, taking a shovel, starts to loosen the plants' roots.

When the Doomadgees were children their mother used to tell them Dreamtime stories, stories about ancestral spirits creating the land, and they'd say, "Oh! You're getting it from library books." At night they would listen as she sat alone, talking "in language" to her father. She believed he came as a crow if anything was wrong. None of her children really understood this blackfella magic until their mother finally took them back to Doomadgee. Here, they learned that their paternal grandmother was Lizzy Daylight. Daylight, the anthropologist David Trigger remembers, was "the grand old lady" of the Gangalidda people, who could sing songs said to have the power to stir up storms, cyclones, lightning, and rainbows.

Elizabeth has loosened the taro roots and she now asks me to pull them out. The job is ridiculously primal. You squat and clutch the stalk and pull as hard as you can and, as you do, slide further into the muddy bed. I squat and pull and an enormous tuberous *thing* covered in muddied roots slowly emerges. As it does, mud splatters all over me. The mud gives off an intense vegetable smell not unlike manure. It is overwhelming. Elizabeth's mother had taught her to do this, and perhaps her mother before her. In the Aboriginal diaspora, people live cut off from the religion and culture of their traditional lands; cut off from the spirits of these lands. Palm Island missionaries tried to stamp out "tribal sorcery and superstition... savage life... medicine men and rainmakers of barbarous nations." For Elizabeth and for her brother, who was much acclaimed for his ability to hunt, traditional food gathering is knowledge missionaries could not destroy.

Elizabeth slices off the stalks with the shovel's blade. The muddy taros are incredibly heavy; their tangled roots look like hair: it's as if I'm filling our bag with human heads. I am now completely covered in mud. Elizabeth is spotless. I realize how far I will have to carry the bag and stand staring at it, gloomily.

"What's that?" Elizabeth asks suddenly. "It's the warning bird calling!"

I strain to hear birdcall.

"It's warning us it's now time to leave." She moves quickly and I pick up the heavy sack and follow. It's impossible to tell how completely she is teasing me. "Thank you very much," I hear her say to any resident spirits. "We're going now."

It's August 2005 before the police involved in Moordinyi's death are required to give evidence at the inquest. People have traveled to Townsville from Palm Island and other communities, they say, to look Hurley in the eye. To enter the courtroom we must all show ID, be electronically wanded, patted down, and have our bags inspected. This heightened expectation seems the antithesis of the police attitude. They sit outside the courtroom in riot gear flicking through magazines. "This is an example," one senior sergeant tells me, "of people trying to look for the worst in a situation."

The lawyers representing the family are keen to hear the evidence of Police Liason Officer Lloyd Bengaroo, who accompanied Senior Sergeant Hurley throughout the arrest. Bengaroo, it is believed, knows more than he is prepared to say.

The day after Moordinyi died, the police videotaped Bengaroo reenacting the events of the previous morning. When they reached the moment when Moordinyi was taken inside the police station, Bengaroo would go no farther. He claimed he waited at the door: "I stood here," he says on the tape, "because I was thinking, um, if I see something I might get into trouble myself, or something... the family might harass me or something, you know...?" The "or something" he refers to is most likely police intimidation.

In an iconic 1980s state-sanctioned Royal Commission into police corruption in Queensland, Tony Fitzgerald Q.C. claimed "an unwritten police code" dominated police culture. "The police code," he wrote, "requires that police do not enforce the law against other police, nor cooperate in any attempt to do so, and perhaps even obstruct any such attempt." Bengaroo also had to observe the code. He was a man caught between two tribes: the blackfella community and the police force.

The Australian federal government's *Royal Commission into Aboriginal Deaths in Custody* recommended each death be treated as a homicide, and that police officers should not investigate other police officers, to avoid "collaboration and dare it be said collusion." But fifteen minutes after the paramedics had pronounced Moordinyi dead, Senior Sergeant Hurley called his good friend, Detective Sergeant Darren Robinson. The two men had served together on the island for the last two years, and Robinson had previously investigated and cleared Hurley of other complaints. After the men spoke, Robinson called Detective Senior Sergeant Kitching of the Townsville Crime and Investigation Bureau. Kitching, it turns out, was also a friend of Hurley's, having served with him in another Aboriginal community, Burketown, near the Gulf of Carpentaria. Robinson then placed a call to Detective Inspector Warren Webber, Northern Regional Crime Coordinator, who also held Hurley in high regard.

It must have been reassuring for Hurley that he—the main suspect—would be investigated by old colleagues and friends. He picked the detectives up from the airport and drove them around to the relevant areas. That night Robinson cooked dinner at Hurley's house for Hurley and those investigating the death. Meanwhile no part of the police station was made into a crime scene or sealed off. No areas were tested to see if there were matches with the blood from Doomadgee's eye. No photographs were taken of Hurley's hands or his boots. The transcript of Hurley's police interview is striking for its camaraderie: Webber refers to Hurley as "mate" or "buddy"; Hurley calls him "boss."

Four days later the autopsy took place. The pathologist's finding that Mulrunji's injuries were consistent with the police's nominated cause of death ("a fall") ignited a riot. Later that day, the Crime and Misconduct Commission took the investigation away from Hurley's associates. Unfortunately, an insider tells me, by then they had already "stuffed things up." Certainly Bengaroo had been persuaded to keep his mouth shut.

> CRIME & MISCONDUCT COMMISSION: Did Senior Sergeant Hurley assault Mr. Doomadgee whilst he was on the floor?
> BENGAROO: I can't recall that one.

Somber, heavyset Bengaroo now walks to the witness box, wearing his police uniform. His long socks are pulled tight to his knees and keys jangle in the pockets of his shorts. His hair is shaved close; his face is pockmarked; and his brow long furrowed. When he sits, there is a roll of fat behind his neck. In a surprisingly soft voice, he swears on the Bible. Later he admits he does not believe in God. A fierce cough plagues him as he gives evidence. I've been told his own eighteen-year-old son was murdered one night on Palm Island over a cigarette.

It is tense in the room. The Palm Islanders are treating this like theater. They boo and moan or whisper encouragement: *yes, yes*.

Everyone knows Bengaroo is skirting the truth. His testimony is full of glaring inconsistencies, obvious evasions. Sometimes he claims he waited outside the station, at others he admits going inside. It is hard to know if he is trying to mislead, or genuinely doesn't understand. When asked directly whether he saw or heard anything improper Bengaroo does not bite. But in the following exchange with the family's lawyer, Senior Counsel Peter Callaghan, he says something that at least sounds like the truth.

> CALLAGHAN: You told [Moordinyi] to walk on down the road for his own safety—what did you mean by that?
> BENGAROO: I told him to walk down the road or he's getting locked up. For his own safety. I just told him to walk down the road or he'd get locked up.
> CALLAGHAN: And the reason you did that was for his own safety?
> BENGAROO: Yes.
> CALLAGHAN: And a safe place is somewhere away from you and Senior Sergeant Hurley?
> BENGAROO: Yes.
> CALLAGHAN: It wasn't safe being near the two of you, for him?
> BENGAROO: It wasn't, no.

Moordinyi was arrested because his swearing was deemed a public nuisance, but Bengaroo admits he did not actually hear this swearing. Nor does he know what legally constitutes a public nuisance. He has never been trained in the matter. Andrew Boe, appearing for the Palm Island community, says to Bengaroo, "There's a lot of swearing that happens on Palm Island, isn't there?"

> BENGAROO: Yeah, plenty.
> BOE: Everywhere you go, people swear?
> BENGAROO: Yes.
> BOE: Have you ever arrested a person for swearing at a person other than a police officer?
> BENGAROO: No, I didn't.
> BOE: Police swear on the island, don't they?
> BENGAROO: Pardon?
> BOE: You've heard police swear on the island.
> BENGAROO: Yeah. Everybody swears.
> BOE: Ever heard of a police officer being arrested for swearing?
> BENGAROO: No.

Bengaroo admits there were no noticeable swellings or abrasions on Moordinyi when he was arrested, and claims he cannot explain how the deceased received a black eye or his other injuries. After Moordinyi was discovered dead, it occurred to Bengaroo, he claims, that the family should be notified, but Hurley told him to "keep quiet."

Later, an older woman told me Bengaroo reminded her of a member of the Native Police who, until the late 1890s, were the subordinate allies of white police and responsible for blood-curdling killing sprees of indigenous people. Other women tell me they feel sorry for Bengaroo: he's spent his years being the white police's "errand boy," holding the police van's doors open as another blackfella was arrested. He must have felt like a stooge and hated anyone who called him on it. Cameron Doomadgee shamed Bengaroo that morning. But it wasn't like he hadn't been shamed before.

> CALLAGHAN: Have you heard that sort of thing before over twenty-one years?
> BENGAROO: Plenty of times.
> CALLAGHAN: Probably something like that, most times you arrested someone?
> BENGAROO: Most times—yeah, most times.
> CALLAGHAN: [And] whilst you might have been upset, it wasn't the sort of thing that would really distress you?
> BENGAROO: No, it wasn't.

At the end of the day, Lloyd Bengaroo stands in the hallway, surrounded by six police officers. They are all smiling. The scene is collegiate, congratulatory: he has done the right thing. I follow Bengaroo and his escorts as they step into the elevator.

"Safest lift in Townsville," one young policeman tells me.

"Not if you swear," I answer.

* * *

When, amid much excitement, Senior Sergeant Hurley arrives, it's through a back door to avoid photographers. He is indeed a tall man; at six-foot-seven-inches he could be straight from central casting as the sheriff. His police uniform is carefully pressed. Each crease is visible. He is clean shaven, tanned, calm, polite. It goes to make him a good witness. He calls Terry Martin, Counsel Assisting the Deputy Coroner, "sir" and looks him straight in the eye. He keeps very still.

MARTIN: Do you have friends who are Aborigines?
HURLEY: Yes, sir.
MARTIN: Do you have anything against Aboriginal people?
HURLEY: No, no. I wouldn't have, I, I wouldn't go to those communities if I had something against Aboriginal people, I, I couldn't serve in those communities.

Martin does not ask him *why* he goes to "those communities." Why choose to be despised? Previously I had spoken to a highly regarded police inspector who had served on Palm for six years. Early in his tenure he'd been viciously beaten but decided not to be transferred and won great respect. "I saw violence mainstream people can't understand." And living on an island is "like living in a fishbowl," he said. "There's no escape." Still, he claims those were the best years of his life. He had a sense of being able to make a difference. His days, he explained, would seem more vivid, more intense; somehow, life was closer to the surface.

But there might also be a darker appeal. Becoming a cop is a way for a man without a lot of education to gain a lot of power. "I was like the King of the Island," the inspector recalled. I suggested this was the temptation some officers succumb to: the community is their fiefdom. "No," he said, perhaps not understanding my meaning. "It was just that it was my place." But can you step into this dysfunction and desperation and not be corrupted in some way? Not made, in some way, mad? In a community of extreme violence, must you become violent? If you are despised, as the police are, might you not need to be despicable sometimes?

Martin takes Hurley back to the morning of November 19, 2004. Within the first few minutes the senior sergeant claims privilege against self-incrimination. None of the testimony he gives will be admissible should he ever be charged in relation to the death.

At length, Hurley describes Lloyd Bengaroo's feelings after Moordinyi challenged him about "helping the blacks." "His pride was hurt," he says. "Lloyd takes his job very seriously [and] I could see Lloyd was upset about what had happened." For the time being Hurley would have the court believe that he arrested Moordinyi to save Lloyd's honor. But in a place where alcohol consumption dominates life, Martin asks Hurley why he could not have said, "Look, mate, you've had too many, you're yelling out in the street, come and we'll give you a lift home." Moordinyi was not known for being violent or a troublemaker, and he could have been taken to a safe place to sober up, rather than to the police cells.

Belligerence shows just beneath the senior sergeant's surface. You can see him thinking: "What would you know about being a copper in this hellhole?" Hurley changes his story. He says there was a chance Moordinyi might have re-offended, and seeing as moments earlier he'd arrested another man for swearing at the police, he wanted to be evenhanded.

Martin then leads Hurley to the moment Moordinyi punched him. The senior sergeant claims he was not angered by this but "annoyed." And in this state he struggled with Moordinyi, until both men tripped through the station's doorway.

> MARTIN: You didn't land on top of him?
> HURLEY: Well, I now know that medical evidence would suggest that. That I landed on top of him. If I didn't know the medical evidence, I'd tell you that I fell to the left of

him. The medical evidence would suggest that that wasn't the case... I mean, life doesn't unfortunately go frame by frame, and if it did, I would've been able to give a hundred percent accurate version. But the version I gave was my best recollection and the most truthful. It was the truth that I thought.

Martin reminds Hurley that in three previous interviews he said he fell to the left of Moordinyi. This is what he said on the afternoon of Moordinyi's death; the day after; and a few weeks later. There would now seem to be only two possible explanations for Moordinyi's black eye and massive internal injuries, Martin claims: that Hurley had indeed fallen on top of him, or that Hurley had struck a series of forceful blows. Since he has repeatedly denied the former—until knowing of the medical evidence—could the latter be possible?

> MARTIN: Just think back, was there a flash of anger whereby you got up first and drove your knee into him, and said something like, "Have you had enough, Mr. Doomadgee?"
> HURLEY: No, that's not correct.
> MARTIN: Clip to the jaw and then you know, with all due respect to the Court, you fell arse-over-tit through the doorway, but it didn't make you angry enough to get up and...?

Hurley, naturally, denies it. But why did Moordinyi have a black eye? Why did he have such terrible injuries? And, a question Martin also does not ask: why was Roy Bramwell allowed to leave the police station? A man was dying in a cell because he may have sworn at police, and this other man—who had just beaten three women unconscious—was allowed to walk free.

The senior sergeant has an extremely good chance of never standing trial. I now know that even a year after he has given this testimony there will still be no finding as to what caused Moordinyi's death. And I suppose this is the terrible joke of the country's much vaunted racial reconciliation project: that the lives of these two men—Hurley and Moordinyi—are supposed to be weighed equally.

In the courtroom I notice the women from Palm Island. Some of them look much older, twenty years older, than they are. All of them are mothers with lost sons. Mothers with sons in custody; sons who've died in custody; sons who've been beaten by the police. They sit in the airless room emitting a low drumbeat of heartache. The Doomadgee sisters sit among them, waiting for something to happen. "This just drag, eh," Valmai says, but she believes her brother is watching over her. "It's like he there telling me to keep pushing, don't give up." Next to her sits Elizabeth who is trying, I imagine, to love her enemies.

Father Tony, the island's Catholic priest, tells me among families ravaged by alcoholism and violence a completely different concept of forgiveness exists. He was with Elizabeth recently when she spoke at a Townsville church service. She told the story of her brother's death and a policeman stood up and started to cry. He said he'd seen terrible things done to black people and how sorry he was. "He cried brokenhearted," Elizabeth told me. She went over and hugged him: "Brother, I forgive you."

9 February 1999

████████████████

New Orleans, LA 70113

Ray Charles

████████████

Los Angeles, CA 90018

Dear Ray:

You won't remember me, but I'm from a long time ago.
I was a "GOFER" at the Latin Casino, Cherry Hill,NJ, in
1961 & 1962. I was the kid that was so in awe of you that
I pussyfooted around you. I didn't want to disturb or
distract you.

Anyway, I see that you're coming to New Orleans on
Apr 24 & 25 for the Jazz and Heritage Festival. So, as a
friend suggested, instead of staying at the DEW DROP INN,
why don't you stay with me? It's a small, rental place,
but I do have a spare bedroom; it'll make a good hide-out.
And on the plus-side, I'm nothing fancy, but I'm a good
cook. Let me know what your food/beverage preferences
are--even if you don't stay here. You might want to drop
in, have a bite, and maybe even play a game of chess.

Little Eddie

P.S. There's one thing you might remember about me. In
1974, on Okinawa, At Camp Zukeran's Gym, you put on a USO

"SMOOCHED AGAIN!!"

show hosted by the Marines. Before you could get to the
dressing room outback after the show, my wife and her girl
friend kissed you.

Ray, get ready to be smooched again!!

We can set it up before your show at the Municipal
Auditorium, and I'm not warning the smoocher ☺ !!

HATE TO BE ALONE

by STEPHEN ELLIOTT

ON THE FOURTH DAY together we broke up. We had planned this for a while. Not the breakup, but the four days. Her husband wanted to spend a week with her over Christmas in Chicago, get her out of the Bay Area, and so she wanted to spend four days with me when they returned. That was the deal they worked out.

We had been dating for over five months and her marriage was falling apart. Eden was in one of those open marriages, the kind where you see other people, the kind of marriage everybody says doesn't work. Except her husband didn't see other people. Which was fine because they had different desires but then I came along and we fell in love and in the nine years she'd been with her husband she had never fallen in love with someone else. Her husband told her he felt ripped off. She told me he hated me but I didn't think it was my responsibility. It was the situation that was killing him. I was incidental. Anyway, I had my own problems.

We spent almost the entire four days in bed and when we broke up there were condoms on the floor, latex gloves covered in lube, a rattan cane flecked with blood. There was rope spread under the desk and near the closet and attached to the bed frame. There was a roller box full of clamps and clothespins and collars and wrist cuffs and a gas mask and a leather hood pulled from under the bed so we had to step over it when we got up to go to the bathroom. There was a strap-on dildo and holster sitting on top of a box of photographs next to the door, a purple silicone butt-plug near the radiator.

Love is a hard thing to explain. I didn't mean to fall in love with a married woman. I had successfully not fallen in love so many times that when Eden told me she was married I didn't even flinch. We were in a café and she was wearing all black. It was the first time we met. She mentioned her husband, showed me her wedding ring, said he was away for a couple of days. "I tell him everything," she said. "I told him we were meeting for coffee." She wanted to be sure I understood that he was her primary, that whatever happened with us I could never be first in her life.

Two and a half weeks later I sat on her kitchen floor while she sliced eggplants, soaking them in salt and transferring them to the stove. The flames licked the bottom of the pot and I was careful not to move. I didn't want to get in the way. She leaned down and took my face in her hands.

"Look at me," she said. "I love you."

"What did you say?"

"I said I love you."

"I love you, too."

* * *

The breakup didn't come from nowhere. I had lost my mind in the week she was in Chicago. I called friends I hadn't seen in years just so I could tell them my story: that I was in love with a married woman and I slept with her once a week and the other six nights I slept alone. My thoughts were consumed with her and I couldn't do my work. My savings were nearly depleted. I saw her three other days each week while her husband was at work and on days we spent apart we spoke for an hour on the phone. When I went to her house I always made breakfast. Sometimes I saw her on the weekend as well and we went dancing and she came back to my house to sleep over an extra time. I told my friends I saw her more than her husband did, as if that counted for something.

They said, "Get rid of her."

I said, "What if it's me? What if I'm not capable of love?" And what I meant was that I was thirty-four years old and I hadn't been in a serious relationship in ten years. I had never been in love. I had minimal contact with my family. There was no one in the world who depended on me in any way.

Before we broke up she told me the story of meeting her husband. They had been neighbors in the Haight District. It was the neighborhood that had been the capital of free love and counterculture forty years ago and is now populated with fashion boutiques and street hustlers, junkies sticking themselves against the frosted windows and smearing their open sores on the meter in front of a bar shaped like a spaceship.

She had had a boyfriend and lived with him downstairs and her would-be husband lived upstairs with his wife. There were six apartments and a small backyard. Occasionally the couples watched a movie together.

Years later he divorced his wife and Eden was no longer with her boyfriend and he called and asked would she like to go see a band.

He didn't try anything that first date because he's a gentleman, with his short dark hair and innocent face. He's tall and thin, handsome, straight shouldered, and from a good family with a good name. He works in a brokerage, wears a suit to work and a black leather jacket. He asked her on a second date and then asked what her deal was. She explained that she was seeing someone, but the guy had moved to Seattle. So now they were still together but she was with other people as well. She said she liked seeing other people. She didn't believe in constraining her love, in not fulfilling her desires. She was never going to be monogamous again; she had tried and it made her unhappy. This was Northern California, a woman's body was her own and people didn't have to abide by the old rules if they didn't want to. He'd fathered a child since the last time they'd met. He asked if he could be one of those other people she was seeing and she said yes. Six months later they were living together and then they were married and she became a mother to his son.

We had almost broken up on the first of our four days. I picked her up at her house, badly damaged and trying to hide it. Why was I so sad? I thought it was the holidays. And my girlfriend had been gone, unreachable, away with her husband. And we'd had a fight before she left. And my friends were also out of town. But maybe I'm just a sad person. I make decisions assuming that I'm probably going to kill myself anyway. It's just a matter of time. That's my big secret.

I rang the bell and waited. When she didn't answer I sat in the corner of her porch. I heard the cat scratching at the door. Christmas was over; it was cold and the streets were wet. It was eight in the morning and the fog was stuck on the hills. I was on time but not early because her husband left for work at seven-thirty and he and I had already run into each other too many times, had too many awkward conversations. They owned a house, a small blue two-bedroom ranch-style home built in the backyard of a larger house. After ten minutes I rang the bell again.

"Hi," she said. She wore a silk gown that hung easily over her shoulders, meeting her body again at her hips. Music was playing somewhere inside.

"I've been here ten minutes."

"I didn't hear you."

Their bedroom was different from mine, dominated by a king-size bed with a short space between two large dressers. Her husband's laundry sat in a small pile in the corner and I waited there while Eden showered.

She had been miserable in Chicago where the streets were cold and her feet hurt from walking the city. She told me about it while we crossed the bridge. They'd been to the library and the museum, the Art Institute, and Clark and Division. They'd taken a train to Addison and seen Wrigley Field. I was from Chicago and I thought they had missed everything.

Later that day, in my room which is just a yellow space I rent in someone else's apartment and is filled with everything I own in the world, before the box full of sex toys was all the way out from under the bed and maybe there was just one or two gloves on the floor, she told me she didn't think it could work. And we broke up. But then she changed her mind. In the morning she broke up with me again, and again changed her mind. I told a joke about Arabs sending threatening email in order to get the federal government to come out and dig up their yard for them. We never left the bed.

On the third day we didn't break up. She caned me, then tied me spread-eagle to the bed and got on top of me. She placed her hand over my face. "Don't come," she said. I closed my eyes and felt her palm against my lips.

And then we laid in bed talking about how much we loved each other and the various things we had done together. The list included Nashville and honky-tonk bars and packed lunches on cliffs overlooking the San Francisco Bay. We'd been to readings and parades and movies and shopped for organic produce at an Asian grocery in Berkeley. We always held hands. We'd been dancing and we danced together well. We spent hours on the phone agreeing on the political issues of the day. Beneath it was this: we were sexually compatible. She liked to hurt people and I liked to be hurt. She liked it when I cried and I wanted to cry all the time.

She turned me over and tied my arms forward. "I'm not going to go easy," she said. She tied rope around my ankles and thighs to keep my knees bent and greased her strap-on and slid it inside of me and fucked me violently. "I want to hear you."

When we were done she said, "I did all the things you like today."

"You did," I told her. She asked me why I thought she did these things and I said because she loved me and I told her I loved her, too.

We went out that night, the only time in four days we left the bed. We went to a noodle house with small round tables and I looked at other couples on dates or just eating dinner. Everyone was in pairs; no one was eating alone. There were couples who had just met, trying to impress each other, afraid of what the other might think when he or she saw them whole. Each person in each couple had their needs. I wondered what those needs were and if they were being met. There was a candle on every table and each base came to a point. The tables stuck in rows like daggers in the floor.

From the noodle house we went to a bar. There were people

I knew playing darts. One of them was moving to France. "I'll be gone six months," he told me. He was going to finish a novel he'd been working on for years. I didn't want to know about it. I thought the bar was cold and empty and there was too much open space.

Then on the fourth day we broke up for real.

It was 1:40 in the afternoon and the curtains were open. We could see my neighbor sitting at a computer in a square of light on the fourth floor of the large apartment building across the street. Eden asked if I remembered when we first got together. I walked her home and we kissed on her stairs. I slid my hand up the back of her leg, lifting her skirt. She told me early on how she was territorial and jealous and I had said I could be monogamous to her. I told her I remembered. She said now she was consumed with jealousy. It wasn't a matter of me seeing other women, she was burning with the idea that I might desire them, which I didn't deny. She had never felt this kind of jealousy before.

Her jealousy was irrational and unfair. She was married. But that wasn't the point. Somewhere in Chicago, in the crunch of that city's hard winter, the word *divorce* had risen between her and her husband and they'd slept in a hotel room on Michigan Avenue with their backs facing each other. But she looked at me and my room and didn't see a future here and neither did I. There was nothing but an unmade bed we couldn't seem to get out of.

I didn't know what I wanted because I had never been in a relationship like this. I didn't know what it would do to me. I didn't say what I thought, which was that this was about other things. That we both wanted our lives back and we had run our course together and there was nowhere left to go. I wanted to write and she wanted to save her marriage and

I wanted to find someone who would love me all the time even though I doubted I would. Even though I knew that being with her part time and sharing her was more than I would ever get full time with someone else. But we had stopped growing. Everything had stopped. We were stuck and there was nowhere for us and there was no acceptable change. The depression that lifted when we met had returned and engulfed me and was getting worse.

Our four days were two hours and twenty minutes from ending. She was meeting her husband at Union Square. They were going to go shopping, and then see a movie. I wondered what that would be like then realized it wasn't something I was interested in at all. I wished it would snow, just one time. It was New Year's Eve tomorrow and she wanted to get groceries so on New Year's Day she could have a traditional breakfast with fish and rice, friends invited over to start the new year correctly. Earlier in our relationship she mentioned that she hoped I could come over for New Year's and be comfortable with her husband and he with me. But we never got to that point. I never fully joined with her husband who has stayed true to his wife these nine years while she went through a parade of men looking to see if it was possible to love two men at the same time and finally deciding on me. Maybe it was the sex. We fucked like animals. She rarely had sex with her husband. He wasn't into the kinky things we were into. He hadn't grown up eroticizing his childhood trauma the way I had. And he had married a sadist.

We had two hours and twenty minutes and she said she couldn't see how to make this work and I agreed. Then I waited a heartbeat and I said, "So we're breaking up?" We were both still and I felt a wave wash across me and for a moment I couldn't breathe. She grabbed me closely and I buried my face inside her hair.

"I can't leave you," she said.

"I don't want to be without you," I said.

"Then don't be."

But five minutes later I asked what was going to happen and she said we were done and I nodded my head. Still we stayed in bed and I pressed my lips against hers, placed my hand on her ass, ran my palm over the contours of her backside. I kissed her deeply and cried more. I couldn't make any sense of it.

"Don't cry," she said. I'd cried in front of her so many times over five months. At first I had been embarrassed but then I realized she liked it so I cried freely. I was shocked by my own propensity for tears. I never knew I had so many of them and they were so close to the surface. I would cry when she was hitting me and she wouldn't even stop. She would beat me the whole way through until the tears were gone and I relaxed again and I came back to her. She said she wanted to provide a space for that little boy inside of me. But now she didn't want me to cry anymore and I tried to put the tears back into wherever they came from and I succeeded and then they came again and then they stopped.

Still I knew I was making my own decision. There were things I could say to keep it going and I wasn't saying them. I was once again jumping from a burning building, abandoning what seemed like an unsustainable situation, something I had been doing since I ran from home when I was thirteen. I never went back. I never did. I've been running away my entire life.

I reached into the tub next to the bed and grabbed a condom from a paper bag. I fucked her hard and fast and unlike I had ever fucked her before. She began to scream and then her own tears came. This was our due. We were breaking up and we were entitled to this sex and we were going to have it. I slammed into her with everything I had. It was like fucking in a storm. I gripped her legs, the flesh of her thighs. I sniffed at her neck. "C'mon," I said, and she screamed and shook with orgasms. Then we rolled over and she was on top of me with her fingers in my hair and one hand on my throat. We were still fucking. She pinched my nipple hard, she reached down between my legs. It didn't matter. I wasn't going to come.

"I want to come," I said.

"Okay," she whispered.

"I can't come inside you."

She got off of me. We were running out of time. I lay next to her and masturbated quickly and came into the rubber. She pulled the rubber off of me, tying a knot in one swift motion, pulling the end with her thumb and forefinger, striding across the room while I watched the naked triangle of her legs tapering into her ankles.

She tried to call her husband. She didn't want to meet him downtown, she wanted to meet him at home. But he had already left the bank. There were three pillows bunched at the top of the bed, two blankets and a sheet thrown to the side.

"I have to shower," she said.

"He's your husband," I told her. "You don't need to shower for him. He's seen you dirty before."

"I'm not showering for him," she said. "I'm showering for myself." I looked at the two unwashed cereal bowls next to the bookshelf.

I followed her into the bathroom. My shower is small, barely room for the two of us. We used the chocolate-scented soap she bought me. She was always buying me fancy soaps. This one was composed of dark-brown-and-white blocks and thin lines and the bar separated into its parts while we were scrubbing.

"I have to go," she said.

"I can't walk you to the train," I told her. "I don't want to break down at the station."

I got dressed while she dressed. I pulled on my jeans and an undershirt and a T-shirt. I laced up my gym shoes.

"Why are you getting dressed if you're not walking me to the train station?" she asked.

"I don't know," I said.

It was raining and I offered her my umbrella. I lose my umbrellas so I never buy expensive ones. The umbrella cost six dollars. I considered giving her my necklace but I knew she wouldn't wear it. She turned down the umbrella. She was going to get wet. We moved toward the door of my room. She was wearing her long blue wool coat.

"Don't go," I said suddenly. I didn't know where it came from and my hand was in the pocket of her coat and her hand was along my neck and the back of my head. I could have turned into an animal, a dinosaur. I could have grown a giant tail and swung it and broken the windows and the table legs and smashed the bed to pieces.

"Walk me out," she said.

I walked her downstairs, out the front to the entryway to the building. I lit her cigarette on the steps. We kept having one more kiss. She was going to be very late to meet her husband. But he would probably be relieved. His ordeal was over. He would make rules next time, communicate better, draw lines in the sand. There would be no sleepover nights with the next boyfriend. No boys in the house when he came home. But for the foreseeable future he would have to hear about me and comfort his wife while she romanticized our love and cried in his arms.

You concentrate on your time alone—you never think about how hard it is to be in bed with someone else, thinking about you, she said once.

She opened the gate and stepped onto the sidewalk and the rain hit her immediately. It blew horizontally in sharp little beads. I ran down the stairs and grabbed the gate and watched her walk to the corner. I waited for her to turn around. She never looked back. She crossed south and then the light changed. I've lived here too long, I thought, wondering why I wasn't somewhere else. I let go of the steel gate and it fell against my shoulder. I watched as Eden became smaller, walking east in front of the housing projects a short distance to the station and the train, which would take her home.

April 1, 1999

Mr. Ray Charles

███████████████

Los Angeles CA 90018

Dear Mr. Charles:

Scout ████████ will officially receive the rank of Eagle Scout, the highest and most prestigious rank in Scouting, at an Eagle Court of Honor to be held at 1:30 p.m. on Saturday, May 15, 1999, in the Old Chapel of the First Presbyterian Church of Arlington Heights. The First Presbyterian Church is located at the corner of Dunton and Eastman Streets in Arlington Heights, Illinois.

Boy Scout Troop 32, the oldest active Boy Scout troop in Arlington Heights, would be honored if you would attend this most auspicious ceremony. Keep in mind that only 2½ percent of *all* Boy Scouts attain the rank of Eagle Scout.

If you cannot attend the ceremony, we would appreciate it if you could send Mark a short congratulatory letter acknowledging his achievement. Your letter may be sent to:

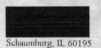

Schaumburg, IL 60195

Thank you for your attention to this letter and for your support of Scouting.

Sincerely,

Eagle Ceremony Coordinator
BSA Troop 32

"AUSPICIOUS CEREMONY"

Matt Rota

THE PRAM

by RODDY DOYLE

CHAPTER ONE

ALINA LOVED THE BABY. She loved everything about the baby.
The tiny boyness of him, the way his legs kicked whenever he
looked up at her, his fat—she loved these things. She loved to
bring him out in his pram, even on the days when it was raining. She loved to sit on the floor with her legs crossed and the
baby in her lap. Even when he cried, when he screamed, she
was very happy. But he did not cry very often. He was almost a
perfect baby.

The baby's pram was very old. Alina remembered visiting
her grandmother when she was a little girl. She had not met her
grandmother before. She got out of the car and stood beside her
father in the frozen farmyard. They watched an old woman push
a perambulator toward them. The pram was full of wood,
branches and twigs and, across the top of the pram, one huge

branch that looked like an entire tree. This old woman was her grandmother. And the baby's pram was very like the old pram she saw her grandmother push across the farmyard. Her father told her it had been his pram, and her aunts' and her uncle's, and even the generation of babies before them.

Now, in 2006, in Dublin, she pushed a pram just like it. Every morning, she put the baby into the pram. She wrapped him up and brought the pram carefully down the steps of the house. She pushed the pram down the path, to the gate. The gateway was only slightly wider than the pram.

—Mind you don't scrape the sides, the baby's mother had said, the first time she had brought the pram to the steps and turned it toward the gate and the street.

Alina did not understand the baby's mother. The mother followed her to the gate. She took the pram and pushed it through the gateway. She tapped the brick pillars.

—Don't scrape the sides.

She tapped the sides of the pram.

—It is very valuable, said the mother.

—It was yours when you were a baby? Alina asked.

—No, said the mother. —We bought it.

—It is very nice.

—Just be careful with it, said the mother.

—Yes, said Alina. —I will be careful.

Every morning, she took the baby for his walk. She pushed the pram down to the sea and walked along the path beside the seawall. She walked for two hours, every morning. She had been ordered to do this. She had been told which route to take. She stopped at the wooden bridge, the bridge out to the strange sandy island, and she turned back. She did not see the mother or the father but, sometimes, she thought she was being watched. She never took a different route. She never let the pram scrape a wall or gate. She was drenched and cold; her hands felt frozen to the steel bar with which she pushed the pram, despite the gloves her own mother had sent to her from home. But still, Alina loved the baby.

The little girls, his sisters, she was not so sure about. They were beautiful little girls. They were clever and lively and they played the piano together, side by side, with a confidence and sensitivity that greatly impressed Alina. The piano was in the tiled hall, close to the stained-glass windows of the large front door. The colored sunlight of the late afternoon lit the two girls as they played. Their black hair became purple, dark red, and the green of deep-forest leaves. Their fingers on the keys were red and yellow. Alina had not seen them play tennis—it was the middle of December—but the mother assured her that they were excellent players. They were polite and they ate with good manners and apologized when they did not eat all that was on their plates.

They were not twins. They had names, of course, and they had different ages. Ocean was ten years old and Saibhreas was almost nine. But Alina rarely—or, never—saw them apart. They played together; they slept together. They stood beside each other, always. From the first time Alina saw them, three weeks earlier, when she arrived at Dublin Airport, they were side by side.

The next morning, Alina's first working day, they came up to Alina's bedroom in the attic. It was dark outside. They were lit only by the light from the landing below, down the steep stairs. Their black hair could not be seen. Alina saw only their faces. They sat at the end of the bed, side by side, and watched Alina.

—Good morning, said Alina.

—Good morning, they said, together.

It was funny. The three young ladies laughed. Alina didn't know why she did not like them.

CHAPTER TWO

Every morning, Alina brought the baby for his walk. Always, she stopped at one of the shelters at the seafront. She took the baby, swaddled in cotton and Gortex, from his pram and held him on her lap. She looked at the changing sea and bounced him gently.

She spoke to him only in English. She had been instructed never to use her own language.

—You can teach the girls a few words of Polish, the mother told her. —It might be useful. But I don't want Cillian confused.

The shelter had three walls, and a wooden bench. The walls had circular windows, like portholes. Alina held the baby and lifted him to one of these windows, so he could see through it. She did it again. He laughed. Alina could feel his excitement through the many layers of cloth. She lifted him high. His hat brushed the roof of the shelter.

—Intelligent boy!

It was the first time he had laughed. She lowered him back into his pram. She would not tell the mother, she decided. But, almost immediately, she changed her mind. She had the sudden feeling, the knowledge; it crept across her face. She was being watched.

She walked as far as the wooden bridge, and turned.

Every morning, Alina saw mothers, and other young women like herself. These women pushed modern, lighter baby-conveyances, four-wheeled and three-wheeled. Alina envied them. The pram felt heavy and the wind from the sea constantly bashed against its hood.

One thing, however, she liked about the pram. People smiled when they saw it.

—I haven't seen one of those in years, one woman said.

—God almighty, that takes me back, said another.

One morning, she pushed past a handsome man who sat on

the seawall eating a large sandwich. She kept pushing; she did
not look back. She stopped at the old wooden bridge. She
would never bring the pram onto the bridge. She looked at its
frail wooden legs rising out of the sludge. The mutual contact,
of old wood and old pram; they would all collapse into the ooze
below. She could smell it—she could almost feel it, in her hair
and mouth. She walked quickly back along the promenade.

The handsome man was still there. He held up a flask and
a cup.

—Hot chocolate? he said. —I put aside for you.

He was a biochemist from Lithuania but he was working in
Dublin for a builder, constructing an extension to a very large
house on her street. They met every morning, in the shelter.
Always, he brought the flask. Sometimes, she brought cake.
She watched through the portholes as they kissed. She told him
she was being watched. He touched her breast; his hand was
inside her coat. She looked down at the baby. He smiled; he
bucked. He started to cry. The pram rocked on its springs.

One morning in February, Alina heard her mobile phone as
she was carefully bringing the pram down the granite steps of
the house. She held the phone to her ear.

—Hello?

—Alina. It's O'Reilly.

O'Reilly was the mother. Everyone called her by her sur-
name. She insisted upon this practice. It terrified her clients,
she told Alina. It was intriguing; it was sexy.

—Hello, O'Reilly, said Alina.

—The girls are off school early today, said O'Reilly.
—Twelve o'clock. I forgot to tell you.

—Fine, said Alina.

But it was not fine.

—I will be there at twelve o'clock, said Alina.

—Five to, said O'Reilly.

—Yes, said Alina.

—Talk to you, said O'Reilly.

—Your mother is not very nice, Alina told the baby, in English.

She could not now meet her biochemist. He did not own a mobile phone. She would miss her hot chocolate. She would miss his lips on her neck. She would not now feel his hands as she peeped through the porthole and watched for approaching joggers and buggy-pushing women.

She arrived at the gates of the girls' school at ten minutes to twelve. They were waiting there, side by side.

—But school ends at twelve o'clock, said Alina.

—A quarter to, said Ocean.

—We've been here *ages,* said Saibhreas.

—So, said Alina. —We will now go home.

—We want to go along the seafront, said Ocean.

—No, said Alina. —It is too windy today, I think.

—You were *late,* said Saibhreas.

—Very well, said Alina. —We go.

The biochemist waved his flask as she approached. Alina walked straight past him. She did not look at him. She did not look at the little girls as they strode past. She hoped he would be there tomorrow. She would explain her strange behavior.

That night, quite late, the mother came home. The girls came out of their bedroom.

—Guess what, O'Reilly, they said, together. —Alina has a boyfriend.

CHAPTER THREE

O'Reilly grabbed Alina's sleeve and pulled her into the kitchen. She shut the door with one of her heels. She grabbed a chair and made Alina sit. She stood impressively before Alina.

—So, she said. —Tell all.

Alina could not look at O'Reilly's face.

—It is, she said, —perhaps my private affair.

—Listen, babes, said O'Reilly. —Nothing is your private affair. Not while you're working here. Are you fucking this guy?

Alina felt herself burn. The crudity was like a slap across her face.

She shook her head.

—Of course, said O'Reilly. —You're a good Catholic girl. It would be quaint, if I believed you.

O'Reilly put one foot on the chair beside Alina.

—I couldn't care less, she said. —Fuck away, girl. But with three provisos. Not while you're working. Not here, on the property. And not with Mister O'Reilly.

Shocked, appalled, close—she thought to fainting, Alina looked up at O'Reilly. O'Reilly smiled down at her. Alina dropped her head and cried. O'Reilly smiled the more. She'd mistaken Alina's tears and gulps for gratitude. She patted Alina's head. She lifted Alina's blond hair, held it, and let it drop.

Alina was going to murder the little girls. This she decided as she climbed the stairs to her attic room. She closed the door. It had no lock. She sat on the bed, in the dark. She would poison them. She would drown them. She would put pillows on their faces, a pillow in each of her hands. She would lean down on the pillows until their struggles and kicking ceased. She picked up her own pillow. She put it to her face.

She would not kill the girls. She could not do such a thing—two such things. She would, however, frighten them. She would terrify them. She would plant nightmares that would lurk, prowl, rub their evil backs against the soft walls of their minds, all their lives, until they were two old ladies, lying side by side on their one big deathbed. She would—she knew the phrase—scare them shitless.

—Once upon a time, said Alina.

It was two days later. They sat in the playroom, in front of the bay window. The wind scratched the glass. They heard it also crying in the chimney. The baby lay asleep on Alina's lap. The little girls sat on the rug. They looked up at Alina.

—We're too old for *once upon a time,* said Ocean.

—Nobody is too old for *once upon a time,* said Alina.

The wind shrieked in the chimney. The girls edged closer to Alina's feet. Alina thought of her biochemist, out there mixing cement or cutting wood. She had not seen him since. She had pushed the pram past the shelter. Twice she had pushed; three times. He had not been there. She looked down at the girls. She resisted the urge to kick their little upturned faces. She smiled.

—Once upon a time, she said, again. —There was a very old and wicked lady. She lived in a dark forest.

—Where? said Ocean.

—In my country, said Alina.

—Is this just made up?

—Perhaps.

She stood up. It was a good time for an early interruption, she thought. She carried the baby to his pram, which was close to the door. She lowered him gently. He did not wake. She returned to her chair. She watched the girls watch her approach. She sat.

—From this dark forest the wicked lady emerged, every night. With her she brought a pram.

—Like Cillian's? said Saibhreas.

—Very like Cillian's, said Alina.

She looked at the pram.

—Exactly like Cillian's. Every night, the old lady pushed the pram to the village. Every night, she chose a baby. Every night, she stole the baby.

—From only one village?

—The dark forest was surrounded by villages. There were many babies to choose from. Every night, she pushed the pram back into the forest. It was a dark, dark shuddery place and nobody was brave enough to follow her. Not one soldier. Not one handsome young woodcutter. They all stopped at the edge of the forest. The wind in the branches made—their—flesh—creep. The branches stretched out and tried to tear their hearts from their chests.

The wind now shook the windows. A solitary can bounced down the street.

—Cool, said Ocean.

But the little girls moved in closer. They were now actually sitting on Alina's feet, one foot per girl.

—Every night, said Alina, —the wicked old lady came out of the forest. For many, many years.

Did she take all the babies? asked Saibhreas.

—No, said Alina. —She did not.

Outside, a branch snapped, a car screeched.

—She took only one kind, said Alina.

—What kind? said Ocean.

—She took only—the girls.

CHAPTER FOUR

—Why? Ocean asked.

—Why? Alina asked back.

—Why did the old lady take girls and not boys?

—They probably taste better, said Saibhreas.

—Yeah, Ocean agreed. —They'd taste nicer than boys, if they were cooked properly.

—And some girls are smaller, said Saibhreas. —So they'd fit in the oven.

—Unless the old lady had an Aga like ours, said Ocean. —Then boys would fit, too.

Alina realized she would have to work harder to scare these practical little girls.

—So, she said. —We return to the story.

The girls were again silent. They looked up at Alina. They waited for more frights.

—It is not to be thought, said Alina, —that the old lady simply *ate* the little girls.

—Cool.

—This was not so, said Alina.

—What did she do to them?

— You must be quiet, said Alina.

—Sorry, said both girls.

They were faultlessly polite.

Alina said nothing until she felt control of the story return to her. She could feel it; it was as if the little girls leaned forward and gently placed the story onto Alina's lap.

—So, she said. —To continue. There were none brave enough to follow the old lady into the dark forest. None of the mothers had a good night's sleep. They pinched themselves to stay awake. They lay on top of sharp stones. And the fathers slept standing up, at the doors of their houses, their axes in their hands, at the ready. And yet—

—She got past them, said Ocean. —I bet she did.

—Why didn't they have guns? said Saibhreas.

—Silence.

—Sorry.

—And yet, said Alina. —The old lady pushed the pram—

—Excuse me, Alina? said Saibhreas.

—Yes?

—You didn't tell us what she did with the babies.

—Besides eating them, said Ocean.

—You do not wish to hear this story?

—We do.

—And so, said Alina. —The old lady took all the baby girls. She carried every baby girl deep into the forest, in her pram. Until there were no more. Then she took the girls who were no longer babies.

Alina saw that Ocean was about to speak. But Saibhreas nudged her sister, warning her not to interrupt. Alina continued.

—She crept up to the girls in their beds and whispered a spell into their sleeping ears. The girls remained sleeping as she picked them up and placed them in the pram. She pushed the pram past the fathers who did not see her, past the mothers as they lay on stones. The wicked old lady took girls of all ages, up to the age of... ten.

Alina waited, as the little girls examined their arms and legs, wondering how the old lady had done this. She watched Ocean look at the pram. Above them, a crow perched on the chimney pot cawed down the chimney; its sharp beak seemed very close. The wind continued to shriek and groan.

—But, said Alina.

She looked from girl to girl. Their mouths stayed closed. They were—Alina knew the phrase—putty in her hands.

—But, she said, again. —One day, a handsome woodcutter had an idea so brilliant, it lit his eyes like lamps at darkest midnight. This was the idea. Every woodcutter should cut a tree every day, starting at the edge of the forest. That way, the old witch's forest would soon be too small to remain her hiding place. Now, all the men in this part of my country were wood-cutters. They all took up their axes and, day by day, cut down the trees.

—But, Alina, said Ocean. —Sorry for interrupting.

—Yes? said Alina.

—What would the woodcutters do afterwards, if they cut down all the trees?

—This did not concern them at that time, said Alina. —They cut, to save their daughters.

—Did the plan work?

—Yes, said Alina. —And no. I will tell.

She waited, then spoke.

—Every morning, and all day, the old lady heard the axes

of the woodcutters. Every morning, the axes were a little louder, a little nearer. Soon, after many months, she could see the woodcutters through the remaining trees.

She looked down at Ocean.

—One night she left. She sneaked away, with her pram. So, yes, the plan worked. But—

Again, she waited. She looked across, at the pram.

—She simply moved to another place. She found new babies and new little girls, up to the age of... ten.

—Where? said Saibhreas.

—You have not guessed? said Alina.

She watched the little girls look at each other. Ocean began to speak.

—You forgot to tell us—

—I did not forget, said Alina. —You wish to know why she took the little girls.

—Yes, please, said Ocean.

—Their skin, said Alina.

She watched, as the goosebumps rose on the arms and legs of the little girls in front of her.

CHAPTER FIVE

It was dark outside, and dark, too, in the room. Alina stood up.

—But the story, said Ocean.

Alina went to the door and walked behind the pram. She pushed it slowly toward the girls. She let them see it grow out of the dark, like a whale rising from a black sea. She let them hear it creak and purr. She heard them shuffle backward on their bottoms. Then she stopped. She stepped back to the door, and turned on the light.

She saw the girls squinting, looking at her from around the front of the pram.

—Tomorrow I will continue, said Alina.

They followed her into the kitchen. They stayed with her as she peeled the potatoes and carrots. They offered to help her. They washed and shook each lettuce leaf. They talked to fill the silence.

Alina left them in the kitchen, but they were right behind her. She went back to the sitting room, and stopped.

The pram had been moved. She had left it in the center of the room, where the little girls had been sitting. But now it was at the window. The curtain was resting on the hood.

Alina heard the girls behind her.

—Did you move the pram? she asked.

—No, said Saibhreas.

—We've been with you all the time, said Ocean

Alina walked over to the pram. She wasn't so very concerned about its mysterious change of position. In fact, she thought, it added to the drama of the interrupted story. The little girls lingered at the door. They would not enter the room.

Alina picked up the baby from the pram's warm bed. He still slept. O'Reilly would be annoyed.

—I pay you to keep him awake, she'd told Alina, once.

—In this country, Alina, the babies sleep at night. Because the mummies have to get up in the morning to work, to pay the bloody childminders.

Alina walked out to the hall. She heard the car outside; she heard the change of gear. She saw the car lights push the colors from the stained-glass windows across the ceiling. She felt the baby shift. She looked down, and saw him watch the colored lights above him.

—Intelligent boy.

The engine stopped; the car lights died. Alina turned on the hall light. The little girls were right beside her.

—Your mother, I think, said Alina.

—Our dad, actually, said Ocean.

—How do you know this? Alina asked.

—Their Beemers, said Ocean. —Mum's Roadster has a quieter engine.

—It's the ultimate driving machine, said Saibhreas.

The lights were on, their daddy was home, and the little girls were no longer frightened. But Alina was satisfied. The lights could be turned off, and their fear could be turned back on—anytime she wished to flick the switch.

She walked the next morning and thought about her story. She pushed the pram past the shelter and hoped to see her handsome biochemist. He was not there. She pushed into the wind and rain. Seawater jumped over the wall and drenched the promenade in front of her. She turned back; she could not go her usual, mandatory distance. She felt eyes stare—she felt their heat—watching her approach. But there was no one in front of her, and nothing. She was alone. She looked into the pram, but the baby slept. His eyes were firmly closed.

The little girls had their hair wrapped in towels when Alina continued her story that afternoon. They'd had showers when they came home from school because they'd been so cold and wet.

Alina closed the curtains. She turned on only one small side light.

The baby slept in the pram, beside Alina's chair.

—And so, said Alina.

She sat.

The little girls were at her feet, almost under the pram.

—Did the old witch come to Ireland? Ocean asked.

Alina nodded.

—To Dublin, she said.

—There are no forests in Dublin, Alina, said Saibhreas.

—There are many parks, said Alina.

—What park?

Alina held up her hands.

—I must continue.

—Sorry, Alina.

Alina measured the silence, then spoke.

—Soon, she said, —the squeak of the pram's wheels became a familiar and terrifying sound late at night as the old lady pushed it through the streets of this city. It was a very old pram, and rusty. And so it creaked and—

Beside them, the pram moved. It did not creak but it moved, very slightly.

The girls jumped.

Alina had not touched it.

The baby was waking. They heard a little cry.

Alina laughed.

—Strong boy, she said. —It was your brother.

Ocean stood up.

—Maybe O'Reilly's right, she said.

—Yes, said Saibhreas.

She crawled away from the pram.

—What did O'Reilly say? Alina asked.

—She said the pram was haunted.

Inside the pram, the baby began to howl.

CHAPTER SIX

Alina stared at the pram while, inside, the baby kicked and screeched.

—Aren't you going to pick him up? said Ocean.

—Of course, said Alina.

But, yet, she did not move. It was like she'd suddenly woken up in a slightly different room. The angles weren't quite right. The baby's screech was wrong.

She stood up. She approached the rocking pram. The movement did her good. The room was just a room.

She looked into the pram. The baby was there, exactly as he

should have been. He was angry, red, and rightly so. She had been silly; the little girls had frightened her.

She turned on the light and the pram was just a pram.

—The pram moved today, said Saibhreas.

She said this later, in the kitchen.

—I should hope so, said O'Reilly. —It's supposed to bloody move. I pay a Polish cailín to move it.

Alina blushed; her rage pushed at her skin. She hated this crude woman.

—It moved all by itself, said Ocean.

Alina stared down at her chicken. She felt something, under the table, brush against her leg. Mr. O'Reilly's foot. He sat opposite Alina.

—Sorry, he said.

—Down, Fido, said O'Reilly.

She looked at Alina.

—Lock your door tonight, sweetie.

—I do not have a key, said Alina.

—Interesting, said O'Reilly. —What happened with the pram?

—The baby cried, said Alina. —And so, the pram moved some centimeters.

—And why, asked O'Reilly, —did Cillian cry?

—O'Reilly? said Ocean.

—What?

—The pram moved before Cillian cried.

—Yes, said Saibhreas. —It's haunted, like you said.

Alina sat as the little girls told their mother about the wicked old lady and her pram full of kidnapped babies, and how the wicked old lady had pushed the pram all the way to Ireland.

—Enough already, said O'Reilly.

She turned to Alina.

—That's some hard-core storytelling, Alina.

—She takes the skin off the babies, said Ocean.

—Who does? said O'Reilly. —Alina?

—No, said Saibhreas. — The old woman.

—My my, said O'Reilly. —And look at the fair Alina's skin. How red can red get?

Alina stared at the cold chicken on her plate. She felt the shock—O'Reilly's fingers on her cheek.

—Hot, said O'Reilly.

The little girls laughed.

—We'd better call a halt to the story, Alina, said O'Reilly. —It's getting under your skin.

The little girls laughed again.

The following morning, Alina pushed the pram along the promenade. She had not slept well. She had not slept at all. O'Reilly's fingers, Mr. O'Reilly's foot—Alina had felt their presence all around her. She'd gotten up and torn a piece of paper from a notebook. She'd chewed the paper. Then she'd pushed the pulp into the keyhole of her bedroom door. She'd lain awake all night.

She walked. The wind was strong and pushed against the pram. It woke her up; it seemed to wash her skin. It was a warm wind. Gloves weren't necessary. But Alina wore her gloves.

The pram was haunted. O'Reilly had said so; she'd told her little daughters. Alina did not believe it. She knew her folklore. Prams did not haunt, and were never haunted. And yet, she did not wish to touch the pram. She did not want to see it move before her fingers reached it. She'd put on her gloves inside the house, before she'd lowered the baby into the pram. She did not want to touch it.

Not even out here, in bright sunshine, away from walls and shadows.

The pram was not possessed. A dead rat could not bite, but Alina would wear gloves to pick one up. That was how it was with the pram. Today, it was a dead rat. Tomorrow, it would simply be a pram.

She took off one of her gloves. She stopped walking. The pram stayed still. Alina put her bare fingers on the handle. She waited. Nothing happened. She felt the wind rock the pram on its springs. But the pram did not move backward or forward.

She removed her other glove. She pushed the pram. She pushed it to the wooden bridge, and back. She would continue her story that afternoon, despite O'Reilly's command. She would plant the most appalling nightmares and leave the little imps in the hands of their foul mother.

And then she would leave.

She pushed the pram with her bare hands. But, all the time, and all the way, she felt she was being watched. She put the gloves back on. She was being watched. She felt it—she *knew* it—on her face and neck, like damp fingers.

—One night, said Alina, that afternoon. —The old lady left her lair in the park and made her way to a tree-lined street.

—Our street has trees, said Ocean.

Outside, the wind cracked a branch. The little girls moved closer to Alina.

CHAPTER SEVEN

Alina looked down at the little girls.

—The old lady crept along the tree-lined street, she said. —She hid behind the very expensive cars. The SUVs. This is what they are called?

The little girls nodded.

—And the Volvos, said Alina. —And... the Beemers.

Alina watched the little girls look at each other.

—She looked through windows where the velvet curtains had not yet been drawn.

Alina watched the girls look at the window. She had left the velvet curtains open.

She heard the gasp, and the scream.

—The curtains!

—I saw her!

Alina did not look. She leaned down and placed her hands beneath the little girls' chins.

—Through one such window, said Alina, —the old lady saw a bargain.

Alina held the chins. She forced the girls to look at her. She stretched her leg—she had earlier measured the distance from foot to pram—and raised her foot to the wheel.

—She saw *two* girls.

They heard the creak.

The little girls screamed. And so did Alina. She had not touched the wheel. The pram had moved before her foot had reached it.

Alina almost vomited. She felt the pancakes, the *nalesniki* she had earlier made and eaten, and the sour cream; she could taste them as they rushed up to her throat. Her eyes watered; she felt snails of cold sweat on her forehead. The little girls screamed. And Alina held their chins. She tightened her grip. She felt bone and shifting tongues. She could feel their screams in her hands. And the pram continued to move. Slowly, slowly, off the rug, across the wooden floor.

Alina held the faces.

—Two little girls, she said. —And, such was her wicked joy, she did not wait until they slept.

The pram crept on. It rolled nearer to the window. She heard the baby. She watched his waking rock the pram.

—The old lady found an open window, said Alina.

The baby screeched. And then other babies screeched. There was more than one baby in the pram.

The girls screamed, and urinated. And, still, Alina told her story.

—Through the window she slid. And through the house she sneaked.

The pram was at the window. The screeching shook the window glass.

—She found the girls quite easily.

The girls were squirming, trying to free their jaws from Alina's big fingers, and trying to escape from the wet rug beneath them. But Alina held them firm. She ignored their fingernails on her neck and cheeks.

—She had her sharp knife with her, said Alina. —She would cut the little girls. And she would take their skin, while their mother was neglecting them. Far, far away, in her Beemer.

But their mother wasn't far, far away in her Beemer. She was at the door, looking at her daughters and Alina.

—Hell-oh! she roared. —HELL-oh!

The pram stopped rocking. The little girls stopped screaming. And Alina stopped narrating.

O'Reilly stepped into the room. She turned on the light.

—She frightened us, said Ocean.

The girls escaped from Alina's grip. They shuffled backward, off the rug.

—She hurt us, Mummy.

—We don't like her.

Alina took her hands down from her face. There was blood on her fingertips. Her cheeks and neck were stinging where the little girls had scratched her.

She looked up.

The girls were gone; she could hear them on the stairs. She was alone with O'Reilly and the screaming baby. O'Reilly held the baby and made soft, soothing noises. She rocked the baby gently and walked in a small circle around the rug. The baby's screams soon lessened, and ceased. O'Reilly continued to make soft noises, and it was some time before Alina realized that, amid the kisses and whispers, O'Reilly was giving out to her.

—My fucking rug, she cooed. —Have any idea how much it cost? There, there, good boy.

—I am sorry, said Alina.

—What the fuck were you doing, Alina?

Alina looked at the pram. It was against the wall, beside the window. It was not moving.

—The pram is haunted, said Alina.

—It's haunted because I said it's haunted, said O'Reilly. —I told the girls the bloody thing was haunted to keep them away from the baby when he was born.

—But it *is* haunted, said Alina. —It has nothing to do with the lies you told your daughters.

—Excuse me?!

—I saw it move, said Alina. —Here.

She stamped her foot. She stood up.

—Here, she said. —I saw. And I heard. More babies.

—Jesus, said O'Reilly. —The sooner you find a peasant or something to knock you up the better.

—I felt their eyes, said Alina.

—Enough, said O'Reilly.

—Many times, said Alina. —I have felt their eyes. I know now. There are babies in the pram.

—Look at me, Alina, said O'Reilly.

Alina looked.

—Are you listening? said O'Reilly.

—Yes, said Alina.

—You're sacked.

CHAPTER EIGHT

O'Reilly wondered if Alina had heard her. She was facing O'Reilly, but her eyes were huge and far away.

—Do you understand that, Alina?

—Yes.

—You're fired.

Alina nodded.

—As of now, said O'Reilly.

—Yes.

—You can stay the night, then off you fucking go.

—Yes.

—Stop saying yes, Alina, said O'Reilly.

But she wasn't looking at Alina now. She was searching for a phone number and balancing the baby on her shoulder as she walked over to the window and the pram.

—I'll have to stay home tomorrow, said O'Reilly. —So, fuck you, Alina, and life's complications.

She gently slid the baby from her shoulder and, her hands on his bum and little head, she lowered him into the cradle of the pram.

She heard the scream.

—No!

It was Alina.

—Fuck off, Alina, said O'Reilly.

She didn't turn, or lift her face from the pram. She kissed the baby's forehead and loosely tucked the edges of his quilt beneath the mattress.

She stood up. She looked down at her son.

—There's only one baby in there, Alina.

She had the phone to her ear. She began to speak.

—Conor? she said. —It's O'Reilly. We have to cancel tomorrow's meeting. Yes. No. My Polish peasant. Yes; again. Yes. Yes. A fucking nightmare. You can? I'll suck your cock if you do. Cool. Talk to you.

O'Reilly brought the phone down from her ear at the same time that Alina brought the poker down on O'Reilly's head. The poker was decorative, and heavy. It had never been used, until now. The first blow was sufficient. O'Reilly collapsed with not much noise, and her blood joined the urine on the rug.

Mr. O'Reilly was inserting his door key into the lock when Alina opened the front door.

—Alina, he said. —Bringing Cillian for a stroll?

—Yes, she said.

—Excellent.

He helped her bring the pram down the granite steps.

—Is he well wrapped up in there? said Mr. O'Reilly. —It's a horrible evening.

—Yes, said Alina.

—And yourself, he said. —Have you no coat?

He looked at her breasts, beneath her Skinni-Fit T-shirt, and thought how much he'd like to see them when she returned after a good walk in the wind and rain.

Alina did not answer.

—I'll leave you to it, he said. —Where's O'Reilly?

—In the playroom, said Alina.

—Fine, said Mr. O'Reilly. —See you when you get back.

Alina turned left, off her usual path, and brought the pram down a lane that ran behind the houses. It was dark there, and unpleasant. The ground wasn't properly paved or, if it was, the surface was lost under years of dead leaves, dumped rubbish, and dog shit. But Alina stayed on the lane, away from street lights and detection. She pushed straight into darkness and terror. She held her arms stiff, to keep the pram as far from her as possible. And, yet, she felt each shudder and jump, each one a screaming, shuddering baby.

At the end of the lane, another lane, behind the pub and Spar. Alina stayed on this lane, which brought her to another. And another. This last one was particularly dreadful. The ground was soft, and felt horribly warm at her ankles. She pushed hard, to the lane's end and fresh air. The sea was now in front of her. Alina couldn't hide.

She knew what she had to do.

But now she wasn't pushing. The wind shook the pram, filled the hood, and lifted it off the ground. She heard the cries—the pram landed on its wheels, just some centimeters ahead, and continued on its course. Alina had to run behind it, pulling it back, as the infant ghosts, their murderers or demons—she did not know—perhaps their spirit parents, she did not know, as all of them tried to wrench the pram from her. She heard the wails, and under, through them all, she heard the cries of the baby, Cillian. Her adorable, intelligent Cillian. Now gone, murdered by the infant murdered.

She refused to feel the cold. She didn't pause to rub the rain from her eyes. She held on to the pram and its wailing evil, and she pulled and pushed the length of the promenade, a journey of two kilometers, to her goal, the wooden bridge, the bridge out to the strange island.

They found her in the sludge. She stood to her thighs in the ooze and seaweed. She was trying to push the pram still deeper into the mud. They found the baby—they found only one baby. The quilt had saved him. He lay on it, on top of the mud. The tide was out, but coming back. The water was starting to fill and swallow the quilt. They lifted the baby and struggling woman onto the bridge. They left the pram in the rising water.

July 20,1999

Dear President Ford,

I'm writing to you for a couple of reasons. The first is to tell you what a
great singer I think you are. The second reason is to ask you for photo of
yourself, if you send them out to fans.

Thank you,

~~signature~~

█████████████████

Colton, Ca. 92324

"A GREAT SINGER"

Robert Goodin

THE STRANGE CAREER OF DOCTOR RAJU GOPALARAJAN

by RAJESH PARAMESWARAN

NONE OF US were surprised when we heard Gopi Kumar had been fired from his job at CompUSA. We imagine he came home and bragged to his wife that at any minute his manager would realize what a mistake she'd made and beg him to take his job back. Manju would have breathed out hard and told him, "Go to the unemployment office anyway and fill out the forms" (as Gopi eventually did). But what Manju didn't know—what none of us understood—was that Gopi had already decided to make his living by impersonating a doctor.

In fact, within three weeks of that day, Gopi had signed the lease on a small office in Manvel, a good hour and a half from where he lived, a place where he hoped none of us would run into him. He told his wife he was looking for a job, and later he said he had found one, as a television salesman. But he would come home those days carrying as many books about medicine and surgery as the Doakum County Public Library System possessed. Every evening he pored through them, making margin marks with his pencil, consulting the internet for clarification on difficult points; and Manju would have stood in the doorway and watched, in her weary way.

"You're not supposed to write in library books," she would say. Manju was a secretary in an insurance agency, and it seemed to us she was shy in public, a little insecure—the sort of woman who always wore saris, and who would respond in Tamil when you spoke to her in English. But we also noticed she had grown to be bold at home with him, because when you are married to a man like Gopi, a man who is always going to be a bit oblivious to those around him, you can be a little loud and say what you think and still not risk offending.

"Why not? My taxes pay for them," Gopi might reply.

"As if you pay all your taxes. What are you reading, anyway?"

And then he would turn to her and say, "Mind your own business," or, "Don't you have enough work to do that you don't have to stand there and bother me?" or, "You should try reading yourself one day, you might learn something."

"And you're such a genius yourself," Manju would answer. Or she might instead hold her tongue, deciding it wasn't important enough to continue provoking him.

Of course, when Gopi went to sleep or stepped into the bathroom, Manju would peep into the books herself to see what was engrossing her husband, and this is why some people say that she must have known and chosen not to stop him— that she was just as responsible as he was for all that happened later. After all, Manju herself told the story of the day in India when Gopi had gotten so fed up with the traffic outside of their house that he had assembled a police uniform using his father's old air-force khakis and gone out into the road. He had issued homemade tickets, ripping them up in exchange for boisterously negotiated bribes, stopping only after Manju pretended to call and report *him* to the police. Obviously, they say, Manju knew her husband had a history as a charlatan, and when she looked in those library books, she should have reached the logical conclusion.

But the people who say this don't understand that there was more than one logical conclusion. During their twenty-one years of marriage, as everybody knows, Manju had been unable to have a child, and seeing the books her husband brought home, with their graphic photographs of women's parts, of glistening uteruses and palsied vaginas, of dead, blue-green fetuses and rash-covered nipples, she might just as well have thought her husband was feeling the loneliness of being childless and almost old, and was seeking again a cure for a problem they had long ago decided would have to be left to the whims and the graces of God.

We liked Manju so much, and we miss her. She had a beautiful voice, and always we asked her to sing at our functions. She would sit down with crossed legs and clear her throat and the room would quiet and parents would hush their children. Then the voice would come out of her, low and quavering and full of awe and sadness, singing of beautiful, dark-skinned young Krishna and how she loved him and longed for him, how she lay alone and burned for him but never could be with him. And when she sang like that we would notice a hollow space in our own chests, and we would feel that space filled with a sweet longing we couldn't understand, and our eyes would grow hot and wet. When people talk about Manju and her husband and what they did and what happened to them, they should try to remember that people have depths.

The office space Gopi rented with his and Manju's small savings had previously housed a veterinary clinic, and Gopi would have liked it because it seemed to require little work to convert to a proper medical office. It was a small storefront in a low-rent strip mall on a quiet country highway, separated from other businesses by a grassy field where a dozen long-dead oil pumps stood like big-beaked birds, a field where in the summer grazed cheaply fed hamburger cows.

It was the sort of place where in the mornings young men wearing baseball caps and Stetsons gathered in the parking lot and stood there until the sun grew hot, then move into the thin shade that rimmed the building. Gopi would have seen them when he arrived in the mornings to clean and prepare, their hats bobbing outside his office window as they waited for the pickup trucks that arrived by ones or twos, and for the men inside the trucks to point out the ones they wanted.

One day, Gopi offered one of these waiting men thirty dollars to help clear trash out of the closets and wash the walls. The man seemed happy to do it. His name, as everyone knows by now, was Vicente, and he had a big smile and looked to be about twenty-three. Gopi asked him where he was from, and Vicente answered, "Puebla, Mexico. You?"

"Madras, India," said Gopi.

We picture Gopi and young Vicente sweeping the little poops and pet foods that lay scattered on the floor. They tossed out the rusty small-animal cages stacked here and there and scrubbed the strange stains on the small metal examining table that stuck out from one wall. They followed without luck in the walls and dark closet corners the knocks and noises that Gopi was convinced were the scamperings and squeals of someone's lost and forgotten pet; and when they were finished, the place still smelled stubbornly of urine, but Gopi was pleased.

To make the office seem complete, Gopi ordered over the internet a phone, a scalpel, forceps, scissors, gauze and cotton, rubbing alcohol, bandages of various sizes, rubber gloves, a microwave oven, and, from a friend who worked in a hospital in India, a small supply of prescription drugs.

After two weeks of preparation, Gopi was open for business. At a copy store he had made a small sign advertising the alias he had decided on: DR. RAJU GOPALARAJAN, MD; WOMEN'S DIFFICULTIES AND ALL OTHER MATTERS. Now he would have taped this sign in his window. We imagine he wore a white lab coat from the local uniform-supply store, and the stethoscope that had arrived in the mail that morning, and now he put it on his ears and listened to his own heart. The sound was clear and strong, and Gopi felt overjoyed at how well he had done. Then he danced, just for a minute. Afterward, sitting down behind his desk, he grinned his little-boy grin.

Then there was quiet. No strange creatures stirred in the walls, no one rang on the telephone. And in the quiet and the stillness, the sound of Gopi's own beating heart returned to him, and for a brief moment, the poor man saw himself as if from a distance. He saw himself as we see him, sitting alone in an office on an empty country highway. A doctor? He wondered if he should have started in a smaller way, working from a room of his house, prescribing medicines for his friends, writing doctor's notes for their children. But even that prospect now seemed absurd. His face grew warm with the dawning realization that he had made a ridiculous, a gigantic mistake.

As a tension began to form in his left shoulder and the base of his skull, Gopi tried to remind himself that he had to do this in the biggest possible way, so that people would feel that he *was* a doctor. But the panic remained, and Gopi felt desperately a need for the company of people, so he walked outside and stood among the men on the sidewalk.

"Good morning, fellows," he said to them. His hands were

thrust into the pockets of his lab coat, and his stethoscope draped over his neck.

"Good morning," they said back. Gopi recognized Vicente and some of the other men, and when they saw him now in a doctor's white coat (he would have looked quite smart) one man said something in Spanish, and another said, "You're the doctor?"

Vicente added, "We didn't know you're the doctor. We thought you were making up the office for somebody else."

"I'm the doctor," Gopi said.

"Good morning, Doctor," Vicente smiled, and Gopi's tension disappeared.

Then Vicente's friend rolled up the cuff of his jeans and showed Gopi a rash of ugly white-and-black bumps on his shin, and all the men gathered around to look. And this is how Gopi Kumar, a.k.a. Dr. Raju Gopalarajan, got his first patients.

Like many of us, Gopi had wanted to be a doctor his whole life. Those of us who knew him back home remember how he thought himself a martyr for having abjured the field early on, after seeing the families of friends thrown into crisis by the necessity of paying enormous bribes to the medical school admissions committee. When his friends asked how he had done on the qualifying exams, Gopi, who had done abysmally, felt an indignant pride in telling them his score was irrelevant because he would never subject his father to the burden and indignity of groveling before those goondas.

He quit college and worked for a time as an orderly in a hospital in Madras. It wasn't work fit for a Brahmin, some people said, but he loved hospitals. He found them exciting. He'd had to lie to his father about what his actual duties were: picking up bloody dressings from the floor, handling the warm, wet test tubes of other people's urine. The doctors never liked him much—he didn't cringe and salaam, like the other orderlies, and they hesitated to give him the most menial chores, yet resented any slight resistance he offered when they did.

He met Manju around this time. At lunchtime and after work, Gopi had taken to sitting in the commissary of the college he had once attended, where he still had some friends, and talking to the girls there. He made headway with his imitations of various professors and his intimacy with the ins and outs of the college bureaucracy. And he bragged about the jobs he would one day get, the car and motorcycle and house he would eventually own, and about the life he would find one day in America. He said he had visited America once: the floors there were covered in soft carpets, and cool air and warm air was pumped from the walls, and anyone could become American, it was in the laws, and he knew it, and he would do it. And when he talked like this, in his confident manner, Manju thought he seemed, in a way, magical. It was weeks into their romance before Manju realized that Gopi wasn't a student—he was an orderly in a hospital who came to the campus only to meet gullible girls. But by then, she told herself, it was too late. Manju was in love.

Her mother, of course, would be scandalized. Even some of her friends back then were scandalized. Manju had always been a shy and proper girl, they say; the last person who should have gone in for a love match.

But her friends' surprise was based on a misunderstanding. If they had looked more closely, they would have seen that Manju's shyness was the mask of an intensely interested observer of the opposite sex. She noticed the unnoticeable, skinny, silly-looking boys who sat in her classrooms, and she surprised herself by wanting them. She knew that the answer to her mind's and body's questions could be found in these greasy-haired creatures, because it was they who had made her realize the questions were there. She searched the faces of her married cousins for some sign of difference, of the calm confidence of transcendent knowledge, of satisfaction.

And so she married Gopi, and they moved in with his parents, and Gopi took a job as a salesman so he could save money; and four years later, just as he had promised, they moved to America. And that is also roughly how long it had taken, after the move, for him to lose interest in her, and for her to lose faith in him—four years.

Gopi had jumped from job to job to job, full of schemes. He approached us once for funds to start a Big Boy franchise. If we gave at all, it was out of friendship for Manju; but what became of the project, we never heard. Even Manju couldn't tell us—Gopi refused to share the details of his business ventures with her.

Incredible enthusiasm, followed by wild and ridiculous efforts, followed by boredom and abandonment: it was the pattern he followed in all his endeavors, Manju realized; and it was the pattern he had followed with regard to her.

This, she thought, was the great ocean of the middle of marriage. The home shore had disappeared from sight, and what had appeared as infinite promise became instead a terrifying endlessness, a lonely, crushing isolation of two selves in the world.

For Gopi, of course, lost in his own head, the promise was still there, always on the verge of fulfillment. There was opportunity all around in platefuls, and one only had to take his helping.

Gopi told the man with the rash on his shin that he would take care of him the next day. Then Gopi would have gone home and consulted his library books (which he renewed every two weeks, as he planned to do indefinitely), concluding finally that the rash was either a bacterial infection or a reaction to the sun. He forged a prescription for topical antibiotic, and recommended as well an over-the-counter anti-itch ointment and sunscreen. He charged the fellow thirty-five dollars for the advice, stressing that this price was a discount because this man was the clinic's first patient. Gopi figured the sum was less than half what a regular doctor would charge someone without insurance. Within five days, the rash disappeared.

Soon, Gopi was consulting with the workers on a whole catalogue of minor ailments, and they began also to refer their families and their friends to him. He recruited additional patients in bus stops or at the mall, preferring immigrants who looked newly arrived, Indians if we appeared trusting and un-Americanized. He would strike up a conversation to get a sense of the person and then hand out one of the business cards he'd printed up. In this way, Gopi generated business with surprising speed. People with very serious-sounding problems—old men with severe chest pains, for example—Gopi reluctantly turned away, but those with more minor ailments he gamely treated, or tried to, and after two-and-a-half months he was able to cover his monthly expenses.

Those first months were giddy ones for Gopi. In the evenings, over dinner, he might tell Manju, "I sold seven televisions today."

"Very nice," she might answer. "Bring one home for us one day, that would be something."

"Soon, my dear," he would tell her. "Soon we will have big-screen televisions and nice vacations, too," and he would grin in his unaccountable way, so pleased with himself. "Don't you trust me? It'll happen, Manju, why not, I say? Why not for us?"

Manju had become by this point more or less a sensible woman, but she would find something in Gopi's manner so infectious, so suddenly appealing—almost like the Gopi of old—that she would get up and take her dirty plate to the sink just so he wouldn't see the smile rising irrepressibly to her face.

At night, he would push up against her and bite her playfully on the neck.

"Ouch!" she would yell, and give him a push on the nose. "Don't be stupid."

"Why not? One good reason," Gopi would ask.

And Manju would answer, "What would be the point?"

"The point?" Gopi would laugh. "Now you see the point?" And Manju would finally relent, thinking, "Okay, why not?"

Of course, when Gopi squeezed himself between Manju's pudding thighs, in his mind he saw pictures of Deepika Shenoy, our doctor-acquaintance Dilip's wife; or of his old favorite, Dolly Parton.

"Whose key is in ignition?" he might even blurt, in his exuberance. "Gopi the physician!" And Manju would have snorted a laugh and asked him what he meant, if she could have, but on those first nights, at least, she was too distracted by the discovery that having his warmth inside her should feel so good and familiar, even though so much time had passed.

After he fell asleep, though, Manju would experience an aftertaste of unplaceable resentment. His behavior had the effect, in other words, of sharpening her long-dormant appetite for happiness, without satisfying it. She sensed Gopi's newfound sense of purpose, but didn't understand it. She saw the outline of a different life together, but the content was missing. And in this state of directed longing, of contoured emptiness, Manju began to suspect that she was pregnant.

It was entirely plausible. Manju had confided in some of us years ago that the doctors had only ever said it would be difficult, not impossible. And now, she thought, perhaps a child had finally arrived to pull Gopi back and create the love they had never properly had. Manju could scarcely believe it, but something Gopi had said kept echoing in her mind: Why not? Why not for us?

When she made the doctor's appointment, Manju decided not to tell Gopi, or any of us, until she had gotten an answer for sure. The doctor was kind to Manju, and patient, and interested in listening, and so Manju would have told her all about her body's changes, and the discomfort, and the intermittent sickness. And the doctor examined Manju and took her blood, and a week later called her back for more tests, and after this second visit, she was drawn and pale from the strain of spending long hours in cold rooms, half naked, stared at, pricked, pried open, and fingered by more people than she could clearly remember.

She drove home that day hoping that her husband at least would have done something about dinner. But when she opened the front door Gopi was hunched over a torn sofa cushion, its foam stuffing strewn over the floor.

"What in the world are you doing?" she asked.

"Nothing," Gopi yelled in alarm. "What do you think? Only fixing the cushion." Gopi had sliced it open with a knife and removed its innards, and now he was stuffing them back in and trying to stitch it all up as cleanly as possible. He was practicing. The following day, he was scheduled to perform his first surgery.

Vicente was the patient. Gopi had noticed that the young man had a lump on his forearm the size of a kumquat. Vicente said he'd had it for years, that a doctor had told him it was harmless—simply a fat deposit—and that it would cost nine hundred dollars just to remove it. Gopi said it was an ugly thing and ought to be gotten rid of, and that he would do it for a very reasonable price. Somehow, the boy agreed.

Vicente arrived at the office with a young lady whom Gopi recognized as the woman who always rode in Vicente's car. She was short and thin and wore loose blue jeans, a white T-shirt, and sneakers. Vicente introduced her as Sandra, and Gopi smiled and shook her hand; from the way he behaved, you could not have known how nervous he was. "Mucho gusto," said the woman, and Gopi corrected her. "I'm not Spanish, I'm Indian," he said. "But that's okay. Se habla Español. Right, Vicente?"

Sandra made a noise that sounded to Gopi like "Hmph."

"Do you want to watch?" Gopi asked her, indicating the examining room. Sandra looked to Vicente, who translated the question for her. She laughed and shook her head. "Oh, no," she said. She sat down in the waiting room.

As they walked into the examining room, Gopi asked Vicente. "She your wife?" Vicente grinned, embarrassed. "Not yet, Doctor. Can't afford to get married yet."

If any of us had seen him then, we might for a moment have doubted that this was the Gopi we knew, and not a surgeon long used to taking knives to human flesh. He smiled and spoke so calmly that Vicente himself was not at all nervous when Gopi told him to sit in a chair and roll up his sleeve and lay his arm on the examining table.

The novocaine had come in the mail from India months previously, but Gopi had not had occasion to use it until now. He opened the box and found his hypodermic, then filled the syringe with the drug, eyeballing the measurement. He injected Vicente in three places around the lump and stared gravely, waiting for the arm to numb.

After eight or ten minutes, Gopi poked the arm with his finger.

"Can you feel that?" he asked.

"Only a little," Vicente replied.

Gopi didn't want to take any chances. He refilled the hypodermic and injected the young man again. After a few minutes, he directed Vicente to close his eyes.

"Am I touching you or not?" Gopi asked him.

"Don't think so," said Vicente.

"Now?"

"Uh uh."

Finally, Gopi touched Vicente's arm. "How about now?"

"Nope."

Now Gopi couldn't help himself. He giggled. Then he thwacked Vicente with three of his fingers. "Did you feel that?" he asked.

"I heard it," said Vicente. "But I didn't really feel it."

"Okay then." Gopi squirmed his fingers into latex gloves and swabbed Vicente's arm with iodine. He had sterilized the scalpel by putting it into a bowl of water that had been microwaved on "high" for fifteen minutes, and now without hesitating and without giving himself time to grow afraid, he sank the blade into Vicente's skin.

The blade sank softly. Gopi sliced a thin line along the center of Vicente's lump. Blood welled slowly from the line, and Gopi wiped it with cotton gauze. Vicente didn't appear to feel anything. It was magical, Gopi thought; it was impossible. Gopi cut smaller, horizontal lines at each end of the vertical one, and then he took a breath and with his gloved fingers pried up a flap of skin. The lump was loosely anchored, and Gopi unmoored it with tentative scalpel cuts until it slipped out, slick and rubbery, into the palm of his hand. Gopi showed it to Vicente, who took one look and slumped down in his chair.

Gopi tried to catch Vicente up as he fainted, but in doing so he dropped the lump. It slid along the floor, and Gopi dropped Vicente to stop it with one foot. He picked up the lump and put it in the sink, making a mental note to flush it in the toilet later. Then he lifted poor Vicente off the chair as best he could and shoved his limp body onto the metal examining table, which seemed designed to hold, at most, a large dog. Vicente's legs dangled off awkwardly above the knees.

"Needle and thread, please, nurse," Gopi chuckled to

himself, and then he picked up the surgical needle that he had laid out earlier on a tray, already strung with clear catgut medical suture.

Vicente woke up halfway through the stitching, and Gopi talked to him reassuringly. "Feeling better?" he asked. "Don't look. Almost done." Gopi tied a little knot and appraised his handiwork. The sutures were cragged and haphazard, but Gopi marveled that a man whose mother and wife had never let him so much as stitch a button on his own shirt could have done such a relatively clean job. Gopi covered the wound with a bandage. He washed his hands and took Vicente's cash, and advised him to go home and take lots of Tylenol. Then he gave Vicente a firm handshake, making the poor man wince.

"See me back in a month?" Gopi said.

When the two men came into the lobby, Sandra stood up. Her face was blanched.

"Qué pasó?" she asked.

She and Vicente spoke to each other in quick overlapping sentences, and Gopi interrupted. "Why is she excited? What happened?"

Vicente turned to Gopi. "She heard the commotion in there," he said. "She thought something bad happened. That's all."

"Nothing wrong," Gopi said in English. He took Sandra's hand in his. "He's a good boy. Take care of him."

Sandra frowned. As she and Vicente turned around to leave, Sandra cried out again: the back of Vicente's shirt was covered with Gopi's bloody fingerprints.

After they left, Gopi sat down. We see him as the adrenaline slowly ebbed, and he began to realize what he had just done. He had used a knife to cut into another man's body, and the man had been helped, not harmed. He had performed a surgery, and what's more, while doing so he had not had a self-conscious thought. He had become a doctor, unselfconscious, and at this realization, Gopi floated with elation. He floated above himself and understood that he was enjoying a delicious and slightly terrifying dream. And in this state of queasy exhilaration, Gopi walked outside, eager for the calming society of the men in the parking lot. But they had left already, so he visited the dry cleaner next door, hoping to make conversation with the teenaged-looking girl who worked there ("Where do you get so many hangers?"). She had gone to lunch, so Gopi walked in the gravel by the side of the long road until he reached the field of grazing cows. He talked out loud to the dumb, death-destined animals, and somehow this calmed Gopi down.

When he went home that night, before making love to his wife, he asked her, "How is it we came to be here, you and me, all alone in this country? Isn't it strange? That we thought certain thoughts that led to certain actions, and a lot of other things happened just by chance, and the net result is me lying here on top of you?"

"It is strange indeed," replied Manju, who, we would learn, had gotten some news from her doctor that day, and unbeknownst to Gopi, was experiencing her own private wonder.

At temple, on the festival of Krishna's birthday, Dr. Dilip Shenoy surprised Gopi by beckoning him over to sit at his table in the lunch hall.

"Sit with me, Gopi," Dilip said, with uncharacteristic friendliness, and Gopi wondered if this was a sign of the uncanny success of his deception—the unfriendly doctor now instinctively recognized Gopi as one of his own.

Dilip poised his thin fingers against his styrofoam lunch plate. "How are you, Gopi?" Dilip said. He had a long, serious face, and his gray hair plumed up softly. "Let's talk. What's going on?"

"Just the usual," Gopi said.

"Really? Nothing new?"

Dilip's intent stare, his tone, began now to strike Gopi as odd."But how are *you*, Dilip?" Gopi asked.

"Let us not talk about *me*," Dilip replied. He smiled, just a little. "Because, Gopi, it seems that you are the much more interesting fellow."

Inside the temple, Manju was looking at the boy Krishna in the altar, the black stone Krishna with wide gold eyes and a wise grin, blowing with his blood red lips into the flute he held there. A lovely, playful Krishna; a mischievous, hilarious Krishna; and all at once, Manju thought, a terrible, mocking Krishna, grinning at all the capricious misery he had spun.

"Krishna, Guruvayoorappa," Manju prayed. She clasped her hands and clenched her eyelids and moaned the words quietly, trying in vain to muster the fever of trust and abandon to which she could sometimes move herself at this spot.

Manju looked around at all the other people in the temple, she looked at us chatting and praying, and thought how strange it was for us to behave as if all this were so normal. Her doctors would have given her months, maybe weeks, and now she looked at us as though we were a million miles away.

We didn't know what she was going through—she never once mentioned the word cancer—nor did she have a husband she could trust or tell, who could share the weight of her dying and make her less alone. She was by herself, floating far above us, and when she turned back to lord Krishna it was with grief but also with this lonely, exhilarating anger. "Is there really no hope?" she asked him in silence. "All my life you have given me only what you have wanted to give me and not what I have asked for. But that's another way of saying you have not been there and that you have never listened to me. Is there any sign to show that you are still with me, or that you ever have been? That after loving you so much my whole pointless life, you haven't abandoned me to die?"

It was Deepika Shenoy, finally, who had the presence of mind to walk softly up to Manju and put her arm around her, and to whisper in her ear and dab the tears discreetly with a corner of Deepika's own green silk sari. She took Manju out to the lunch line in the dining hall and made sure she got a little bit of everything, and brought her to sit down with their husbands, and by then Manju was looking reasonably calm.

We ask ourselves at what point it became inevitable, and perhaps it was then. Gopi looked up from his food and was grateful for the new company. He greeted Deepika and complimented her on her sari. She had always been Gopi's triple-deluxe dream; it was embarrassingly obvious. Looking at this dream Deepika, Gopi wished Manju would eat better, smile more, wear some jewelry. Deepika laughed at something someone said and put her hand on her shaking bosom. It was a gesture that normally would have made Gopi giddy with pleasure, but now he managed only a wan smile.

Then Manju tried in her way to make small talk, but her husband interrupted her as usual.

"Not now, Manju," Gopi said, because Dilip had reached his hand into his shirt pocket and pulled out a business card, and was talking now, oblivious of the women.

"My nephew was driving to our place last weekend from College Station," Dilip was saying. "You see, he studies hard, just like I did. People like us slog for years. Don't you find us silly? He was driving home and he stopped at a gas station, where someone gave him this business card." Dilip paused now to stare intently at his acquaintance; but Gopi's eyes stayed fixed on his plate. "Someone who looked very familiar gave him *this card,*" Dilip repeated, extending the business card, clipped between two bony fingers, toward Gopi.

Gopi refused to touch it. And Manju looked at her husband and looked at the card. And at last, she herself took it from Dilip's hand.

"*Doctor Raju Gopalarajan, MD,*" Manju read slowly. "*Medical Doctor Specializing in all things specially Women's Health Matters.*"

Dilip finally turned, exultant, to Manju. "But you already know Doctor Gopalarajan, don't you?"

Manju shook her head no.

"You don't?" Dilip gave her a mordant smile. "But he's the great doctor specializing in Women's Health Matters. One of the most difficult specialities in the world, and he is an absolute master."

"Aha?"

Dilip raised his finger in mock severity. "If something cannot be cured," said Dilip, who had always been more insinuation than action, and who, after scaring Gopi, was content to leave things there at that. "If something cannot be cured," Dilip said again, turning back toward Gopi, "then ask Gopalarajan, and Gopalarajan will find the cure!" Was there any hope for poor Manju, for either of them, after that?

The next morning, when Gopi's office phone rang—it's hard to believe, but in a way it isn't—he didn't even recognize his own wife's voice, at first.

"Who's calling, please?" he asked, and she spelled her name as he had heard her spell it so many times to others.

"M like Mary A-N like Nancy J-U-K-U-M like Mary A-R."

Gopi had not prepared for this moment, but for a few seconds his quick wits came to his aid. He drew in his breath and almost without thinking asked, "Something wrong with you, madam?" He spoke in a gruff tone he hoped his wife wouldn't recognize.

"Yes," Manju said. "That's why people call doctors, isn't it? Can I make an appointment, please?"

Gopi was surprised to find that Manju's voice, transmitted over the anonymizing phone, had an authority he had never appreciated in real life, and Gopi felt suddenly uncertain of his ability to bluff through the situation.

"Hello?" Manju asked.

The silence grew, and now Gopi panicked. He hung up, and when the phone rang again, he ignored it.

He had only a few minutes to wonder what in fact was wrong with his wife when he was interrupted again, this time by Vicente and Sandra walking in through the door. They held each other's hands stiffly.

The look in their faces struck Gopi with alarm. "Sorry to bother you, doctor," Vicente said. "But seems like, maybe, there's a problem."

"I did everything well," Gopi said. "What problem? Everything is fine." Sandra's face turned red, and Vicente looked at her, then at Gopi. And then Vicente began to cry.

"He has pain," Sandra tried to explain, as she and Gopi waited for Vicente to compose himself.

Gopi saw that the young man had tied a white cloth around his forearm, and the cloth was soaked through with some dark fluid, and his hand and fingers below were plumply swollen.

When he unwrapped the bandage in the examining room a few minutes later, the smell hit Gopi so hard he staggered to the door and leaned out of it for a few moments. When he came back, he tried to breathe through his mouth. He already knew from his reading what had to be done, and that there was no time to waste. As Sandra stood anxiously at the far end of the room, Gopi anesthetized Vicente's arm and began to cut away the blackening flesh. He cut and he threw the sloppy matter into the trash can and closed the lid, but still the stench didn't go away, so Gopi cut more. Blood oozed from the cavity in Vicente's arm, filling the hole and spilling to the floor. Gopi spooned out the blood with a plastic cup and cut quickly before the hole filled again. Sandra held her hand to her mouth and cried, and Gopi told Vicente, "Tell her to stop moaning, won't you?" but Vicente's eyes were half closed and his head was nodding backward and he didn't say anything. Gopi cut more and became very frightened when finally he encountered a length of white bone.

After he and Sandra laid Vicente in the back of his car, Gopi watched Sandra drive away (on her way, we know now, to the Manvel General Emergency Room). Then he stood on the pavement, damp and terrified, and let his head slump down to see the footprint-spattered trail of red leading from inside the examining room all the way to the parking lot, to terminate there, at Gopi's feet. Inside, minutes later, he didn't notice the sound of the front door opening, or hear the footsteps leading to the examining room door, or see his wife walk in until she was two feet away from him.

Manju and Gopi stared at each other in silence. She studied her husband's bewildered eyes and looked at the lab coat he was wearing. She saw the gore-caked instruments, and she remembered Dilip Shenoy's odd expression at the temple the day before, and the voice on the phone when she had tried to make an appointment. She clutched harder the library book she held in her arms, and remembered Gopi's strange jokes in the bedroom, and the increasingly implausible stories about his advancements in television sales. And she remembered the lies Gopi had told everyone all his life.

And Gopi—exhausted, for once guileless—quietly pried the book from her trembling hands, bookmarked and dog-eared, and stared dumbly at the picture it showed: a woman's ovaries, bloated and blistering, laid out on a dissecting table, with a label that read INOPERABLE. The dull fear in his eyes was obvious to Manju.

"What's the matter?" Manju asked. She wiped her nose with the back of her hand. "You're such a famous doctor. Can't you help me? Hm?"

Gopi was unsure, for a moment, if his wife was credulous

or mocking, but something in her tone seemed to demand an answer. "I can try," he said simply.

There are those who will never accept what must have happened next. They don't understand what Manju saw in Gopi, for a few moments, here at the dying-ember end of our story. But there is a reassuring certainty to some unlucky lives, which is to say that fear has no place for persons already doomed; and a kind of calmness descended on Manju, seeing her husband covered in some other man's blood, seeing him drained and frightened. And isn't it possible that Manju herself found in Gopi's examining room the iodine and the novocaine, the knife and the needles? Manju herself lay down on the examining table, just as the Manvel General doctors, having gotten the details from Sandra, were phoning the police station.

Gopi was still nervous, no doubt. It took him some time to fathom the hopeless clarity of the situation. But Manju's calmness would have calmed him, and soon he understood there was no help for either of them outside of that room. The news stations had even somehow picked up the story—didn't some of us hear the name on the radio and wonder who this doctor was, and if maybe we had met him at a function somewhere? And on his own, without asking, Gopi picked up the scalpel, knowing the red and blue lights would soon be shimmering through the cracks in the window blinds. We are with them as he picked up the scalpel and looked in Manju's eyes, knowing what the police would have no choice but to do when they came through the door and saw him doing what he was about to do.

But now those anxious police officers were still miles away along the highway. Vicente's friends had left for work already. The dry cleaner's clerk was late as usual. Only the skinny cows in their dirt-patch field could know what noises came from that desolate office building, and so there are some who will always have doubts—who will cling to their versions with the same shiftless confidence with which those cows stood waiting under the midday sun, dulled to their own fate or anyone else's—and who will never believe what happened when Manju looked down, and followed the sure movements of Dr. Gopalarajan's fingers, and smiled.

Ms ████████████

    Please thank Mr Charles for his 2 beautiful
autographed photos & thank-you for your letter.

    I gave the black & white one to my ailing
mother. She loves Mr Charles. I would like another
black & white photo. Please have him sign it as:
WHAT I SAY? & his name. I can't tell you how much
it would mean to me. I will not bother you again.

████████████

Campbell, California 95008   Kitten

"MY AILING MOTHER"

Leif Parsons

MAJESTY

by MIRANDA JULY

I AM NOT the kind of person who is interested in Britain's royal family. I've visited computer chat rooms full of this type of person and they are people with small worlds, they don't consider the long term, they aren't concerned about the home front; they are too busy thinking about the royal family of another country. The royal clothes, the royal gossip, the royal sad times, especially the sad times, of this one family. I was only interested in the boy. The older one. At one time I didn't even know his name. If someone had shown me a picture I might have guessed who he was, but not his name, not his weight or his hobbies or the names of the girls who attend that coed university of his. If there were a map of the solar system, but instead of stars it showed people and their degrees of separation, my star would be the one you had to travel the most light-years from to get to his. You would die getting to him. You could only hope that your grandchildren's children would get to him. But they wouldn't know what to do; they wouldn't know how to hold him. And he would be dead; he would be replaced by his great-grandson's beautiful strapping son. His sons will all be beautiful and strapping royalty and my daughters will all be middle-aged women working for non-profit earthquake-preparedness organizations. We come from long lines of people destined never to meet.

All my life I have had the same dream. It's what they call recurring; it always unfolds to the same conclusion. Except for on October 9, 2002. The dream began as it always does, in a low-ceilinged land where everyone is forced to crawl around on their hands and knees. But this time I realized that everyone around me was having sex, a consequence of living horizontally. I was furious and I tried to pry the couples apart with my hands, but they were stuck together like mating beetles. Then suddenly I saw him. Will. In the dream I knew he was a celebrity but I didn't know which one. I felt very embarrassed because I knew he was used to being around cute young girls and he had probably never seen anyone who looked like me before. Then gradually I realized he had lifted up the back of my skirt and was nuzzling his face between my buns. He was doing this because he loved me. It was a kind of loving I had never known was possible. And then I woke up. That's how I used to end all my stories in school: And then I woke up. But that wasn't the end, because as I opened my eyes a car drove by outside and it was blaring music, which usually I hate and actually I think it should be illegal, but this song was so beautiful; it went like this: *All I need is a miracle, all I need is you.* Which exactly matched the feeling I was having from the dream. And then, as if I needed more evidence, I opened the *Sacramento Bee,* and there, in the World News section, was an article about Prince Charles's visit to a housing estate in Glasgow, a trip he took with his son, Prince William Arthur Philip Louis. And there was a picture. He looked just as he had when nuzzling my buns, the same lovely blond confidence, the same nose.

I typed *royal family* into a dream interpretation website, but they didn't have that in their database, so then I typed *butt* and hit INTERPRET and this came back: *To see your buttocks in your dream represents your instincts and urges.* It also said: *To dream that your buttocks are misshapen suggests undeveloped or wounded aspects of your psyche.* But my butt was shaped all right, so that let me know that my psyche was developed and the first part told me to trust my instincts, to trust my butt, the butt that trusted him.

That day I carried the dream around like a full glass of water, moving gracefully so I would not lose any of it. I have a long skirt like the one he lifted, and I wore it with a new sexual feeling. I swayed into work; I glided around the staff kitchen. My sister calls these skirts "dirndls." She means this in a derogatory way. In the afternoon she came by my office at QuakeKare to use the Xerox machine. She seemed almost surprised to see me there, as if we had bumped into each other at Kinko's. QuakeKare's mandate is to teach preparedness and support quake victims around the world. My sister likes to joke that she's practically a quake victim because her house is such a mess.

"What do you call that exactly, a dirndl?" she said.

"It's a skirt. You know it's a skirt."

"But doesn't it seem strange that the well-tailored, flattering piece of clothing that I'm wearing is also called a skirt? Shouldn't there be a distinction?"

"Not everyone thinks shorter is more arousing."

"Arousing? Did you just say arousing? Were we talking about arousal? Oh my God, I can't believe you just said that word. Say it again."

"What? Arousing."

"Don't say it! It's too much, it's like you said *fuck* or something."

"Well, I didn't."

"No. Do you think you might never fuck again? When you said Carl left you that was the first thing that came into my mind: She will never fuck again."

"Why are you like this?"

"What? Should I be all buttoned-up like you? Hush-hush? Is that healthier?"

"I'm not that buttoned-up."

"Well, I would love to go out on that limb with you, but I'm going to need some evidence of this unbuttonedness."

"I have a lover!"

But I did not say this, I did not say I am loved, I am a person worth loving, I am not dirty anywhere, ask Prince William. That night I made a list of ways to meet him in reality:

1. Go to his school to give a lecture on earthquake safety.

2. Go to the bars near his school and wait for him.

They were not mutually exclusive; they were both reasonable ways to get to know someone. People meet in bars every day and they often have sex with people they meet in bars. My sister does this all the time, or she did when she was in college. Afterward she would call me and tell me every detail of her night, not because we are close—we are not. It is because there is something wrong with her. I would almost call what she does sexual abuse, but she's my younger sister, so there must be another word for it. She's over the top. That's all I can say about her. If the top is here, where I am, she's over it, hovering over me, naked.

The next morning I woke up at six and began walking. I knew I'd never be thin, but I decided to work toward an all-over firmness that would feel okay if he touched me in the dark. After I lost ten pounds I would be ready to join a gym; until then I would just walk and walk and walk. As I moved through the neighborhood I reignited the dream, reaching such a pitch of clarity that I almost felt I would see him around the next corner. And upon seeing him I would put my head under his shirt and stay there forever. I could see sunlight streaming through the stripes of his rugby pullover; my world was small and smelled like man. In this way I was blinded and did not see the woman until she stepped right in front of me. She was wearing a yellow bathrobe.

"Shit. Did you see a little brown dog run that way? Potato!"

"No."

"Are you sure? Potato! He must have just run out. Potato!"

"I wasn't paying attention."

"Well, you would have seen him. Shit. Potato!"

"Sorry."

"Jesus. Well if you see him, grab him and bring him back over here. He's a little brown dog, his name is Potato. Potato!"

"Okay."

I walked on. It was time to concentrate on meeting him, plans 1 and 2. I've gone to other schools and discussed earthquake safety, so it wouldn't be the first time. There's a school in the neighborhood, Buckman Elementary, and every year they invite the firemen in to explain how to Stop, Drop, and Roll, and later in the day I come in and talk about earthquake safety. Sadly, there is very little you can do. You can stop, you can drop, you can jump up in the air and flap your arms, but if it's the Big One you're better off just praying. Last year one little boy asked what made me the expert, and I was honest with him. I told him I was more afraid of earthquakes than any person I knew. You have to be honest with children. I described my recurring nightmare of being smothered in rubble. Do you know what smothered means? I acted out the word, gasping with my eyes popping out, crouching down on the carpet and clawing for air. As I recovered from the demonstration he put his hand on my shoulder and gave me a leaf that was almost in the shape of a shark. He said it was the best one; he showed me other ones he had collected, all of them more leaf than shark. Mine was the sharkiest. I carried it home in my purse; I put it on the kitchen table, I looked at it before I went to bed. And then in the middle of the night I got up and pushed it down the garbage disposal. I just don't have room in my life for such a thing. One question is: Do they even have earthquakes in England? If they don't, this is the wrong approach. But if they don't, I have one more reason to want to live in the palace with him rather than convincing him to move into my apartment.

Then Potato ran by. He was a little brown dog, just like the woman said. He tore past me like he was about to miss a plane. He was gone by the time I even realized it had to be Potato. But he looked joyful and I thought: Good for him. Live the dream, Potato.

Forget the school visit. I would step into the pub. That's what they call a bar over there. I would step into the pub. I would be wearing a skirt like the one he lifted in the dream. I would see him there with his friends and bodyguards. He wouldn't notice me, he would be shining, each golden hair on his arms would be shining. I would go to the jukebox and put on "All I Need is a Miracle, All I Need is You." This would give me confidence. I would sit at the bar and order a drink and I would begin to tell a yarn. A yarn is the kind of story that winds people in, like yarn around two hands. I would wind them in, the other people at the counter. There would be one part of the story that involved participation, something people would be compelled to chant at key moments. I haven't thought of the story yet, but for example, I would say, "And again I knocked on the door and yelled—" and then everyone at the bar would chant: "Let me in! Let me in!" Eventually all the people around me would be chanting this, and the circle of chanters would grow as they gathered in curiosity. Soon William would wonder what all the fuss was about. He would walk over with a bemused smile on his face: What are the commoners doing now? I would see him there, so near to me, to every part of me, but I would not stop, I would keep spinning the yarn and the next time I knocked on the door, he would shout with everyone else: "Let me in! Let me in!" And somehow this story, this amazing story that had already drafted half the English countryside, would have a punch line that called upon William alone. It would be a new kind of punch line, totally unlike "Orange you glad I didn't say banana?" This punch line would pull him to me. He would stand before me, and with tears in his eyes he would beg me: "Let me in! Let me in!" And I would press his giant head against my chest and because the yarn wasn't quite over I would say.

"Ask my breasts, my forty-six-year-old breasts."

And he would yell into them, muffled: "Let me in, let me in!"

"And my stomach, ask my stomach."

"Let me in, let me in!"

"And get down on your knees, your Highness, and ask my vagina, that ugly beast."

"Let me in, let me in, let me in."

The sun was collapsing with a glare that seemed prehistoric; I felt not only blinded but lost, or as if I had lost something. And again she appeared, the woman in the yellow bathrobe. This time she was in a little red car. She had not even put her clothes on; she was still wearing the robe. And she was yelling "Potato" so desperately that she was forgetting to stick her head out the window. She yelled into the interior of the car, uselessly, as if Potato were within her, like God. Her vaulted cry was startling, a true wail. She had lost someone she loved, she feared for his safety, it was really happening, it was happening now. And I was involved. I was involved because, amazingly, I had just seen Potato. I ran over to the car.

"He just went that way." I pointed down the street.

"What!"

"Down Effie Street."

"Why didn't you stop him?"

"He was going so fast, it took me a moment to realize it was him."

"It was Potato?"

"Yeah."

"Was he injured?"

"No, he looked happy."

"*Happy*? He was terrified."

As soon as she said this I thought of how fast he was running and understood she was right. He was running in blind panic, in terror. A teenage Filipino boy walked up to the car and just stood there, the way people do when disaster strikes. We ignored him.

"He went that way?" She was trembling.

"Yeah, but that was at least ten minutes ago."

"Shit!"

She roared off, down Effie Street. The boy stayed with me, as if we were together in this.

"She lost her dog," I said.

He nodded and glanced around, like the dog might be right nearby.

"What's the reward?"

"I don't think there is one yet."

"She has to have a reward."

This seemed crass to me, but before I could say so, the red car returned. She was driving slowly now. She rolled down her window and I walked over with a spilled feeling inside. She was in a nightie. The yellow bathrobe had been formed into a little nest on the passenger seat, and in the nest was Potato, dead. I said I was terribly sorry. The woman responded with a look that told me I alone was responsible. I wondered how many other things had flown past me into death. Perhaps many. Perhaps I was flying past them, like the grim reaper, signaling the end. This would explain so much.

She drove off, and the boy and I were alone again. I was only a few blocks from my house, but it was hard to walk away. I didn't know what I would think about when I began moving again. William. Who was William? It felt perverse, almost illegal, to think about him now. And exhausting. Suddenly it seemed as if our relationship took mountains of strength to maintain. She was probably burying the dog in her yard right now. I looked at the boy; he was the opposite of a prince. He had nothing. When my sister was in college she used to sometimes take these boys home. She would call me the next morning:

"I could see it in his pants, it was like half hard, so I could already tell it was big."

"Please stop now."

"But when he took off his pants I almost shit on myself, I was like, Please honey, get that thing up in me, and quick!"

"I see."

"And then he took out this tiny piece of black rope or something and tied it around his cock and I'm like, what's that for? And he just laughed in this nasty-little-boy way. And I put on these tacky panties that I just got, they have a zipper in front that goes all the way around to the back. But he didn't really like those, I guess, because he just pulled them off and told me to do myself. Have you ever heard a guy say it like that? Do yourself?"

"No."

"Of course you haven't. Anyways, I was rubbing and rubbing and I was super wet and he's all rubbing it in my face and I'm going crazy for it and then, you're not going to believe this, he jizzes all over my face. Before I even get it in. Can you believe that?"

"Yes."

"Well, yeah, I guess so. I guess he was really young and he probably'd never seen such white pussy before."

And then my sister paused to listen to the sound of my breath over the phone. She could hear that I was done, I had come. So she said goodbye and I said goodbye and we hung up. It is this way between us; it has always been this way. She has always taken care of me like this. If I could quietly kill her without anyone knowing, I would.

I looked at the boy; he was looking at me as if we had already agreed on something. Just by standing beside him for a minute too long I had somehow propositioned him. I couldn't leave him without some kind of negotiation.

"You could wash my car."

"For how much?"

"Ten dollars?"

"For ten dollars I won't do anything."

"Okay."

I opened my purse and gave him ten dollars and he walked down Effie Street toward certain death and I walked home. In the recurring dream everything has already fallen down, and I'm underneath. I'm crawling, sometimes for days, under the rubble. And as I crawl I realize that this one was the Big One. It was the earthquake that shook the whole world, and every single thing was destroyed. But this isn't the scary part. That part always comes right before I wake up. I am crawling and then suddenly I remember: the earthquake happened years ago. This pain, this dying, this is just normal. This is how life is. In fact, I realize, there never was an earthquake. Life is just this way, broken, and I am crazy for dreaming of something else.

Dear Ray,

Hi, my name is ███ "The Kid" ███ I am a history buff and in love with the old west and United States history in general. I am still in school, but do plan on teaching after I complete my degree in history. My parents started me collecting old comic books and memorabilia when I was a kid. My interests have grown from cowboys and country music, to all fields of entertainment. I believe that whatever is considered entertainment at any given time, is a representation of the culture. This of course has significant historical value. Maybe not today but eventually it will. I would like to have a collection of autographed photos from celebrities to help me chronicle the changes over the past and next 50 years or so. As I do plan on teaching history, I know they will be very useful or at least interesting conversation pieces. I feel you have made a mark on the American culture/history and would love to be able to include you in my collection. Will you please send me one or two autographed photos (from your prime if posable), and sign the enclosed index card for my for my collection? I do not want to ask a personal favor of you without returning the favor. So I have enclosed an autographed index card for you. If nothing else it might help you get a good campfire going someday. Maybe a day that will live on in history. Thanking you in advance.

Sincerely

███ The Kid ███

"A HISTORY BUFF"

Nate Beaty

SNAKEBITE

by ARTHUR BRADFORD

WE WERE RIDING in a car together, Clifford, his wife Jolene, and
I. Clifford was at the wheel and Jolene sat next to him, up front.
I was in the back. We were running late, on our way to the wed-
ding of a friend named Margaret out in the hills of Virginia.
According to Jolene, I was underdressed. I had neglected to
bring a tie and, instead of shoes, I was wearing a pair of sneakers.

"You look like a jackass," said Jolene.

"It's a country wedding," I said. "This is appropriate."

Clifford refused to weigh in on the subject, but I did notice
he was wearing a tie and some nicely polished shoes. I wondered if maybe someone at the wedding might have an extra tie
I could slip on before the ceremony. There probably wasn't
time for that, though. I could put the tie on afterward, but
then everyone would know that I was just taking action after
the fact. I looked down at my ratty sneakers and realized Jolene

was probably right. Why was I always the dumbass who showed up in sneakers?

We were driving on a country road and it was spring, a sunny April day in the mountains. Clifford sped along trying to make up for lost time. The hillsides were green and popping with little white flowers. There were some yellow ones out there, too. Even a person like me, poorly dressed for a wedding and feeling glum about it, could appreciate the beauty of the day.

Jolene said, "Look at this weather. Margaret's a lucky gal. Well, about the weather anyway."

Jolene was not fond of Margaret's husband-to-be. He was a lanky plumber's assistant from Culpeper named Luke. I liked him fine, although months earlier I'd actually advised him not to get married. He had confided in me one night that he was thinking about proposing to Margaret and I told him that they didn't seem as if they were ready for that. The very next day Luke bought a ring from the pawnshop and got down on his knee. That's how much my advice was worth to him. Jolene felt that Luke was a "simpleton."

The wedding was set to take place at a farm. We were about twenty minutes away, nearly there, when we came upon a plump man waving his arms in the middle of the road. His vehicle, an older model Cadillac, was pulled off to the side, and one of his pant legs was rolled up to his knee.

"Don't stop," said Jolene. "We'll be late."

"I have to stop," said Clifford. "He's waving."

"Drive around him."

Clifford slowed down and tried to coast by slowly but the man flung himself onto the hood of our car. Clifford hit the brakes and the man just lay there on his belly, breathing heavily.

"Get off!" yelled Jolene.

"I think there's something wrong with him," I said.

"Good observation," said Jolene. "Speed up, Cliff. We're late as it is."

"Don't do that," I said.

Clifford was trying to think things over. The man on the hood lifted his head and gazed at us through the windshield. His round face was covered in sweat. He had a little brown mustache perched above his small, thin-lipped mouth.

"Help me," he said to us.

"Oh Jesus," said Jolene.

I sensed an opportunity here to make myself useful. I opened up my door and got out to confront this fellow.

"What's going on here?" I asked him.

The chubby man pointed down toward his ankle, the one with the cuff rolled up. "I got bit," he said, wincing. "Snakebite."

I stepped forward and examined the spot on his leg. There were indeed two red small holes, fang marks I suppose, where a snake, or some other small animal, had punctured him. It didn't look like anything very serious to me.

"Does it hurt?" I asked.

"Oh God yes!" said the man. "I think my leg's going numb."

Jolene leaned her head out the window and said, "Tell this person to please get off our car."

The man gave Jolene a pitiful look and slowly rolled off the hood, landing gingerly on his one good leg.

"We're late for a wedding," I explained to him.

"I think I've been poisoned," said the man. "I could really use some help. I can't drive like this. My leg's going numb."

"What did the snake look like?" I asked.

"It had stripes and some colors on its head. A little fellow. I think those are supposed to be the worst kind, the little ones, right?"

"What color was its head?" I knew very little about snakes, but this seemed like a sensible question.

"Orange, I think. Or red. Maybe white."

"Get in the car, Georgie," Jolene said to me. "We're leaving."

The snakebitten man gazed at me with beady, helpless eyes. They were like two raisins set in a mound of dough. "Don't leave me here," he said. "I'll die."

Clifford honked his horn and lurched forward.

"Please," said the man.

I decided to make an executive decision. "Hop in," I said. "We'll find a doctor at the wedding."

Jolene was disgusted. Clifford saw no way out of it and waited until we'd gotten inside before he began to drive. Jolene shook her head and muttered curse words as we picked up speed. She remained unconvinced of our passenger's plight even after we showed her the fang marks on his ankle.

"It looks like you got bit by a mouse. Are you sure it wasn't a mouse? Or a rat?"

"I'm sure, madam," said the man. His name was Wilfred Cotcher. He told us he was on his way to visit a lady acquaintance a few hours south and had stepped out of his car to relieve himself when, as he put it, "the serpent struck."

"Serpent my ass," said Jolene. "I don't believe this shit. We can't just bring a stranger to Margaret's wedding."

"He's dressed for it," I pointed out.

This was true. Wilfred was wearing a light blue suit and, I noted with envy, a sporty tie. I thought about asking him if I could borrow it, but I would have felt bad about putting him at even more of a disadvantage. I realized too late that I should have asked if he had another tie back in his car. That way I could have put it on as we were driving.

Wilfred twisted about in the cramped backseat and began to moan.

"My leg," he said. "It feels like it's full of sand. I can't look at it. Is it turning blue?"

Wilfred lifted up his leg and it was indeed a little blue. There was a bruise developing around the two holes in his ankle.

"Oh wow," I said.

Wilfred's face got pale. "I'm going to vomit," he said.

"Oh, you'd better not," said Jolene.

"I might faint," said Wilfred. "I feel dizzy."

Clifford spoke up. "What shape was its head?"

"Its head?" asked Wilfred. "Do you mean the snake's head?"

"Right," said Clifford. "Was it shaped like a triangle?"

"You mean pointy? Yes. Yes, I believe it was. Is that bad?"

"What about its eyes? Were they colored?"

"They were green. Or maybe yellow."

"Sounds like a cottonmouth to me," said Clifford.

"Is that bad?"

"Well, it's not good."

"Oh Lord," said Wilfred. "I can't feel my leg at all. Am I paralyzed?"

Right as he said that Wilfred lifted up his leg and moved it around.

"It's not paralyzed," I said.

"We need a knife," said Clifford. "Cut an X over the snakebite and suck the poison out."

"What?"

"That's what you're supposed to do. It's in the Boy Scout handbook. You suck out the poison."

"Who sucks out the poison?"

"You," said Clifford. He was looking at me. Wilfred looked at me, too. He was sweating profusely now, nodding his pudgy head.

"I'd be most appreciative," he said.

Clifford opened up the glove compartment and fished out a small penknife. He handed it to me.

"Here you go," he said.

I turned to Jolene for some sort of confirmation that this was a poor idea, but she seemed through with the matter.

"Don't look at me," she said. "You're the dumbass who let him in the car. Go ahead and suck on his foot. Maybe it'll help." She cracked a smile when she said that. This was amusing her. I took the knife from Clifford and flipped open the blade.

"Cut deep enough so that you draw blood," said Clifford. "That way you'll get most of the poison out when you suck on it."

"Is this safe?" I asked.

Wilfred was beginning to shake. "Don't worry," he said. "I can take it."

"I mean the blood," I said. "Is it safe for me to suck on blood? How far are we from the wedding? Maybe I should wait."

Clifford said, "Don't wait another minute. Every second counts when you're dealing with venom."

So now Clifford was an expert on this subject. In all the years I'd known him I'd never once heard him discuss snake venom. Wilfred trembled some more and pushed his beefy leg onto my lap.

"Please, George," he said to me. "I don't want to die. Just get it out, please."

I sized up the spot and tried to hold his leg steady. Clifford slowed down a little and turned to look back as I made the cut. The knife was not as sharp as one would like for such an operation. I had to press down pretty hard just to break the skin. Wilfred let out an anguished howl.

"Oh Jesus!" he cried.

I was making a mess of it. Instead of a neat X I carved a set of ugly gouges around the two original tooth marks.

"Quickly," said Clifford. "Suck it!"

Little curly hairs sprouted up from Wilfred's beefy leg. He was pretty much sobbing from the pain now, and sweating like a hog. His leg felt like a big wet sponge.

"That blood's going to stain your pants," said Jolene.

This was true. A line of blood trickled down Wilfred's

calf and into my lap. I wiped it away with my hand, and then leaned down and shut my eyes. I placed my lips on Wilfred's leg and sucked his salty, musky blood into my mouth. I tried not to taste it, but as soon as it hit my tongue I began to gag. I kept myself there for just a moment longer, to preserve the appearance I was still extracting something, and then I popped my head up and spit Wilfred's blood out the car window. It dribbled against the side of the car in a string of red slime.

"Turn here," said Jolene.

We'd arrived at the wedding. What an entrance! Clifford pulled the car into the middle of a bumpy meadow where everyone else had parked. Wilfred sat there heaving and mopping sweat from his brow. Clifford handed him a handkerchief and told him not to let his blood get on the car seat.

"Did you get all the poison out?" Wilfred asked me.

"I don't know," I said. "Sure. I got it. I think I did."

"Maybe you should try again," said Wilfred.

"I got most of it," I said. "I'm pretty sure."

Jolene stepped out of the car. "Damn it, we're late. Come on, Cliff, the ceremony's already started."

Clifford looked at the two of us, me underdressed and now stained with blood, and Wilfred panting dramatically in the backseat.

"We'll find a doctor at the wedding," said Clifford. "You wait here, Mr. Cotcher. Come on, George."

I got out of the car and tried to smooth out my clothes. There was a big spot of blood on my thigh and some smaller ones on my shirt. I ducked my head back in the car.

"Excuse me, Wilfred?" I said. "Do you think I could borrow your tie, just for the ceremony?"

Wilfred looked very put out by this request. I would have felt bad about asking except that I'd just sucked poison out of his leg. Plus his blood had ruined my clothes. It seemed like a reasonable trade. Wilfred grudgingly loosened his tie and placed it in my hand.

"I'm leaving," said Jolene.

"You should try to relax," Clifford said to Wilfred. "The less your heart pumps, the less the poison can spread."

"What?" said Wilfred.

Jolene grabbed Clifford and the two of them walked away.

"My leg's still numb," said Wilfred.

"We'll find a doctor," I told him. And then I added, "A good one," hoping that this would make him feel better. I trotted off across the meadow to catch up with Clifford and Jolene.

The ceremony was well under way, like Jolene had said. Everyone was sitting outside on hay bales facing the bride and groom. As we got closer we could hear the preacher saying something about the long journey they were about to embark upon together.

Jolene was mortified. "I can't believe we're late for this," she said.

"We didn't miss the vows," I pointed out. I was trying to get my tie on as we were walking.

"Who do we know here that's a doctor?" asked Clifford.

Jolene said, "Clifford, you are not going to disrupt Margaret's wedding to find a doctor for that idiot. He'll be just fine."

Clifford thought about this and, predictably, deferred to Jolene's judgment. We sat down in the back row just as our friend Amanda stood up front and began to play something on her accordion. Luke looked out over the assembled guests and swallowed deeply. He appeared pale and unhappy. Margaret's face was stern and resolute. She looked nice in her white dress, though. And there were flowers in her hair.

Amanda shut her eyes and swayed back and forth with the slow rhythm of whatever hymn it was she was playing on that accordion. The song was interminable. People began to shift about on their hay bales and look at their watches. We were all sweltering there under the sun and I became increasingly worried about Wilfred.

Finally the preacher stepped forward and made Amanda stop. She nodded and took a seat. The preacher smiled out at us and remarked at what a handsome crowd we were. Everyone chuckled. This process was taking forever. I can never understand why they always drag a wedding out like that. We all couldn't wait to get out of the sun and find the bar. It occurred to me that if Wilfred were to die now I would have sucked on his leg for nothing.

The preacher backed up and took the hands of Margaret and Luke into his. He was a bit of a hippie, this preacher, with his stringy gray hair pulled back in a tight ponytail behind his head. He wanted everyone to join in on the blessing. We were supposed to channel good energy toward them, or something like that. I looked out toward the car and saw that Wilfred had gotten up. He was standing there propped up against the car with his head resting in his hands. He peered over in our direction and then began limping awkwardly across the field. His bad leg moved stiffly, as if it were wrapped up in a cast. Eventually he fell down, face-first, and did not get up.

The preacher was about to proclaim Margaret and Luke man and wife, but first he asked us all, "Does anyone here know of a good reason why this couple should not be married here before God? Speak now, or forever hold your peace."

There was a long, uncomfortable silence while people adjusted themselves again on those scratchy hay bales. Amanda stood up and strapped on her accordion, preparing to drone through another hymn. Wilfred was still lying out there on his face and I couldn't stand it any longer. I decided to take advantage of the silence and called out, "Is anyone here a doctor?"

The entire gathering jerked their heads around and glared at me.

"I'm sorry," I said. "I have no objection to the marriage. Sorry about that. I just need to borrow a doctor. It's urgent. There's a man out in the meadow who got bit by a snake. His leg is numb."

Somebody called out, "Was its head triangle-shaped?"

I guess that was a standard question. I said we thought that it was. Someone asked if there was a rattle on its tail and I said I didn't know for sure, but thought not. An older gentleman from up front got to his feet and walked toward me.

"I'm a doctor," he said. It was Margaret's grandfather, Mr. Fiske. He was actually a veterinarian, and he had retired a few years back, but this was no time to be picky.

"I'll be right back," Mr. Fiske said to his family. "Go on without me."

Jolene shot me a look of extreme contempt. "You son of a bitch," she whispered.

Clifford stared down at his feet. Mr. Fiske hobbled up the aisle, trying to move as quickly as he could.

"We'll be right back," I promised. "I'm sorry for the disturbance."

Waves of confusion washed over Luke's face. Margaret bit her lip and prepared to soldier on. Mr. Fiske and I hustled out to the meadow and left all that behind us. I heard the preacher say, "Now, where were we?" and there were a few forced chuckles from the guests.

"I'm sorry about this, Mr. Fiske," I said. "I feel awful for pulling you away."

"It's all right," said Mr. Fiske. "I was falling asleep. I'm afraid Margaret's chosen a retard boy for a husband anyway."

"He's not so bad," I said.

"I didn't say he was bad," said Mr. Fiske. "Just slow. Now where is this sick person?"

"He's right out here," I said.

We soon came upon Wilfred lying facedown in the grass.

I was worried he had expired, but then I saw his large body rise and fall with labored breaths.

"What's gotten into him?" asked Mr. Fiske.

"He's been poisoned," I said. "Or he thinks he has."

Mr. Fiske pushed at Wilfred's fleshy side with the tip of his shoe. "Wake up," he said.

Wilfred stirred a little and lifted his head. "Is it a doctor?" he asked. "Am I dead?"

Mr. Fiske looked at me. "Where did you find this fellow?"

"He was standing by the road back there," I said. "He got out of his car to look around and something bit him. See, look at his leg."

The spot on Wilfred's leg was a bloody mess on account of my handiwork with the knife.

"A snake did that?" asked Mr. Fiske.

"No," I said. "I cut an X over the bite mark and sucked some of the poison out."

Mr. Fiske's face twisted up like he'd just eaten a lemon. "What the hell did you do that for?"

"It's in the Boy Scout handbook."

"That organization is run by a bunch of lunatics. Lunatics and homos. Did you know that?"

"I heard something about that," I said. "Clifford thinks it was a cottonmouth that bit him."

Wilfred rolled over and gazed up at us. "Am I dead? Am I going to die?"

Mr. Fiske shook his head. "No, son. No, you're not." He called everyone "son" no matter what their age. Wilfred here was probably forty years old. Mr. Fiske pulled a silver flask from his breast pocket, unscrewed the cap, and splashed some of the liquor on Wilfred's wound. Wilfred screamed.

"Oh, it stings!"

"I bet it does," said Mr. Fiske. He took a nip from the flask and then passed it to me. "You better have some of this, too, after sucking on that boy's leg."

I touched the flask to my lips and it made them tingle. The liquor went down like hot syrup.

"White lightning," said Mr. Fiske. "Disinfectant." He took back the flask and splashed a little more on Wilfred's leg. Then he made Wilfred take a swig himself.

"Whoa," said Wilfred, after drinking it down. "What was that? Is that medicine? Are you a doctor?"

"I'm a veterinarian," said Mr. Fiske. "And you'll be just fine. Quit your whining and get out of the sun."

We helped Wilfred to his feet and sat him down under a tree. Mr. Fiske gave him another hit off the flask and then told him to try to go to sleep. The ceremony was over now and we walked back to congratulate the new couple.

"Is he really going to be all right?" I asked Mr. Fiske.

"Sure he is."

Mr. Fiske and I each took one last nip from the silver flask and then he placed it back in his coat pocket.

By the time we returned most of the guests had made a beeline for the bar. It was a hard-drinking crowd and that lengthy ceremony hadn't helped things. A few people commented on the blood on my outfit, and I had to readjust my tie and button up my coat. No one seemed too concerned about Wilfred's condition. Luke's father, a wiry little fellow with strange, leathery skin, told me he had chopped the head off of a rattlesnake with an ax one time. When he went to fetch the skull as a souvenir, the detached head bit him right on the hand, "just like in *Old Yeller.*"

I didn't remember that part of *Old Yeller,* but I told him it was a remarkable story. I asked him if he'd cut an X mark over the bite and sucked out the poison.

"Everybody knows that trick don't work," he said. Everyone but Clifford and me.

I went to find Clifford, but he was busy with Jolene and

I didn't want to encounter her ire. A bluegrass band started up and people hooted as Margaret and Luke danced around in front of us. Luke got dizzy and had to sit down. Margaret's father took over and he tried to get the band to slow the tempo but they wouldn't. Then the rest of us joined in and whooped it up until dinner.

I brought a plate of barbecue over to Wilfred but he was still asleep under the tree where we'd left him. He was breathing and appeared okay, so I placed the plate of food beside him and went back to the festivities.

As dinner wound down Luke got up and told us all to be quiet. He held up his glass and said, "This is the most important day of my life so far. I never thought I'd get married. It just wasn't something I thought I'd want to do. But Margaret here convinced me it was a good idea, and well, we'll see how it goes."

Then he got out a guitar and played a Willie Nelson song, "To All the Girls I've Loved Before."

Margaret got up and said she didn't know what to say after that. "I know some of you think Luke isn't good enough for me, but you don't know him the way I do. He's a good man."

Jolene was crying but I wasn't sure what about. Clifford decided to stand up and make a speech as well.

"You two are a real inspiration, and I know you're going to be very happy," he said. "Those of us who are married already really appreciate it when our friends get hitched, too, because now we're all in it together... What I mean to say is, if you stick with it, you will find rewards. Really. Don't get divorced, especially if you have children..."

Jolene was hissing at Clifford now, telling him to cut it short and sit down. She pinched me and told me to go up there and retrieve him, but I was wary of making another spectacle of myself. Clifford rambled on a little while longer. He told us about how he and Jolene have been trying to have kids but he thinks his sperm is shaped wrong and can't swim correctly.

"Some of them have two heads," he said. "Imagine if one of them made it through and then what would happen?"

That's when Wilfred showed up. He wandered up next to Clifford and stood there with a big wide grin on his face. His light blue suit was all crumpled and his shirt was undone and there was a big splotch of barbecue sauce on his chest where I suppose he'd fallen over into the plate of food I'd left for him. He didn't seem to mind this, though. He was more relaxed, and his limp wasn't so bad. He patted Clifford on the back and then gave him a big bear hug. Clifford reciprocated and then sat down, much to Jolene's relief. Wilfred stayed up there, though, gazing out over the bewildered wedding guests with a wide joyful smile.

In a booming voice, Wilfred said, "People, I stared into the cold face of death today. I met the Grim Reaper himself, and here I am, alive to tell the tale. Now, I'm not a religious man, for the most part. I think one god is just as good as another, but today... today I found Jesus. I just want to tell you all that this wedding must be a blessed union because it has already saved one poor wretch like me. I was out there alone, loaded full of the serpent's venom, when along came these fine people."

With that, Wilfred pointed at us.

"They showed me mercy. They sucked the poison from my veins and delivered me from an eternity in Hell! Where's that bride? Where's the groom? I want to thank them personally for bringing on the angels that saved my life!"

Wilfred yanked Luke and Margaret up front with him and they all engaged in a tipsy three-way hug. Luke's father marched up there and joined them and then so did the long-haired preacher. Soon there was a whole bunch of people hugging each other in one happy mass. Even Amanda the accordion player and old Mr. Fiske joined in.

Amanda started playing "Amazing Grace" and Wilfred pushed them all away so that he could sing along. When he was done Luke's father hugged him again and they both fell down.

Jolene didn't know what to make of this. "Oh, Margaret," she said, and got up to powder her nose.

Clifford took a long sip from his drink. His eyes were all glassy in a way I'd seen them get before. Most likely he would have no memory of the night's proceedings.

After dinner they cut open the cake and then there was a big bonfire out back and Luke sang a few more songs and everyone slapped Wilfred on the back, congratulating him on surviving that snake attack. Mr. Fiske pulled out his silver flask again and Clifford took a swig and announced he needed to lie down.

"Help me with him, Georgie," said a voice from behind me. It was Jolene. I help her walk Clifford over toward the hay bales, where we laid him down in relative privacy. I started to walk back to the bonfire but Jolene just stood there looking at me. I didn't want to meet her eyes, but I could tell there was no way around it.

Jolene let out a sigh. "Clifford can't drive now. He'll be out for hours," she said.

"I'll drive," I said.

"Oh no you won't," she said.

"I'm sorry about all this, Jolene," I said. "About Wilfred. Cliff. Luke. Me..."

Jolene shook her head. "Such disappointments..." she said. I wondered which one of us was the biggest disappointment to her, or if it was just all of us put together.

Jolene's eyes got a little wet and she wiped at their edges. She looked very pretty like that. I'm not sure if I'd mentioned how pretty Jolene could be. She was quite a beauty, there was no denying that. It was sort of a shame she'd ended up with old Cliff, actually. At least that's the way I felt about it just then. I wasn't thinking too clearly. I stepped forward and bent down to kiss Jolene. I was going to show her that there were still a few good things left to look forward to. That's what I was thinking. My lips touched hers and she pulled away. It was a terrifically awkward thing to have done. She could have slapped me hard and been justified.

Instead she just said, "Um, George..."

"Oh, hey, I'm sorry."

"Right, of course."

"Let's go back to the party," I said.

"Yes, let's go. You smell like a brewery. All of you do."

I wiped my mouth with Wilfred's tie and we wandered back toward the fire.

Clifford woke up at some point and managed to drive Jolene home. They left without me, which was fine. I didn't want to have to sit in that car with them all the way back. I stuck it out until the end with Wilfred, Luke, Amanda, and that hippie preacher. Margaret had gone to bed long ago. Luke didn't want us to leave and kept making Amanda play songs on her accordion. But finally we just had to go.

Wilfred and I caught a ride back with the preacher. He dropped Wilfred off in front of his vehicle, which was still parked there by the side of the road. Wilfred said he was going to take a nap inside of his car and then continue on in the morning to meet his ladyfriend for lunch.

"I'm going to ask her to marry me," he announced. "And I want you both to be there for the wedding."

"We'd be honored," said the preacher.

"Good-bye, preacher man. And good-bye, Georgie," said Wilfred. "Thanks for saving my life. Both of you."

He gave us each a sweaty embrace and then exited the preacher's truck. After a few steps he turned around and said, "Georgie, I'd like my tie back now."

I removed it from around my neck and handed it to him. It wasn't in very good shape, but he didn't seem to mind. The sun was beginning to peek up over the mountain. Wilfred limped back across the road and then collapsed onto the hood of his car.

Memphis, TN 38141-7860
December 28, 1999

Mr. Ray Charles
███████████

Los Angeles, CA 90018

Dear Mr. Charles,

Several years ago, I began a serious autograph collection of prominent world figures. The main purpose of the collection is to pay tribute to talented individuals and personalize a chronicle of world events. (*Only a handful of people in a world of over 7 billion have been able to successfully meet your accomplishments!*). Since then, I have obtained the signatures of many individuals I admire. Among them are Indira Gandhi, Colin Powell, James A. Michener, Jack Nicholson, Nolan Ryan, Sir Anthony Hopkins, Hank Aaron, Dalai Lama, and Elizabeth Taylor; just to name a few.

I admire your work, and as stated, gather signatures for my own personal collection. I have never publicly displayed them, nor parted with any, for any reason. *I do not do this for commercial gain.* I am a serious collector who would not betray the trust given me by anyone kind enough to honor my request. *Your autograph will never be sold, or traded for any reason.* An autograph personalizes history, and you certainly have made a permanent impact on the world. *You have accomplished something that has taken great determination, dedication, talent, skill, focus and courage.* Regardless of anything else that happens on this planet, your accomplishments can never be undone.

Obviously, I would prefer an autographed photo, but I realize you must be overwhelmed with requests, and I want to honor you - not burden you. Instead, I have enclosed a stamped, self-addressed envelope with a blank 3 " x 5 " card for your autograph, should you decide in my favor of my request.

Thank you in advance for any favorable consideration. *Most of all, thank you for your positive contributions to our world.*

Sincerely yours,

P.S. Do you have a personal quote that helps you through the day?

yes, "There is nothing worse than an autograph seller / trader."

"HANK AARON, DALAI LAMA"

Matt Rota

THE LOST BREED

by YANNICK MURPHY

WE ARE IN SEARCH of a breed that is most likely lost. The breed is the Mucuchies, said to have accompanied Simón Bolívar on his conquests. I have come to help the professor, his wife, and the girl whose brother will die. I will ask people where a dog of this breed might be. I know a little of the language. I know "un poquito."

The Cadillacs should have been jeeps. We had reserved jeeps to travel the bumpy roads, to travel off the roads, through the frailejones plants that grew everywhere around where the farmers lived who kept dogs who might be the mysterious Mucuchies. At the airport, though, they did not have any jeeps for us to rent.

"No, no," I said in Spanish about the Cadillacs. "We must have jeeps. We need jeeps!" But of course I only know "un poquito" and I did not know if there was a word for jeeps, so

I said, "Heaps. We must have heaps!" thinking it sounded Spanish. But still they did not make any heaps magically appear in their lot in the hot sun where the Cadillacs gleamed all in a row.

I have known the girl whose brother will die a long time. I have been to her house. I have sat on the wide porch with her. We have stood side by side cooking in the old farm kitchen where the warped boards lean in toward the stove and food set in the back of the pans cooks faster than in the front. I have known her boyfriend who whenever he is sitting pulls her down onto his lap so she is sitting on him and so I am used to seeing him with his face half covered by her sleeve as he peeks around her when he talks to others. I have not met her brother. But there is one story I know about him. How when they were younger he made a bomb and set it off in the bottom of their empty, leaf-filled swimming pool. The blue tile cracked. The leaves blew up and over the sides of the pool and throughout their New England town as if it were fall again, when really it was winter.

Oh, hell, her name is Alice, and yes, still, her brother will die.

The professor is Duncan, his wife is Charlotte. Duncan loves the price of gas in this country. After filling up the Cadillacs, he wants to fill them up again, just because it is so cheap. Charlotte takes pictures of us. We are standing in the road, asking farmers about their dogs. We are shown a box of puppies, the mother letting us come close. But the puppies look like Saint Bernards. "Mucuchies?" I ask.

"Sí, sí," the farmer says, the stubble on his chin flecked with flaking skin. The air up here is dry. We are close to the sun. Our cheeks turn red in one afternoon. The farmer shows us his terraced fields where potatoes grow that he will sell to burger chains back in our land.

Alice drives. She follows Duncan and Charlotte's Cadillac

as Duncan drives and leads the way as we search for more dogs. I look at the map and read the guidebook. I tell Alice we should visit Pico Espejo, where it says in the guidebook we will find "eternal snow." "Or of course," I say, "we could visit Estado Barinas which is a major hunting place 'with tiggers and dears' or there is also the forest of 'permanent rain.'"

Alice says she is thirsty. She licks her lips. Duncan is not stopping. There are no signs of dogs in the town we are passing through. There is a church made entirely of stones. The church looks like children built it. The stones look like they teeter in the mountain wind. I tell Alice that the guidebook says that every year there is a reenactment in the church. Every year Baby Jesus takes his first baby steps and Mary and Joseph rejoice, but every year Baby Jesus, because he now can walk, gets lost. "The painful Virgin asks for her lost baby in every door. 'My son is lost,'" the guidebook says. "'Where might he be? I cry inconsolably. Take pity on me.' 'Go on,' the people answer her. 'Your baby is not here.'" Then the painful Virgin becomes angry. "Give me back my baby," she says to someone at their door. "You are a thief," she says.

"At last," Alice says when she sees Duncan turning off the road and stopping in front of a store. There are no lights inside. There are no fixtures on the ceiling, no lamps plugged into the walls. The store is only open when there is enough daylight for the customers to see the soda in small bottles, the flat salted fish beneath the glass countertop. The eyes of the fish are covered with grains of crusted salt. Alice buys six of the small soda bottles, and drinks two while paying at the counter. We do not know the money. We lay our bills over the counter, the flat fish now hidden. We let the woman behind the counter take what she wants of our money. She slides out a bill. Her blouse is embroidered with orange, red, and yellow flowers. The flowers are so bright they seem to light up her store and make it easier to see what's for sale. Maybe the woman has been in the reenactment at the church made entirely of stones. Maybe she plays the painful Virgin.

Alice's house has connected rooms. You can walk from the kitchen to the living room to the dining room to the study and back into the kitchen again. It saves time when you are looking for keys you cannot find—you never have to stop and turn around, you just keeping going in circles. Alice's boyfriend continues his conversation while walking through the rooms because he knows that even if Alice misses a word when he is in the room farthest from her, she will hear the rest of what he has to say very shortly and she can easily guess what words she might have missed.

Duncan is at the gas pump smiling, shaking his head, not believing the price. Charlotte is taking pictures of the only dog she has found. It is small and brown and its legs are so short and skinny they look like Slim Jims and when she reaches out it trots away. It is not a Mucuchies. It is not a dog Simón Bolívar would have taken into war. It could not possibly have trudged through eternal snow and perpetual ice on legs like Slim Jims.

We stay in a hotel for the night with a dining room that the guidebook says "overlooks the eternal snow and the perpetual ice." Duncan asks me to ask the waiter where all the dogs are in the town.

"All the dogs have gone," the waiter says.

"Gone where?"

"To the dump," the waiter says. "The dump outside of town. All the food they need is there."

"That's it," Duncan says. "We have to go to the dump at dawn. I bet that's when the town dumps their garbage. I bet that's where we'll spot a Mucuchies," he says.

Driving to the dump at dawn, the Andean mountains are purple, the tops bright white where the sun strikes the peaks before anything else on the land. In the half-light, standing on a hill of garbage that we realize is made completely of plastic coffee stirrers, we see the dogs come. Duncan has night-vision binoculars. "Are they Mucuchies?" we ask.

"Mucuchies, hell, no," he says. "They're mutts. But they have learned a great lesson, they are in perfect harmony with us. They eat our garbage." He continues to watch the dogs, all with the same Slim Jim legs gingerly walking over the hills of garbage, stopping to eat, their heads down, then up, like deer listening for hunters in the woods.

We do not find a Mucuchies. We travel south. Duncan wants to know what kinds of dogs live there. We stop on a bridge and see the bumpy head of a crocodile in the river water. I read aloud from the guidebook, "The rerained water makes an ideal place where to enjoy acuatil sports," "One can see continuous lightning without thunderclaps." The crocodile slides beneath the water. We climb back into our Cadillacs.

There is a place to see birds in the rain forest. We find it on the map. We cannot go as far as the road goes into the rain forest. "If only we had Heaps," I say, "and not these low-riding Cadillacs." We park our Cadillacs on the side where the road begins. We walk a little ways on foot.

Duncan has a bird book. We can hear the howler monkeys. We can see them sitting in the trees. "Look there," Duncan says. On the forest floor is a bright orange bird. Duncan looks through the bird book. "A Cock of the Rock," he says. He taps his finger on the page. "This bird is the rarest in the country." More of the orange birds join the first orange bird. They circle and dance together. "A lek," Duncan says. "A lek of Cock of the Rocks." Charlotte takes a picture. The howler monkeys up above start to throw things at us. Leaves fall down onto our heads and shoulders. We walk back to our Cadillacs with bits of branches and seed pods in our hair. Charlotte protects the camera, keeping it under her shirt.

We get to our hotel in the evening. There are bugs that make ticking sounds as they fly in our room. There is a bug in the bathroom on the floor that Alice thinks I should step on. The body of the bug is as big and thick as a candied date. "You step on it," I say and Alice comes into the bathroom and we stand looking at it and decide we can live with the bug.

In the morning Alice says she could use the beach. It is not too far. At the beach three boys come and sit on a boat with broken boards and they watch us. We are on our backs. We are taking in the sun. After a while, a woman comes and the boys make room for her and she sits with them and watches us. When we go for a swim, the woman tells the boys to stay on the boat with the broken boards and then she lifts up her skirt and walks in the water and watches us. Alice is good. She can ride waves all the way up to shore. All the way up to the woman's brown ankles.

That night we are in our beds. This is when it happens. This is when the phone rings and it is Alice's boyfriend. This is when Alice says, "What?" into the phone and I think how maybe the boyfriend is walking through the connected rooms in Alice's house and she cannot hear the words he has said and she has to guess what the words are that were left in one of the rooms in her house. Then Alice sits up on her bed. Her face is very red. "He is dead?" she says. She has found the missing words. They have reached her now.

He was following his friend in a car on the road. The tire blew on the friend's car and so they stopped by the guardrail. He pulled his car behind his friend's car. He worked the jack. He turned the axle. He did not know a car with a drunk at the wheel would smash into his car and that he would be killed by the force of his own car pinning him against his friend's car. He did not know his sister would be in a hotel room and hear the news and stand at the window, pushing the curtain aside, to watch the continuous lightning strike over a hillside.

Charlotte could do it. Charlotte could sit with Alice on the end of the bed and hold her and rock her. Charlotte had children of her own and Charlotte had shoulders already knowing the feel of a face pressed into them and the strange sound a sob made there in the pit of her arm. Charlotte knew when she felt the bed shaking that it was from Alice lost in crying. I sat on the floor by the bathroom. I looked at the bug that looked like a candied date in the bathroom and then it began to crawl in my direction, as if to come and comfort me.

It was the end of our trip. We returned the Cadillacs we wished were jeeps back to the airport and there, in the rental parking lot, were two brand-new jeeps that probably should have been ours and we wondered how our trip would have turned out different if we had had those jeeps instead of the Cadillacs and Duncan said it wouldn't have been different at all. Alice looked at the jeeps a while and I thought maybe she was thinking how it could have been different, but then she had been looking at things for a long time all day.

She had looked at a picture in the guidebook of the eternal snow a long time without even turning the page while I drove the Cadillac to the airport. She had looked for a long time at an ashtray in a gift shop when we stopped for gas. She looked at it for so long, I was about to tell her to hurry. I wanted to tell her we shouldn't miss our plane, but then she finally took the hoof ashtray and brought it to the counter and paid for it, fanning out the money in her hands to the cashier so he would take what he needed. She bought it for her boyfriend, even though he didn't smoke. She held it in her lap on the ride to the airport. She smoothed down the hair on the leg of the steer so that strands of it covered the hard black hoof.

There were birders on the plane. The birders went through the aisles visiting one another. They pulled out white sheets of paper. They checked off birds they had seen on their trip. Alice nudged my shoulder and then, to one birder standing next to us in the aisle she said, "Excuse me." Then Alice smiled. "Did you get a chance to see the Cock of the Rock?" she said.

"Well, we flew out here specifically to see one, but we didn't. No one's seen the Cock of the Rock on a birding trip for a good ten years," the birder said.

"Really?" Alice said. "We saw one."

"No!" the birder said.

"Really, we saw more than one. We saw a lek," Alice said. The birder gasped.

"A lek!" he said. "My god, where?" he said. We had our map. We showed him where. "But we were there, we went for miles into the heart of that place!" he said.

By now all the birders who could surround our seats were surrounding us. They wanted to know exactly where we saw the bird. Alice told them we had Cadillacs, not Heaps. Alice told them we could not drive into the heart of the place because of the low-riding Cadillacs. She said we hardly drove on the forest road. "We pulled off at the start of the road," she said. "We did not walk far at all," she said. "Maybe twenty yards or so into the trees," she said. The birders' mouths were open. The birders wanted to turn the plane around. They quickly made a plan. The birders would land in our country, they would start another trip. They would rent Cadillacs this time, to hell with the Heaps they had rented. The Cadillacs made all the difference, they reasoned. Alice smiled. "Yes," she said to the birders, "it very well could have been the Cadillacs."

When we landed, Alice's boyfriend was there to pick us up. While we waited for our bags to come off the carousel, Alice's boyfriend sat down, and he pulled Alice onto him so she was sitting on his lap. He peeked around her shoulder to talk to us. He asked Duncan and Charlotte about the Mucuchies breed and Duncan showed him photos of the dump and the dogs at the dump that lived there and who did not have an ounce of blood in common with any dog that may have traveled with Simón Bolívar while he conquered a country.

*   *   *

Years later, Alice's family and mine were invited to a Day of the Dead potluck dinner. Everyone brought the favorite meal of one of their relatives who had died. Other people at the party had spent hours cooking dishes like Chicken Marbella and veal medallions in white wine.

"I'm lucky," Alice said to me in the kitchen. "I have it easy. My brother liked mac and cheese from a box."

Alice and I both had baby girls, and at one point during the dinner they were both hungry at the same time. Alice and I both excused ourselves and got up from the dining-room table and went and sat in rockers in the living room. We both lifted up our shirts at the same time. When our milk let down at the same time, we knew it, and we started to laugh. We could not stop laughing and our baby girls still nursed, securely latched, the closest things to our shaking selves.

Hello,

How are you? I hope you are well.

I've always wanted to write to you. My husband and I are fans.

We have always wanted to see you. If you do decide to come to Tucson we will attend.

Curt and I have sure enjoyed your book and music.

Brother Ray is the only talking book he will read other than the ones on The Beatles.

He agrees about the subjects of institutionalization, braille and the steriotypes society sticks on persons who are sightless.

He prefers the sight guided technique.

The piano store he tunes for doesn't mind guiding him.

He doesn't have a guide dog.

He has tuned pianos for Lou Rawls, Dinah Shore Journey, Frank Sanatra,

He met Elvis and the Beatles.

We both lived in Europe as kids,

His dad, the air force.

My dad, a company did contract work for the V.S. Goverment.

We both were premature babies.

Stay Cool,

██████████

"CAUGHT WITH SPERMICIDE"

P.S. Funny things happen about being visually
impaired
when...
 1. ~~Being~~ Being caught with ~~s~~ spermacide
in place of ~~toothpaste~~ toothpaste on your
brush
2. Ketchup mistaken for jelly on Peanut
   Butter & jelly sandwich
3. Stewed peaches accidentally in place
   of tomatoes for Enchiladas
4. Waiting at the drive thru at the
   Bank ~~of~~ on foot

Nate Beaty

THE BALLOON

by A. NATHAN WEST

I NEVER ENJOYED visiting my grandparents. On the drive up
the mountain that led to their house, the road forked, and it
was necessary to cross the opposing lane of traffic to continue
upward. I was always afraid. My grandparents never remembered anything about me and asked me the same questions
about myself every time I saw them, and they would slip me
embarrassingly small sums of money; approaching from both
sides, veering their faintly wobbling faces toward mine, so
that I could smell Joan's makeup and George's cheap, fumy
aftershave, they would wink as one of them produced a fifty-
cent piece or a dollar bill folded to resemble a peacock. I suppose the rarity of the one and the novelty of the other were
meant as recompense for the many things they could not buy.
Because of my gloomy and scrupulous temperament, I could
only partly smile, my lips turned in, and even this falsehood

troubled me. I would have to turn my eyes away. Since I had enjoyed a brand of meatball soup when I was five, a can was warmed up for me every time I came, and the flavor underwent, through the years, that mysterious metamorphosis from delightful to familiar, tiresome to nauseating. They would each take one of my hands and guide me to their garden, where their favorite old chestnut or walnut grew, I'm not sure which, a billowing green cloud with a rough, scored trunk, as well as certain fruits and vegetables they cared for which meant nothing to me.

Then one year Joan had both breasts removed, and a while later she died. Afterward, my grandfather was left less a person than a custodian of the life they had shared. He couldn't help mentioning her; he continued to rise early, although he often complained that she would never let him sleep in, and he still stepped outside to smoke his pipe. A fragile film of drab dust drifted down onto the shelves and end tables, each day thicker. He kept Joan's piano and the reams of sheet music on top of it, and would have liked, I think, to keep her clothes, too; but one day, when my father wanted to take me into the attic to show me a glass case of beetles he had caught as a boy, we walked past George's bedroom and saw him, eyes closed, his pale pink brow surrounded by a bloodless burst of wrinkles, holding one of Joan's shirts to his face and sniffing it. An hour later, as we were standing by our cars about to leave, my father relayed what we had seen to my aunt Melissa, as if it were a bit of sleazy gossip, then whistled a sustained high note and twirled his index finger in a circle beside his ear. The next time we came, my father and Melissa put Joan's clothes into trash bags to give to the Salvation Army. George asked what they were doing, and my father hissed. "What are you going to do with them? They're not doing you any good. You should at least give them to somebody who needs them."

"I'll do it myself," George said.

"Why should you? Meliss and I have already got it taken care of."

I wonder do we decide to grow old. I saw once on television a frenetic and strangely dressed eighty-year-old man pulling a coal car along a track by a chain attached to a leather bit in his teeth. He claimed that science had yet to prove the link between the dimming of the faculties and aging, and he offered a vitamin powder for sale over the phone; and a kung fu instructor who drew me into conversation while I was waiting for a ride at a service station claimed to have met two-hundred-year-old men in China. It strikes me as regrettable that the aged should bear the blame for their disintegration; yet it is true that a pitiful but not wholly involuntary change overcame my grandfather. He began to wear every day the same slacks, slippers, and white T-shirt, the last becoming finally brown and baggy through overuse. He shaved less, and ended up resembling a stranded mountaineer with rime-caked throat and cheeks. He would leave the television on without the sound, and abandoned most other foods in favor of thin chocolate-covered mints, the empty jade boxes of which were cast away in all corners of the house.

Rather than answer George's sorrows by consoling him, my father himself plunged into melancholy, sometimes for days saying only the barest few words, and when he spoke, he would mourn George's new impairments, which I could not perceive and which he failed to describe or name. When he and Melissa took a drink in the kitchen after shuffling their father back to his room, they would predict his doom, egging one another on like two eager, imaginative children, proposing either Alzheimer's or dementia with crestfallen airs of enthusiastic and improvised grief. Driving home afterward, my father would expel a deep breath in weary disgust and announce,

"George is really losing it." He would shake his head. His chin sometimes shivered, and then tears would scroll down his face.

One day Melissa called my father's cell phone. I could hear her nasal low. "You're not going to believe this," she said.

"What?"

"George wet the goddamn bed last night."

"Jesus Christ."

We drove that afternoon to a Super Wal-Mart on the northern border of the city and bought an enormous square package of Tranquility disposable briefs. I recall looking at the miserable shoppers, many obese and slovenly, and particularly at a girl in her twenties one place ahead of us in line, around whose cart clambered three children, sobbing and begging for candy, and who was six-or-more-months pregnant. In her cart were palettes of multicolored sugar drinks in plastic bottles shaped like tiny casks. The spectacle of her, the thought of George's gathering devastation, and the absence of tenderness that prevailed between my father and me provoked, in regards to the idea of human increase in the world, a sudden, painful unease that has only deepened in the intervening years. It was not comfortable to be seen with the diapers, and, as if to excuse himself, my father took a Twix from the shelves beside the checkout line and placed it first on the belt.

The Tranquilities heralded a series of lamentable presents we bought my grandfather. There was a walker, with two blunt feet in the back and two wheels in the front, so one needn't strain to lift it up. When George, somewhat hurt, said he had no use for it, my father shouted, "Good God, you don't have to use it if you don't want to, just leave it in the damn corner. I just brought it because I care about you and I don't want you to hurt yourself." My father was incapable of moderating the rages that could explode from within him—I never once saw him simply angry or annoyed—and he left the room murmuring obscenities, letting George feel selfish for having defended his own dignity, his eyes straying through the room in search of a consoling detail, like those of an unwelcome ghost. And on his seventy-second birthday, my father handed him a square box wrapped in red foil, about six inches per side. George whined that he had everything he needed, that no one should be hassled at his expense, but a slim red smile extended itself within his white whiskers, cracking to reveal the bluish tips of his teeth.

"Well, open it," my father said.

It was a blood-pressure cuff. George asked what he was supposed to do with it. "Well, duh," my father said, being fond, like many middle-aged people, of using what he took to be the fashionable expressions of the young a few years after they had gone stale. He gave George a brief and humiliating lecture about the dangers of high blood pressure and demonstrated the usage of the cuff. "We've been a little worried about your diet," Melissa said, "and we just want you to keep track of things a little better so we can always know you're all right. We want to have you around as long as possible."

As though to fulfill his duty, George began to display not long afterward the mental defects Melissa and my father had complained of. We went to keep him company a few weeks before Thanksgiving. Melissa had made mulled wine, and we were all drinking and playing board games. Over time, we lost interest in the game, and the chats between moves lengthened and turned to family reminiscences. Melissa squeezed two deep creases between her brows and pressed the fingertips of one hand against her temple—she was trying to think of something—and after a moment she said, "George, what year was it that we moved into this house?"

"Well," George whispered, and cast his squinted green eyes toward a dusty cluster of glass grapes, a kind of bizarre chandelier, that hung from an exposed wood rafter. "It was two years after we got Mr. Whiskers, so it must have been maybe...

1955?" Mr. Whiskers, a fat, complacent tabby, was lying in a half circle on my grandfather's lap, languidly licking his paw-pads and purring mechanically.

Melissa's face froze, her eyes swelled, and she turned her chin counterclockwise in exaggerated shock. My father puckered his lips and lifted his brows. They stared at each other, turning pink as they stifled laughter. George, mistaking their mirth for ambient good feeling, smiled as well. He asked that we excuse him a moment. He shuffled down the hallway toward the bathroom, dragging his slippers, and with each step, a tiny fart escaped him. This was the limit for my father and aunt, who were already drunk. They covered their faces with their hands and burst into teary snorts and giggles.

At last it came to light that Mr. Whiskers, a stout, perhaps even immortal feline, had been with George throughout the latter's life. He would recount to me their adventures together in long, haunting tales that became increasingly fabulous and heroic. He had given himself over entirely to dreaming. One of the last times I saw him, I was sitting on a squat wooden stepladder in his kitchen and he at a seat at the table, stuffing recipes and coupons into green metal cases. My father had left us alone, and George was, I think, trying to "get closer" to me, as we are always resolving to do with one estranged person or another. He was recounting his father's indecision about whether to live on the mountain or in the valley, and he mentioned that he, his parents, and his siblings were exploring the city's neighborhoods, which looked very different then, on a raft made of logs. Mr. Whiskers had twice run it aground near Cress's Cove, and George and his father had sunk thigh-deep in mud pushing it back into the river. "But when we all went to sleep that night, with no light to see by but the stars, Mr. Whiskers drove us back to the very same spot, and when we woke up my father said, 'Well, if he keeps bringing us back here there must be something to it,' and that's where my family settled down."

I remember what happened soon after that with shame.
I had just learned to drive, and my father woke me one morning
and told me to go to Melissa's to pick her up. I asked why, and
he replied, with a preoccupied air, as if he shouldn't have to
speak to me, "It's something to do with George." When
I returned, the three of us went in my father's car, without talking, up the mountain. George was still asleep when we entered.
Books splayed open, underwear, and the gaping gray tubes of
socks covered his bedroom floor. George lay on his side in bed,
the shiny white diaper huge against his small waist and frail
legs, and his tired eyelids, like wet newsprint, thin and softly
shifting. My father shook him by the shoulder. "Dad? Dad,
wake up," he whispered.

Melissa asked my father and me to wait in the kitchen and
said that she would dress him. When she brought him out a
few minutes later, he was wearing a safari hat—I had given it
to him one Christmas, one of those gifts we buy to imitate
affection when we know nothing about a person, and which
I had never seen since—with a thick wool jacket, jeans, and a
pair of hiking boots. He leaned on her straightened forearm
and she walked him outside to the car.

For half an hour we passed over narrow, wooded roads in
the city's outskirts, through dilapidated suburbs where weeds
like green wheat grew to head-height and hid the facades of
houses from view. I saw dead animals, rusted, abandoned cars,
and other signs of decay. My father turned onto a gravel path
lined by elephant-gray, leafless trees, the low boughs of which
screeched against the roof of the car. He stopped in a clearing
beside a pond uncreased by wind that glowed white in the
dawning sun, and through the windshield, a few yards away,
I saw the vast red dome of a hot-air balloon.

"What are we doing?" George asked.

They left the front seats to help him from the car, and he
gave a single, futile elbow-jerk before allowing his pride to

perish. "What are we doing?" he asked again. My father, staring away with a stoic pout, grasped again the freed elbow, and Melissa, beginning to sniffle and wipe her eyes, slipped her mittened hand in George's. "Oh, Dad, please be strong," she said.

And as he had with the blood-pressure cuff, my father began to give directions—to avoid power lines, to gain or shed altitude by adjustment of the flow of propane—and he pointed upward into the balloon's throat, past the brass plates overhead and the spitting jet that flushed out bloated ribbons of flame, toward the flap in the top that might be opened in case of emergencies. While Melissa helped George in, my father discussed the history of the balloon as a mode of travel, held his chin reverently between his thumb and two fingers while thinking of the cotton vessels the pre-Incas might have flown over the Nazca plains in Peru, and commented that balloon races, so-called, were not really races at all, but contests of accuracy, with pilots dropping objects onto targets from the sky. He ended with a rousing quotation on flight that he may have memorized for the occasion. George, kneeling in the basket, began to cry. Only his face, puppetlike, was visible above the lip. My father stroked his cheek with a palm and we cut the cords that held him to earth. "I love you," George shouted as the balloon began to lift. We could see his face looking down at us from the basket, a wan swatch touched with gold, wounded by the deepest incomprehension; ignorant, as I was, of where he was going and why. At length the white face was no longer distinguishable from the drifting dot, and then the red dot, too, disappeared, swallowed whole by the clouds.

04-835 Warszawa 94
Poland

Warsaw,4.10.99.

Maestro
RAY CHARLES
U S A

Dear Maestro,
    I would like to ask of You kindly,with respect,for a favour.Excuse
me,please,my resolutenes,my poor English...I am writing very late.But
scarcely,now,when Cold War,Iron Curtain,communism/censorship,etc,/is
over I can write outside Poland safely.And now,when I found in CELE-
BRITY DIRECTORY Your,Maestro,correct address it is beyond my power.
    Since 1950 year collecting of autographs of eminent personages,who
are leaving indelible sign on world's destiny through their political
consequence or eminent artistic,scientific or technical talent,is my
life's passion.
    You are my the Greatest Fascination,Dream Legend of Music,King of
World's Jazz,IMMORTAL...
    Therefore I would be feeling especially honoured and proud if I co-
uld supplement and to add splendour my collection with Your,Maestro,
authentic/as a shake hand!/autograph or a photograph with an inscrip-
tion.
    Kingdom for it - PLEASE !!!

                              Respectfully Yours

"MAESTRO"

Robert Goodin

LAST WORDS

by HOLLY TAVEL

IT WAS NOT I who killed the last remaining Slaty-Crowned Bulbul, says the Hyacinth Macaw, though I was there when it happened. I flew far away from the place of my birth, across and through and under skies, and over and under moons. The fat figs dropped down. I opened my beak to catch them on my tongue, but they slid past and plunged into the sea, making no sound. My eye turned with the tides.

The Hyacinth Macaw is lying, of course. Such stories! It was born here in Pickettsville and has lived here all its life. Of that I am certain. We have not known each other very long. I won it in a bet, from a lowlife. The next morning it was delivered in a panel van by one of the lowlife's associates, a man wearing women's sunglasses and no shirt. Shaky-kneed, he climbed up my front lawn and deposited there a sagging cardboard box with holes in the top. The box shuddered. A monkey sat in the van's passenger seat holding a small plastic radio. I waved at the monkey from my front porch, having always been fond of monkeys. The monkey turned, squinting into the sun, and drawing its lips back over its teeth, spat, in my general direction, something wadded and fuzzy.

The Hyacinth Macaw says: Once, a great many years ago, I belonged to a Galician brigand named Iago Otero Souza. Iago Otero Souza when he walked made a sound like wooden wheels bumping over stone. He was made largely of wood, except for his teeth, which were fashioned of hammered bronze. Oh! What adventures we had together, Iago Otero Souza and I! In the evenings he took off his wooden leg and I climbed inside. When we made land at the port of Oran I rode not upon his shoulder but atop his lacquered head. My name then was Xurxo Ponte, and I had my own quarters on board the galleon ship. Iago Otero Souza used to say to me of a silent starless evening, *Xurxo Ponte, one day I will open my mouth and swallow up the sea. The world will fall to its knees. All will tremble before me. Kings and emperors, sultans and tsars will ply me with all the jewels and riches of the world, with twilit maidens and tender boys, with these things they will try to make me give back the sea. But, ah! Mermaids will live in my belly, Xurxo Ponte, and sea-dragons in my generous loins. I will be the greatest pirate who has ever lived! The pirate who stole the sea!*

Iago Otero Souza, I would say, you are not a pirate but a poet.

Iago Otero Souza would laugh rusty bells and his body would make a sound like wooden wheels rolling over stone.

You will see, Xurxo Ponte, you will see, he would say.

Then he would rap me lightly on the head with his great

gold-banded knuckle and feed me pomegranates. The pomegranates of the moon!

I say to the Hyacinth Macaw: Macaw, your stories are very
amusing. But that is simply not possible. No, no, no, Macaw.
That was not you, but another of your kind.

The Hyacinth Macaw says: There is no difference.

For the first few weeks I had the Hyacinth Macaw it did not say
anything at all. At the pet store in town I purchased a large parrot cage, a deluxe model, and from the organic produce vendor in
the market square I purchased bushels of tropical fruit, which
I stored in the garage. I placed branches and twigs in the
Macaw's cage, beaded toys, a large mirror. For several days, before
I was able to acquire these things, the Macaw lived on top of the
refrigerator. When I went to get something out of the refrigerator, a head of lettuce or a bottle of juice, it would be sitting there.
We avoided making eye contact. I walked through the rooms of
my house. I sat on a garden bench, afraid to go inside. I did not
know what to do with such an ostentatious frivolous thing,
whose ostentatious frivolity made my shabby gray secondhand
furniture appear even more shabby and gray and secondhand.
The mechanical movements of its head disturbed me, swiveling
on its neck as though turned by an invisible hand. The hard,
glossy eye, the crustaceous beak. I read once, in some book or
other, that birds are closely related to reptiles. Whenever I looked
at the Hyacinth Macaw I could not help but see, beneath the
bright and carefully arranged feathers, the dull slickness of scales.

I say: It is all very entertaining, this talk of piracy on the high
seas. But that simply cannot be, Macaw. Perhaps you mistook

the lowlife for a pirate, and the panel van for a galleon ship? Perhaps you only imagined these things, while you were inside the cardboard box—the wooden wheels bumping over stone, the rusty bells? It is an understandable mistake, Macaw, I say. But enough is enough. The Macaw, lifting a palm nut to its beak, cleanly slices the shell into two neat halves, and says:

Once, a Great Conference of Vanishing Birds was held. It was held on a very small and nameless island in the Pacific Ocean. Each of these birds was the very last, or very nearly the last, of its kind. It was on that very small, very white island that the Slaty-Crowned Bulbul met its ultimate demise. This was, you must understand, nearly one hundred years ago. At that time I was living with my mate and child many miles and moons away in a hollow of a Manduvi tree. We had yellow days and green days. On yellow days thousands of us, all alike, would gather at the clay lick to lick up all the clay. The sound of us spread out over the cliffs and along the river where the people who lived nearby crouched, dark and low. One day I did not go with the others to the clay lick but stayed, instead, in the Manduvi tree. I was nursing a minor headache after eating some soft bitter berries I had discovered in a hole dug by the locals. A bad monkey came along and jeered at me. *Arara azul,* said the bad monkey, *you are a very great fool.* And he slunk away trailing his stink behind him like a kite, laughing.

I say to the Macaw: Macaw, you know that I enjoy your stories. But you are, according to the avian veterinarian we visited, if you will recall, just last week, less than ten years old. A young parrot! You have never lived in a hollow of a Manduvi tree near a river, nor flown above cliffs, nor visited a clay lick, and you have never, I am sorry to say, had a mate, Macaw. Besides, everyone knows that monkeys are not bad, but delightful. What's more, they cannot help the stink. Macaw: it is not their fault.

The Hyacinth Macaw says: I don't believe the berries had anything to do with it, despite what certain monkeys would say. I waited for my mate and child to return. When they returned, bursting with clay from the clay lick, I would nudge the dry clay from their beaks to cure my headache. I heard the susurration of footsteps among the fallen leaves, but it was not a human who appeared just then, in a sudden clearing, but a bird, the strangest bird I had ever seen. It was quite ugly and dull-looking, and I trembled in my hollow, for I believed that the bird must be a kind of god, though I had never heard of any bird-god, or of any birds believing in gods or of any gods appearing to birds. The only gods I had ever heard of or known about belonged to the low-crouching humans, and their gods did not scare us in the least.

I say to the Macaw: Macaw, I have to go to the market now. The cupboard is bare. While there I will buy some grapes for you. Would you like the purple grapes or the less-purple ones?

Both, says the Macaw.

I cannot afford both, I say. I am not rich, and it is expensive enough to keep you as it is. Now then. Purple or less purple?

Both, says the Hyacinth Macaw.

Not both, I say.

All right. Less purple.

Less purple it is, I say.

And pomegranates, says the Hyacinth Macaw.

Later in the week, I purchase, from the hardware store in the center of town: one dozen bags of plaster of Paris mix, a hammer and a box of assorted-size nails, several large, thick blocks of styrofoam, screws, wood glue, liquid cement, half a dozen sheets of plywood, a large roll of brown paper, a drill, one hundred square feet of low-pile carpeting, ten gallons of paint in different shades of brown and green, an awl, a crowbar, a handsaw and sawhorse, a power generator, a home water-filtration system, and a shiny red wheelbarrow.

The Hyacinth Macaw says: Above me, the sky was as smooth and pale as an egg. Bocaiuva nuts fell from the heavens, and the day was very yellow. The ugly, dull-looking bird, from the sudden clearing, said to me: *I am called Dodo, and have been dead these two hundred years. My real name has long been forgotten by everyone, including myself. I was buried in an automobile graveyard in Peoria, in the great and shining land of Illinois. A band of hard-worn and gleaming conquistadors from the seventeenth century showed up the next day and unburied me. My legs were cut off and became handles for umbrellas opened by Englishmen in light drizzles, my beak became the spittoon of an old wayfarer, my feathers stuffed the nuptial pillow of a child bride, my bones were ground to the finest dust and sifted into the sands of Mauritius where they remain to this day. A pirate danced on my grave; a monkey fell out of a tree. A fog stole in to observe, silently. I come to you as neither ghost nor memory, but as a palimpsest upon which is printed, in darkest red ink, a likeness of myself in profile, and a mark that spreads beyond my boundaries and consumes, like a rot, the heart of the bird it has chosen. I am ugly and stupid, it is true, but my mark is indelible. Beware the mark of the Dodo!*

Yes, I see, I said to the bird called Dodo, but what is this mark you speak of? Even as I spoke the words I felt the mark hovering around me like a black-winged moth, and recoiled deeper into my hollow. I decided then and there to have nothing more to do with soft bitter berries, or with bad laughing monkeys and their ilk.

When the last bird of its kind has vanished from the earth, said the Dodo, *the mark will be all that is left of it.* To be sure, says the Hyacinth Macaw, this explained nothing, or very nearly nothing, and I waited for the Dodo to say more. In the near distance a great streak of brilliant blue cut the sky in half, and the day was turning from yellow to green. It was a flock of others of my kind, returning from the clay lick. There were so many of us!

The Dodo said: *Hyacinth Macaw, fly to the smallest and whitest island in the Pacific Ocean. Fly to the top of the highest tree and wait. Observe quietly. Soon the birds will gather on the island. Each of them has seen me, or a likeness of me, in spreading red ink, or in blue, and each one, stupider than the last, has come to know his own name, thanks to me, the stupidest of all! Each one carries upon him my mark, and the knowledge of this mark, though he himself cannot see it.*

The Dodo had become a shimmer, and I looked up into the convex shadow of a black wave that had appeared, and the ground thundered beneath me, says the Hyacinth Macaw.

It occurs to me that I am beginning to believe the Hyacinth Macaw's lies.

One night a dark shape crawls across the window. The Hyacinth Macaw stretches and cocks its head to one side, and blue-purple feathers ripple, one by one, along its outstretched wings. I part the curtains and see, on my ransacked front lawn, next to my car up on blocks, in a damp wedge of moonlight, the lowlife, the lowlife's associate, and the monkey, with bottles of whiskey and ratchety music coming from the small plastic radio. The monkey is the only one still standing. I peer through the window while dialing the number for the local police. The voice on the other end of the line says: *Yes. Yes. Is this an emergency?*

While I wait, in my bathrobe, for the police to arrive, I occupy myself reading from a book I have recently purchased entitled *The Care and Training of Your New Parrot.* On the cover of the book is a photograph of a Rainbow Amazon with a nut in its beak, looking right at me. The Hyacinth Macaw sits on the table with the bowl of plastic fruit, its talons curling and uncurling like a slow breathing. From the front lawn I can no longer hear the radio music. By the time the police arrive the lowlife, the lowlife's associate, and the monkey are long gone.

Can you describe this monkey? they say, the two policemen, standing in my living room eyeing the Hyacinth Macaw nervously.

It sounded like a yodel yodeled from the bottom of a deep well, I say.

The monkey? says the first policeman, bursting at the seams.

The music, I say.

And the lowlife? says the second policeman.

I've seen him around, I say.

It was an ordinary monkey, I say.

Well, says the policeman.

I tack to the wall in the dining room a large map of the world. I show it to the Hyacinth Macaw, who cleans a talon, feigning boredom. I am beginning to believe its lies, but also to know its tricks. Right here, I say, pointing, is the general location of the Brazilian Pantanal, and your so-called Manduvi tree. I mark it with a black magic marker. And here—I point to a tiny white dot a great distance away—is, if my calculations are correct, the approximate location of the island where the Great Conference was held, or so you claim, I say. When I mark the white dot with the black magic marker it disappears completely.

The Hyacinth Macaw says:

We came from all the corners of the world,

each a palimpsest in a stage of erasure,
each one well on his way to becoming imaginary,
each of us a variation on a theme.
The Fasciated Tiger-Bittern's legs were a drawing of legs,
The Spectacled Cormorant's filoplumes were a drawing of filoplumes,
The Labrador Duck's waddle was a drawing of a waddle,
The New Caledonian Wood Rail's head was a drawing of a head,
The Canarian Black Oystercatcher's head was beginning to become see-through,
The Grosbeak-Weaver's head was completely see-through,
The Rufous-Sided Towhee was half live Rufous-Sided Towhee and half drawing,
The Orange-Breasted Flowerpecker was an orange breast, floating, nothing more,
The Slaty-Crowned Bulbul was all there but not for long.

One day a small manila envelope arrives in the mail, badly torn and dirtied, and bearing no return address. I take the envelope inside my house and open it. It contains a cassette tape, a very cheap brand, with a label on one side that says "Sounds of Amazonia." In the hall closet I manage to locate an ancient tape recorder I purchased long ago at a neighborhood garage sale. I place the cassette tape in the tape recorder and press play.

The Hyacinth Macaw says:
The Guadalupe Flicker's beak had faded completely away and so it could not speak;
The Chatham Island Bellbird's legs had faded completely away and so it could not walk;

The Forest Spotted Owlet was a mere sketch of a Forest
Spotted Owlet;

The Mangareva Kingfisher was a pair of bones walking
hand in hand;

The Bourbon-Crested Starling was a vague idea of a starling;

The Carolina Parakeet was half para half keet;

The Réunion Solitaire was patiently awaiting its own return.

The next day, and for the next several days following that one,
I am forced to call in sick to my job, because the Jungle
Room—which I am building in the room that used to be the
spare bedroom, before the earthquake which left half of my
house sitting eight feet lower than the other half—has become
overripe. I only meant to put in a few trees, made from plywood and sheets of paper painted various shades of brown and
green, but now I find myself with the sudden inclination to
put in a volcano, although I am fairly certain there has never
been a volcano in the Brazilian Pantanal.

The Hyacinth Macaw says: I flew for a month and a day, until
I saw a pattern of marks dotting a white circle, and the sky
turned to sea, and I knew I had found the island the Dodo had
spoken of. I circled the island twice, and from below a flutter of
voices, faint at first, then louder, bird voices, swirled up and surrounded me like buzzing wasps. What a cacophony! Each bird
held tightly to his name, and each believed that he alone knew
the secret of undoing the terrible mark, the mark that would
consume, like a rot, the heart of the bird it had chosen. Some of
the birds were bright and brilliant colors, some were the color of
tree bark, and some were the color of the moon. I hid behind a
fallen palm tree and watched as, each in turn, they spoke.

I have begun, while the Macaw has been speaking, to doodle,

in a small black notebook open on my lap, a sketch of the island, with a single palm tree growing almost horizontally across it, and along the length of the palm tree a series of shapes suggesting the outlines of birds.

The Fasciated Tiger-Bittern said: *We must go to the salt flats; we must lick up all the salt and become so salty the shadow hunters will no longer desire to hunt us for food.*

The Labrador Duck said: *What we must do with the eggs: We must protect the eggs in a new way. We must swallow them whole so that they hatch inside us and grow there; then to die will only be a molting.*

The Orange-Breasted Flowerpecker's orange breast said: *The problem is our shapes are all wrong. Corners! Sharp corners! That's what we need! Corners and armorlike plates! Remember the ancestors! Remember the ancestors!*

The Bourbon-Crested Starling said: *We must shed our feathers and grow very large. There is, I have heard, a root that can make this happen. It grows inside the island of the Ruby-Breasted Blue Lupine. The island is not far from here. We can fly there in a day!*

The Orange-Breasted Flowerpecker's orange breast said: *Pterodactyl! Pterodactyl!*

The Forest Spotted Owlet said: *Listen up! In the forest stands a pane of glass. Once caught in it, a bird's reflection cannot escape. Then he cannot fly far. The pane of glass pulls him back. Again and again he flies into the pane until there is nothing left. Who among us will smash it? Who among us will speak for the birds?*

The Mangareva Kingfisher said: *We must swim, and those of us who cannot swim, must swim. We must swim to the shipbuilding yards where they build the great ships. Then we must little by little chip away at their rudders, with our beaks, from underneath. No more ships, no more humans!*

The Canarian Black Oystercatcher said: *Who will speak for the birds?*

The Grosbeak-Weaver said: *Slaty-Crowned Bulbul! Your time has come!*

The Slaty-Crowned Bulbul said: *I will not speak for the birds!*

The Spectacled Cormorant said: *You, you must speak for the birds!*

The Rufous-Sided Towhee said: *Towhee! Towhee!*

I sit in the wobbly chair with the notebook and my special pen and say: Not that I believe you, Macaw. But. Had it to do with his slaty crown? If I had to guess I would say that the slaty crown had something to do with it. Was it, after all, on account of the Bulbul's slaty crown?

The Spectacled Cormorant said: *Slaty-Crowned Bulbul, we are only a group of very small and foolish birds, and though you and I have not known each other very long, I can tell that you are perhaps the most foolish among us. But because you have retained a solidity of form, and because of the grandeur of your slaty crown, this task has fallen to you—to go among the humans and tell them what transpired here today. You must speak for the birds!*

The Slaty-Crowned Bulbul said: *Spectacled Cormorant, my voice pings against a pane of empty sky. The sky is too empty, and the sea too wide. This island is made of quicksand, and my name will not save us, nor my slaty crown!*

The Bourbon-Crested Starling said: *Slaty-Crowned Bulbul! Speak, or you will die on this island! Your kind will vanish from the earth, never to return!*

The Mangareva Kingfisher said: *I am only a pair of bones, and my voice, if you can hear it at all, sounds as sweet and faint as a dream dreamed under a blue summer sky.*

The Grosbeak-Weaver said: *Slaty-Crowned Bulbul! Your time has come!*

The Slaty-Crowned Bulbul said: *I will not speak!*

I spend many hours each day outlining plans for the Jungle Room, painting scenes of dense forest receding into morning mist, building replicas of acuri, bocaiuva, and Manduvi trees, reconfiguring the electrical and plumbing systems, and so on. At the small card table where I eat my meals, I spread out an array of library books I have obtained featuring images of macaws in different stages of flight, half-hidden in cages of fluttering leaves, nestled in hollows, lifting nuts to their black beaks, their black tongues rolling out. I carefully cut out the macaw images, tracing the outline of each with a sharp knife. Between these activities and my trips to the hardware store in the market square, the library, the pet store in the center of town, and so on, I find myself arriving late to work most days, and finally forgetting to go in at all. In the ceiling of the Jungle Room there is a hole the size of a fist, and a bucket directly beneath it to catch the rain which falls day and night during the rainy season. The bucket fills up before I have a chance to empty it, and water fills the room ankle-deep, seeping under the door and into the rest of the house.

The Hyacinth Macaw says:

The argument lasted for the rest of that day, and most of the next one. Though the birds were little more than shards and fragments, their anger bound them together and gave off a blue-white glow, and the very island shook with its force. The Bulbul had been marked, but had not yet begun to disappear—and this I believe was the thing above all others which made the birds rise up against him. I flew to the top of the highest tree and from there I watched as the birds came at him. I heard no cry, nor the awful beating of feathers against the air. Only a terrible stillness settling over the island like a fog. When the fog dissipated there was nothing left of him but a pinkish seep of blood, of Bulbul blood. That and a bone, and a tuft. The blood seeped slowly into the white sand of a nameless island as the century came crashing down around it. Did I weep? No, not for the Slaty-Crowned Bulbul. He could have spoken for the birds! I knew also that the bird called Dodo had never nor would ever shed a tear for man or beast. His bones are glass, they live behind glass in a great hall, and a placard bears his name. The museum children, powdered and starched, parade in and cry from behind velvet stanchions: *Towhee! Towhee!*

I say to the Hyacinth Macaw: Macaw, I have a surprise for you I think you will like. I have been making something for you, in the spare bedroom—that is to say, the room that used to be a spare bedroom, before the earthquake—and it is almost ready, Macaw. All these weeks I have spent building it for you, spending every last penny of my savings, forgetting to go in to work, making trip after trip to the hardware store in the center of town, for you, for you, and it is finally ready, Macaw. Almost, that is. I don't want to spoil the surprise, but I think you will enjoy spending time in there.

The Hyacinth Macaw says: I do not know how long I was gone, but it must have been a very long time, for when I returned to the Manduvi tree my child was no longer a child. The bad monkey was long dead, though there were others just like him, laughing, jeering, and trailing their stinks behind them like kites. Time passed, my mate gave forth an enormous egg, and a new child replaced the old one. One day I did not go with my mate and child and the others to the clay lick but stayed, instead, in the Manduvi tree. I was nursing a minor headache after eating some bitter-tasting nuts I had discovered in a hole dug by the humans. I died soon afterwards. A low-crouching human happened along, and plucked out all my feathers. A monkey happened along, and made off with my head. A Spanish conquistador, on his way to kill all the local humans and burn down their villages in the name of some god or other, took what was left and roasted it over an open fire and ate it while cursing the heavens. My mate and child returned from the clay lick and found in my place a fat conquistador asleep and snoring in a waning shadow, and a blue-purple feather trapped in a light breeze, drifting silently down. Later that day they were, both of them, eaten by a condor.

I say to the Macaw: About the surprise. I went to the library and found many pictures—of others of your kind, and of bad laughing monkeys. I spent many painstaking hours making handcrafted replicas of the flora and fauna indigenous to southeastern Brazil. I'm no artist, so be kind. I was not sure what kind of clay to get, so I purchased a variety. You will have to let me know.

The Hyacinth Macaw says: Once, a great many years ago, I belonged to a Galician brigand named Iago Otero Souza. Iago Otero Souza when he walked made a sound like wooden wheels bumping over stone. He carried on his neck an enormous soggy pear of a head to match his enormous soggy pear of a belly. One day Iago Otero Souza, without any warning whatsoever, swallowed the sea. The world fell to its knees. All trembled before him. Kings and emperors, sultans and tsars plied him with all the jewels and riches of the world, with twilit maidens and tender boys. Mermaids lived in his belly and sea-dragons in his generous loins. But Iago Otero Souza forgot one thing: a man may swallow the sea, but no man may contain it! One second ticked by on Iago Otero Souza's pilfered timepiece, dangling from its golden chain. The chain went slack; the sea flowed out, taking Iago Otero Souza, his hammered bronze teeth, his lacquered head, his laugh like rusty bells, all his spoils and treasure, his galleon ship, his crew of wanted criminals, two twilit maidens and a Tunisian cabin boy with it. I was there, perched upon his wooden leg. I rode for many days upon the waves and saw: the pomegranates of the moon! They dropped down, and a man floated by on a hollow log.

I say: Macaw. Allow me to present your Jungle Room. Right this way, Macaw. I have created, to the best of my ability, an exact replica of your native habitat. Watch your step, Macaw. Careful of the river. You'll notice that the river, as I refer to it, is actually more of a creek or crick or rivulet, and, on account of its flow being powered by a generator hidden in the wall, isn't quite as silent as perhaps your river was, but is quite dark, thanks to my having painted the bottom of the trough—it took me weeks to figure out the logistics of an effective drainage system—a uniformly matte black. As we wend our way through the palm forest, please note that the trees are roughly half-scale, the tallest being well over twenty feet. This presented a problem, as I'm sure you can imagine, until I came up with the simple solution of removing a large portion of the roof. Feel free at this point in the tour, Macaw, to examine the meticulous detail with which I have rendered the forest floor, the clay lick, the flooded plains, the clear sparkling lake, and a representative assortment of wildlife, all of them smiling and friendly, all of them bidding you welcome, Macaw. Please notice, as well, the different-colored lightbulbs overhead, one yellow and one green. We will have yellow days on Tuesdays, Thursdays and Saturdays, and green days the rest of the week. And this is only the beginning, Macaw. You will notice that there are many images of others of your kind scattered here and there, and that I have made a number of hollows in the trees. Over here, Macaw. I am aware that in your jungle there was never a volcano, and I hope you will forgive me, but I simply could not resist putting one in, geographically inaccurate though it may be. I am aware, also, that strictly speaking your native habitat in the Brazilian Pantanal was not a jungle but a dry forest, the name "Jungle Room" therefore presenting something of a misnomer; however, I'm sure you will agree that "Jungle Room" has a nice ring to it. I will leave you now, Macaw, to get better acquainted with your new home.

The Hyacinth Macaw sits in the Jungle Room on top of the plaster of Paris volcano, and says: It was not I who killed the Slaty-Crowned Bulbul, though I was there when it happened. With one curled talon I nudged the place where the Bulbul had been and a cloud of feathers, sticky with blood, rose. I opened my beak and my black tongue rolled out. I flew straight up, across and through skies, and over and under moons. The Dodo did, after all, shed a single tear, for its own sorry fate. When I looked down at the sheer surface of the island, all that was left of the Slaty-Crowned Bulbul was a very white bone and its slaty crown, all tufty.

From the sky I called down to it: The mark of the Dodo is upon you!

The bone said nothing. The crown gave a little twitch and called back: *Who?*

Dear Ray Charles,

Please have your Business Manager Read this to you as this is Curtis Close as I hope you had another Bullet to Bite. As I am a lyrics writers to sell you a song known as Curtis Close. My fees are $1500.00 and you need the music Notes written for them. This is Country Music with a duet Possible. My address is ███████████

I am a former Beatles who did the Let Be Song and Lonley Hearts and did George Benson's Give Me the Nights. Songs. My Body Gaurd is Singer Tony Orlando if you wish to contact him for some of my work. Continued on an ahtther Paper.

You Can Lave another Payment in Check in another Name to Protect Your address and Private Life

(Continued)
My
Social Security Number
███████████

"MY BODYGUARD"

Curtis Close

Ray Charles Song "The Love of My Life"

I Love to tell my story about my Life.
then Remember those things that bring
the Love of life.

I have wonderful moment of a normal
time and it only cost a dime
to pay my rent. Then to have all
my paycheck Lent out by weeks end,
and then to Bend the Rules
of the Love of my Life
and tell the story to my Kids
Who forBid to Lie and get a bad
ed-grade at school as they are No fool
And then possible remember the love
of Mom And Dad and the Entire
family around the fire at Night.
and then to Light the Candle
of love from Above. tell Me the
Story of life and Rember those
moments.

Leif Parsons

I FEEL FREE

by GREG AMES

I'D BEEN DATING Karen for two weeks, maybe three, when she told me an ex-lover was stalking her. "Relentlessly," she said. They'd broken up over a year ago, she insisted, but Trang just couldn't take a hint. He followed her everywhere, threatened her with a bowie knife, and had even kicked another man repeatedly in the mouth with his combat boots. Major reconstructive surgery. "He's huge," she said. "And crazy."

I didn't feel an immediate urge to speak. I am not a big man, and any comment from me, I believed, would only emphasize the disparity in our physiques.

"I don't want to freak you out or anything, Bobby," she said, "but Trang's probably parked across the street right now, in that doughnut-shop parking lot, watching us with his high-powered binoculars."

I glanced at the window. "Interesting," I said. I didn't want to appear weak or excitable. "With binoculars?"

"Last night I felt him watching us have sex," she continued. "When my bra came off, I could feel him cursing. He was pounding his fists against his steering wheel, vowing bloody revenge. He was scraping his knife against a small gray stone, sharpening the blade." She shuddered. "That knife is so sharp."

"Come on, Karen." I laughed, still thinking it was a joke, a test. "How could you possibly know that?"

"I just know," she said. "I know Trang."

Online dating was new to me. My friend Diamond Doug Ronson had suggested it. He said, "I know three people personally, *three,* who met their wives on the internet."

Advice on dating from a married man always rankled me. I suspected that Diamond Doug knew he had made a terrible mistake and now wanted all his friends to do the same.

I said, "Hell no. Put my face online. 'I like chocolate and literature.' No thanks."

"Listen," he said. "I'll ask one of these guys which website he used and I'll send you the link. Totally discreet. Couldn't hurt to try, right?"

I told him that I would consider it, primarily to shut him up. If I agreed, then we could talk about baseball. There were two interesting pennant races to break down and analyze.

The website, I learned the following day, was called *GetInvolved!.com*—an online dating forum "for singles who want serious commitment now."

I ignored Doug's email for over a month, scorning the whole idea of meeting another person through the computer, until I heard from an old friend that my ex-girlfriend Teresa was engaged to a jazz drummer. The wedding was set for June. My solitude proved unbearable then. I had eaten a thousand meals alone in the last year or two. Many of those meals were choked down on street corners, standing with a plastic fork in my hand. My cheek bulging with lo mein, I watched couples pass hand-in-hand, laughing. That was no way to live. Finally I drafted a profile, outing myself as a SWM, 32, NS, who was "independent" and "friendly but shy."

At first Karen was so lighthearted and flirtatious. Our first date was an Italian restaurant somewhere in Prospect Heights. When we walked in, the hostess squealed and pulled Karen into a big hug. "You look great! No more bags under your eyes." She gave Karen's breasts a friendly squeeze. "Putting some weight back on!" I didn't like the sound of this. Why was this woman fondling my date's bosoms? The hostess turned to me. Her dark eyes glimmered. "So you're banging Karen? I know this bitch from Riverward. Were you there, too? Over in the men's ward?" I shook my head no. "Come this way," she said and sat us by a side window.

While we perused our menus I asked Karen about Riverward. She said it was a rehab in Pennsylvania. I didn't pursue the topic.

After dinner, we took a midnight walk through Prospect Park. It was pleasant but not especially memorable or passionate. We kissed good night before she drove home to her place in Canarsie. "I'll call you," I said, but I wasn't entirely sure about that. A recovering addict living out in Canarsie was not exactly what I was looking for.

But the following evening Karen showed up at my apartment building with take-out Chinese and a Scrabble board. Personally I believe one should always call first—dropping in unannounced is kind of rude—but I let her in anyway, despite my annoyance. Surprisingly, we had a lot of fun that night. Later that week she helped me to decorate my apartment. It was true that I hadn't done much to personalize the space since

I'd moved in. I had simply ignored its unloveliness. The thin, frayed carpet fell somewhere on the color spectrum between beige and turd brown. The walls were flat white and scuffed, unpainted during my tenancy. I had tacked up only one print, "Nude in the Tub," by my favorite painter, Pierre Bonnard, who I imagined as a private man, somebody like me. Karen brimmed with ideas about interior decoration. She was always knocking down walls in her mind.

My apartment featured a small washer/dryer setup. When she saw them, Karen was thrilled. "Are these new?" she said. The landlord had installed them the previous year. He had also raised the rent a hundred bucks, but it seemed like a fair deal at the time. "These aren't even coin-op," she said, hugging me.

Karen transformed corners with low tables and spider plants and driftwood sculptures. Walls came alive with bright tapestries. She even added a phone line for herself. I admired her creativity and enthusiasm. Day after day she continued to add little touches to the place. Plastic geraniums. Candelabra. I strolled around my apartment like a tourist. On my bare white walls Karen had hung photographs of herself having fun in not-so-distant locations. One showed her at Canarsie Pier, another at the cemetery. She stood next to fishermen and tombstones, beaming. I wondered who was working the camera. The unknown photographer's shadow sometimes fell across her face, darkening her features.

Karen was temporarily unemployed, so she did most of her interior decorating while I was at work. I'd come home at night to find another surprise waiting for me. "Isn't it exciting?" she'd ask. Or she'd say, "It'll grow on you."

On the mantel above the fake fireplace I kept a black-and-white portrait of my parents. A wedding photo from 1967. Karen exiled them to the bathroom. Arms around each other's shoulders, they laughed from their cold perch on the toilet tank. They watched me urinate and floss. But the mantel wasn't barren. In

Mom and Dad's place stood a framed eight-by-eleven photograph of a man I'd never met. He was not smiling. He just stared out of his plastic frame with cold, expressionless eyes.

"Karen, who is this?" I said, peering into the frame. The man's dark hair looked like it had been trimmed with a scythe.

Karen didn't hear my question, though. She was power-drilling a series of holes into the ceiling so that she could hang some Boston ferns.

"Karen," I called out in a louder voice. "Who's this dude on my mantel?"

She turned off the drill, flipped up her protective goggles, and joined me on the opposite side of the room.

"Oh, that's just Trang," she said, taking my hands in hers. She kissed me. Then she trailed her lips across my cheek to my left earlobe. "It's an old photograph," she breathed in my ear. "It's just there to remind me how awful and domineering he was."

Pulling away from her, I took a closer look at that photo. He had a scar above his lip that seemed to connect his nose to his mouth. He was an ugly man.

"Are you kidding me?" I said. "The stalker Trang?"

"He was so terrible," she said, eyeing his picture on the mantel. "Such an animal."

"Take it down," I said. After all, I didn't have any photographs of my ex-girlfriend Teresa on display.

"It's cute that you're jealous, Bobby, but let's leave it up for a few days and see if it grows on you. If you still don't like it, I'll whisk it away and you'll never see it again. Does that sound like a fair deal?"

"It sounds insane," I said.

My married buddy Diamond Doug Ronson, the reformed wild man, otherwise known as Pass the Jug, I Wanna New Drug, and Doobie Doug, often talked about the compromises he needed to make with his wife Liz. Frequently he just gave in, surrendered outright, because he knew most things weren't worth the fight. "You have to choose your battles," he said. "Otherwise you'd find yourself fighting over everything. Who's got the energy for that? Man, here's my advice: just let her have what she wants. What the fuck do you care?"

Still, I had to draw the line somewhere. "No way," I said. I took down the photograph and buried it in a drawer. It had been a test of some sort, I decided, and I felt like I had passed.

For a few nights Karen and I got along great. We made meals together and talked about our lives. She was funny, articulate, thoughtful. Karen talked openly about her former addiction to cocaine, detailing where it had taken her and what she had done to recover. She considered abstinence her greatest achievement in life. Chopping onions on a cutting board, I marveled at her courage and discipline. I found myself comparing my experiences to hers, embarrassed that I had never been arrested or locked up in a women's detention center.

One evening I returned from work and found damp clothes scattered all over the living room. There were mounds of moist fabric on the steaming radiator, wet jeans draped over drying racks, T-shirts clinging to the backs of wooden chairs. Soggy gray underpants drooped above every doorframe, like mistletoe in a surrealist painting. Men's dress shirts hung from newly hammered nails in the walls. The washer and dryer were both shuddering. I did not recognize any of the clothes. They weren't mine, and they didn't seem to belong to Karen.

I unbuttoned my collar and stripped off my jacket. I waded through the humid air. Sweat beaded on my forehead. "Karen," I called out, "it's really hot in here." All the windows were steamed. I wiped my forehead with a tissue. "Is the heater on? What's the deal with all this laundry?"

"It *is* hot in here," said a strange man seated on my couch.

Startled, I jumped back and raised my fists reflexively. "Who are you?" I said. His face looked familiar to me, but I couldn't place him. He wore a black T-shirt, khaki slacks, and brown leather sandals. He stared at me without speaking. I couldn't see the scar over his lip from that distance, and he had a shorter haircut—high and tight, military style.

I felt my jaw muscles tensing. "I asked you a question, man."

"I suggested she open a window." He waved his hand, indicating the futility of the request. "She wouldn't listen."

Karen came into the room carrying a sloshing pitcher of margaritas. Lime wedges seesawed in the yellow liquid like capsized boats. "Hi there, sweetie," she said. She placed the pitcher on the coffee table and rushed toward me. She rammed her tongue into my mouth. "I missed you," she said.

I tasted Nicorette and tequila. Abruptly I disengaged my mouth from hers and said, "Who is that, Karen?"

"Him?" She followed the angle of my pointed finger. "Oh, that's just Trang."

"In the flesh," he said.

"Actually, he was just leaving," Karen said, pointedly. "Weren't you?"

"No, I don't think so," Trang said, then he winked at me. "That's news to me, in any case."

"It's ridiculous," I said. "This is beyond ridiculous. It's absurd."

Trang had one slender leg crossed over the other. He wasn't nearly as big as Karen had described, but his narrow face suggested a fierce and nasty intelligence. Both of his ropy-muscled arms were slung over the back of my couch. His posture vaguely suggested crucifixion. "What's up?" he said to me. "How was work?"

Karen squeezed both my hands in hers. "Oh, now, listen, Bobby, before I forget: we really need to have that old dryer looked at... Bobby! Pay attention. Stop staring at Trang. What are we gonna do about the dryer? It's been giving me trouble all day."

I wiped a rivulet of sweat off my cheek. The apartment was as humid as a greenhouse. "Wait. What's wrong with the dryer? It's brand new."

Trang said, "This is a nice little pad you have here, Brent."

"I told you his name is Bobby!" Karen stamped her foot. "Can't you remember anything? *Bobby*."

Yawning, Trang flicked a piece of lint or a cat hair off his knee. He leaned forward and poured himself a goblet full of margarita. Then he poured one for Karen. Both rims were crusted with salt. "Whatever," he said. "You say tomato, I say Brent. Let's call the whole thing off."

As I approached the couch I felt my foot strike against something. Trang's mouth fell open. With astonishing quickness he leapt up and stood face-to-face with me. At my feet a steel briefcase lay on its side. "You should watch where you're going," he said. Trang reached down and picked up the case with both hands. He hugged it to his chest. "This is off-limits to you," he said, and returned to his seat.

"What are you two up to?" I asked Karen. "Is this some kind of scam?"

"Bobby, no!" She seized my hands again. "You and I are together. Trang is a distant memory. He means nothing to me. He just came over to drop off my clothes."

As crazy as it may sound, I wanted to believe Karen. I really did enjoy her company. She laughed a lot and talked about things I'd never thought about before. She kept the apartment clean. Despite her eccentricities, Karen made the place feel more like a home. And I hadn't been involved with a woman in well over a year. Sometimes after sex, Karen blew gently on my skin to dry the sweat. Her long hair tickled my skin as she moved slowly down my body, cooling my chest and thighs and the bottoms of my feet with little puffs of breath, and I liked that almost as much as the sex itself. No one else had ever done that for me before. It seemed to me such a tender, thoughtful act of affection. Now I found myself even more attracted to her, knowing that another man was still in the picture. Her smile seemed brighter; her eyes were more luminous.

"I believe you, Karen," I said. "I was just surprised. That's all."

While Karen and Trang drank margaritas in the living room, I retreated to the bedroom. Alone, I resumed reading a biography of Tolstoy. At least a week had passed since I'd last looked at it. Before I could read an entire page, though, Karen barged in and sat on the bed's edge. "What's the matter, Bobby?" she asked. "Are you depressed?"

"No, it's just... well. Trang," I said, my eyes still focused on the page. "I think you're still in love with him."

"Bobby, that's crazy. I kicked him out. Told him, 'Don't come back.'"

"I'm not going to be a watchdog in my own house," I said. "I don't have the energy for that. If you're going to screw around behind my back—"

"You're adorable!" She kissed my cheek. Then she eyed the cover of my book. "'The Russian Master: Leo Tolstoy,'" she said. "Did you ever read any Larry McMurtry? You should check out McMurtry if you're so into Tolstoy."

The Tolstoy biography was informative and reasonably interesting. Not the best book I'd ever read, but I was enjoying it. My office work exhausted me. All day long I packaged and sold recruiting manuals for marketing networks. Half the time I had no idea what I was talking about. I had to learn the job on the fly. So I certainly didn't want a lot of stress at home, too. A good book and a few beers made for a perfect night.

Karen slid even closer to me, sucking her cough lozenge. "That McMurtry. Boy, he's something else. What a way with words."

I shut the book on my index finger to save my place. I don't know why I liked Karen so much, but I did. Maybe it was something in her eyes, the trusting and childlike quality in them. "He's good?" I asked her.

She waved the question away. "Just read him. You'll see. You'll see what I mean about old McMurtry."

After a moment of charged silence, Karen stood up and left the room. She shut the door quietly behind her.

For the next hour I read about Leo Tolstoy's dramatic experiences in the Caucasus. He fought bloody skirmishes with mountain tribesmen. He went days without eating. He was a rugged, intelligent man who would change the course of world literature. I immersed myself in his story, trying to gain strength and guidance from it. My life lacked drama and danger. Sometimes I longed for it. At my office we made a point of avoiding any conflicts. Aggression wasn't "conducive to productivity."

Soon my bedroom door swung open again. "Knock knock, Lonesome Dove," Karen said. She carried a stack of clean clothes into the room. I tried to keep reading, but the sentences blurred and became incomprehensible.

Humming a song under her breath, Karen yanked open dresser drawers and slammed them shut. "We—are—family," she sang, wagging her head. "I got all my sisters and me."

"Karen, please," I said, not looking up from my book. "I'm trying to read."

"Sorry, Bobby."

She approached the bed, sat down, and took a long look at the book's cover. "Still working on that one, huh?"

"Well, I've been a little distracted," I told her.

Nodding affably, Karen posed a question. "You think Sir Leo Tolstoy liked to shampoo that big beard of his?"

"I don't know how he behaved in the bathtub," I said. "And for the record, Karen, Tolstoy was a count, not a knight."

My tone was more acerbic than I'd intended. But Karen didn't seem to notice. She leaned closer to inspect the book's cover. She tipped the book back with her hand, preventing me from reading it. "What a beard, huh?"

I smelled her peach-scented shampoo. "Karen," I said.

Ignoring me, she gently stroked the image of Tolstoy's cottony beard with her forefinger. "He looks crazy," she said. "And I've seen some kooks, boy. He fits the profile."

Against my will I looked down at the photograph, or daguerreotype, or whatever it was. He was in his most pious religious phase then, an old man wearing some kind of white gown and seeker's sandals.

I said, "He was obsessed with God and vegetarianism and humility when that was taken."

"Yeah, I bet he was," Karen said agreeably, "but you know he spent some quality time on that beard each morning. Probably used a top-notch conditioner and some French oils, too. Scrubbed it up good." She paused. "But you know Trang's the same way. Some nights he'll spend a couple hours polishing up those snow globes he carries around. He really takes his time with it."

"Snow globes," I said. "You're kidding."

"He's pretty intense about it."

Karen walked out of the room humming. I couldn't even enjoy my damn book after that. No matter what the biographer wrote about the Russian master's selflessness and his talent for humanity, I imagined Tolstoy lathering his beard with imported French or Italian conditioner, smiling at his brilliant face in the mirror, while behind him Trang held a snow globe up to the light and dabbed at it with a cloth.

I didn't know a great deal about Karen, but a few memories

she shared with me indicated that she had had a pretty rough childhood. This endeared her to me. My childhood was not sweet either. My folks moved a lot, from one dead town to another. I never made any close friends. Almost every day I fought after school. Karen had a look that I recognized from all those forgettable places; she was a watcher, the girl who stood off to the side, cupping a cigarette, pretending she had seen it all before. She could probably destroy my entire life in three months. She could break it down into sections and then smash it into smaller pieces, right before my very eyes. And maybe I wanted to feel myself come completely undone at the hands of a damaged, mysterious woman. Otherwise, how could I have been sure I was still alive?

Later that night, after Karen and I had eaten dinner, Trang returned with a rented DVD for us to watch. "It's a classic," he said, waving it over his head. In his other hand he carried the snow-globe case. Karen explained in a whisper that this rented DVD was a peace offering. She said that it was very difficult for Trang to be friendly with me. He was making a concerted effort to be civilized. Trang had had a very rough life, she said. He needed love and tolerance.

"What's the movie called?" I said miserably.

"Okay, Curious George, I'll give you a hint," Trang said. "The cast includes such luminaries as Dudley Moore, Liza Minnelli, and Sir John Gielgud... Does that ring a bell?"

"No," I said.

My couch only seated two people comfortably—it was more of a loveseat, actually—and we had a hard time deciding who should sit where. After a brief negotiation, Karen decided to get down on the floor, which left Trang and me side by side on the loveseat.

"Cozy, no?" he said to me.

I moved my knee away from his.

The movie was called *Arthur*. It was pretty lame, not that

funny or clever, but Trang and Karen laughed all the way through. I honestly couldn't understand what they saw in it. Afterward, Trang called it a brilliant socioeconomic parable. He walked out the door, still chuckling to himself. "Oh, that Arthur," he said. "What a lark, what a plunge!"

"Karen, we need to talk," I said later that night. "This doesn't seem to be working out."

"What doesn't, Bobby?"

"This," I said. "Us."

Karen cried. She buried her face in her hands and cried. "And I've been so happy. Please. Don't do this. Don't end this."

"You've been happy?" I said, surprised. "You like how things are going?"

"I'm in love," she said. "Can't you see that?"

I was touched. She was in love? How could I have been so oblivious?

Alone in the bedroom, I thought about my relationship with Karen. What kind of future did we have together? I weighed the pros and cons. There was companionship, clean laundry, and Trang. Was it an ideal situation? No. I wouldn't say that. How much did I have in common with Karen? Close to nothing. But the sex was phenomenal. Having Trang around would make that a little more difficult, of course. There were obvious complications. But this was what you had to expect when you shared your life with another person, especially a woman in her thirties. Baggage. Hell, I was no prize myself. And if you wanted a romantic relationship to succeed, then you needed to understand the logistics of surrender and sacrifice. Nothing good came without a struggle. I decided to stick it out for another week.

"Can I offer you a piece of advice?" Trang said the following morning. He was seated at the kitchen table, drinking my coffee. He had the Job Market section of the *Times* spread before him. When I didn't reply, he forged ahead anyway. "You're a pussy," he said. "And you've got no nuts."

"What?" I said, cinching the knot of my plaid flannel bathrobe. "Stand up. Say that again."

I'd been in scraps before. For four straight years I fought at least once a week after school, surrounded by a ring of leering, bitter faces, the up-front cruelty of kids, and I actually began to look forward to the afternoon's final bell. Even though I hadn't chosen it for myself, this had become my identity: I was a brawler. At three-thirty, I stood in the center of the circle with a bloody lip, refusing to go down. A perfectly landed punch to the jaw would end it. Somebody was going to lose. I had brought my right knee down on more than one blood-spurting nose. I had elbowed people, hard, in their kidneys. I had been made to eat dirt. For years I had thrived on fear. It fueled me. "I'll fight right now," I said to Trang. Even though it had been almost a decade since I'd last thrown a punch, I warmed instantly to the idea. "Stand up, Trang. Let's have some fun."

"Holy cow," he said with a grin. "Don't shoot the messenger, amigo."

At that moment I wanted to grab Trang by the shoulders and throw him out the door. I wanted to smash in his face. But I remembered what Karen had said about reconstructive surgery. And how Trang had once kicked a man in the head, repeatedly. I wondered if a confrontation was worth it.

"Let's examine your relationship with Karen," he said. "You're playing this thing all wrong, my friend. I'm just trying to help you here."

"I don't need your help."

"Yes, you do. Women want to believe that we—men—are much more calculating and dangerous than we really are." He lowered his voice. "Usually I try not to disavow them of this misconception, if you know what I mean."

I felt tired, lightheaded. "What are you talking about?"

He leaned forward on his elbows, preparing to let me in on a secret. "Sometimes you gotta play the savage." He glanced over my shoulder, then continued in a lower voice: "Beat your chest a little, Brent. You're too nice and a chick'll walk all over you. Where do nice guys finish?"

"Last," I said grudgingly.

"That's right." He glanced over my shoulder again. "Every now and then you gotta jack up their heartbeats. Women are like little rabbits. Make them think their life is in jeopardy, and then you rush in and save the day. They're so relieved, so aroused, they forget you put them in peril in the first place."

"You have a pretty low opinion of women," I said.

That night the living-room windows were all steamed up again, but at least the wet clothes had disappeared from the chair backs and walls.

"I made baked ziti," Trang said with a triumphant smile. He emerged from the kitchen carrying a steaming casserole dish. He wore an apron that said COOKIN' WITH GAS. His face was flushed. "I made enough for all of us."

I joined Karen by the washer-dryer combo. She was frantically adding figures on a small notepad. "Yes, sir. Have it for you by tomorrow," she said into the phone. "That's thirteen-fifty, total. Okay. Yes. Bye." She hung up. "Hi, Bobby." She stepped forward for a kiss. "How was work?"

Before I could reply, the phone rang again. She flipped her hair to the side and lifted the receiver to her ear. "Karen's," she said. "This is Karen speaking."

"Hey," I said. "We need to have a serious talk."

"Watch your foot, Bobby," she said, pointing at my shoe. "Careful."

I looked down. My toes had grazed the steel briefcase by

accident. "Jesus," I said. "Why doesn't he store that in a safer place? If it's so important to him."

Luckily, Trang couldn't hear us. He was in the kitchen putting the finishing touches on his baked ziti.

After dinner, I overheard Trang talking long distance to a collector out in Vancouver. He described the delicate hand-blown glass of his collectibles. He talked about the quality of the glitter in the newer models—shaved porcelain and bone chips had, of course, been the industry standard for decades—and he reminded the man that distilled water, which could be found in the best globes, evaporated much more slowly than plain tap water. I still had a hard time believing that he was serious. Soon Trang was shouting, pacing in the living room. Enraged, he gesticulated with his free hand and called the man a novice, a world-class shithead. The snow globes from Graceland and Alcatraz were from his dead grandmother's private collection; he wouldn't let them go for cheap. They were exceedingly rare. "Go look them up in the red book," he shouted. "Stop wasting my time, you clown." He tossed my cordless phone onto the couch.

Our apartment was crowded at night. Strangers passed through the living room with their hands buried in potato-chip bags. Others arrived and peered into the fridge. Were they friends of Karen? I couldn't keep up. They seemed to know where to find everything: the various soups and spaghettis, the paper plates and plastic ware, the remote control.

One evening an elderly woman with a gold front tooth informed me that we needed more toilet paper. "Yo, Brent," she said. "You gotta start buying the cheap T.P., baby. Single-ply. No more of that scented or quilted stuff that leaves the dingleberries." Then she hobbled out the front door.

There was so much I didn't know about Karen. And what scared me was that she would continue to reveal herself to me over months, years, decades. If we ever decided to get married, all these strange people would become my extended family. It was almost too much to handle. Shaken, I called my former ally, Diamond Doug, even though I knew he couldn't hang out with me anymore. Long gone were the days when the two of us could just spontaneously head off to the bar together, throw darts all night or just watch *SportsCenter* on the TV suspended above the bar.

I began to tell him about my bizarre houseguest but Doug interrupted me and launched into a horror story of his own. His in-laws were visiting from Illinois. They were outrageously tall, annoying Midwesterners who sometimes stayed for ten days. They slept in his guest room, ate all his food, smiled incessantly.

"It makes my life a living hell," he said. "Consider yourself lucky, bro."

"It's not like that over here," I told him. "Really. It's crazy."

"You'll get used to it," he said.

"No, I won't."

"Dude, I've heard all this from you before. 'Her ankles are too thick.' Or, 'She doesn't read enough books.' You want to be alone forever? If you do, that's cool. Be alone. You'll be another Saint Francis of Assisi, feeding seeds to all the birds. But if you don't want to be alone, whacking your pud to cyber porn and sobbing into your pillow every night, stop sabotaging this relationship before it even starts. I'm sick of your bullshit."

"You don't understand, Doug. This one is different. She—"

"Oh, I understand. Believe me, I fucking understand. Nothing surprises me anymore. I have seen it all. Trust me on this one. You won't find anyone better than this Karen. She sounds awesome. And soon you'll have two or three kids before you know it. And after a while you won't even notice the insanity. *What?*" Now he was talking to his wife in the background. "No, it's not Fran, honey. It's Bobby. Okay, okay. *Okay.*"

"Doug," I said, my voice cracking. "Please. I need help. This is moving way too fast for me."

"Listen, Bobby. I gotta go. Wife's waiting for a phone call. Hang in there."

I was scared, angry, confused. Maybe Karen and I needed to go to couples counseling.

Almost every night Trang listened to one of my Cream CDs at full volume. His favorite track, evidently, was "I Feel Free." He'd stand at the stereo and press repeat, so that he could listen to that song ten or fifteen times in a row. There was a time when I had really enjoyed that album, too, so I understood his excitement. Jack Bruce had a wonderful singing voice. But my musical tastes had changed radically in the eighteen years since I had purchased the CD. Hearing it over and over was beginning to enrage me. It was an insidious form of torture.

"Slowhand," Trang said, bobbing his head to the music. "Slowhand was in this band." We were home alone together. It was a Friday night and Karen was out returning clothes to her many relatives around the city. "Eric Clapton's nickname is Slowhand," Trang added.

Averting my eyes from an air-guitar solo, I took out my journal. I still hoped that one day I would write something beautiful, something profound and illuminating about human nature. With a tiny pencil I scribbled: *Trang likes Cream.*

I sat there staring at my words.

Trang stood next to one of the speakers, cocked his head to the side, and pressed his ear to the woofer. "What a lark, what a plunge!" he shouted over the music. "Cream was a power trio. Bass, drums, and guitar. Man, those suckers rocked. Case closed."

I shut my journal. "Where are you from, Trang?"

"What?"

"Where. Are. You. From?" I shouted.

"Canada," he hollered back.

"How long have you been in New York?"

"Feels like forever." He was getting ready to press repeat.

"You were born in Canada?"

"Not exactly. It's a long story."

We said nothing after that. I listened to "I Feel Free" about four more times, then I retreated to the bedroom, shut the door behind me, and inserted foam earplugs into my head.

Toward the end of his life, Tolstoy moved away from his beloved Yasnaya Polyana, his sprawling family estate, to live an ascetic life in a monastery. He renounced his birthright as a member of the aristocracy. "I will live simply," he proclaimed. "Without resources. God will guide me." Ten days later, Tolstoy died of heart failure in a railroad station in Astapovo. A porter found him dead on a rickety cot. "He looked just like any other corpse," the porter said to a journalist. "Sort of desiccated, like an old pear. We get corpses here all the time. At the time I didn't know he was Lev Tolstoy, God rest his soul."

An hour later, when I came out of the bedroom for a snack, I found Trang standing on my loveseat holding a hairbrush to his lips. The stereo was cranked as high as it could go. Even with the foam plugs jammed into my ears, I felt Jack Bruce's voice thumping like a fist on my sternum.

"Bo, bo, bo, bo, bo, bo, I feel free!"

I stood in the doorway and watched the following scene: Karen emerged from the bathroom still wearing her slick yellow raincoat. Her dark hair was yanked back in a tight ponytail. She emptied her pockets, pulling out great wads of wet bills, which she stacked on the coffee table. After counting her earnings, she watched Trang.

He swayed his hips sensuously, side to side. "Feel when I dance with you," he lip-synched, eyes clamped shut. Trang held the hairbrush in both hands. "We move like the sea. You, you're all I want to know. I feel free."

A smile bloomed on Karen's face, spreading from her mouth to her eyes. She blushed. She stripped off her soaked raincoat and watched him intently.

"I can walk down the street, there's no one there," Trang serenaded her, the hairbrush clutched in his left fist. His right hand was pressed, fingers splayed, against his chest. "Though the pavements are one huge crowd. I can drive down the road, my eyes don't see, though my mind wants to cry out loud. Though my mind wants to cry out loud!"

Watching him, Karen smoothed a few wet curls of hair back with her fingers. Her face flushed. With dilated eyes she looked at Trang as she had never once looked at me. He turned his body fully toward her. I didn't need to watch his lips to know what he was singing. I knew the lyrics by heart. Standing on my couch, Trang smiled down at her. His joy was pure. "You're the sun and as you shine on me, I feel free... I feel free... I feel free."

When the song was over, Karen laughed and blew kisses at him. She clapped her hands softly, soundlessly.

It was a hot, humid night. The streets were still slick from an earlier rain. Karen and Trang sat out on the front steps, drinking malt liquor from forty-ounce bottles. He had dragged the stereo over to the windowsill, so that they could listen to his song from outside. I think he also had the remote control. This would soon be my family, I realized. When you moved in with a woman you didn't get involved with only her. You got involved with all the people in her life—her girlfriends, her relatives, and her ex-lovers. She carried them all around inside her, a battalion of ghosts.

While they fraternized on the stoop, I walked out of my bedroom to make myself a snack. The kitchen light was on. Nobody appeared too concerned about my electric bills; I certainly didn't care anymore. The music was cranked.

There was no ham, cheese, or tuna left. No bread or mayo. Karen hadn't gone shopping in a week. The vodka and gin bottles were both empty.

On the breakfast table was the steel briefcase, its lid open. I stepped closer and looked into it. Inside were eight pristine glass orbs, each one snug inside its purple foam cutout. The case alone was worth a grand or two, Trang had claimed the day before, stopping me outside the bathroom to explain the history behind its acquisition. He had found it in a pawnshop in Niagara Falls. The proprietor had no idea what he held in his possession. Trang paid him fifty bucks and laughed all the way to the casino. The steel briefcase had once been owned by Umberto Granaglia, the world famous Bocce master. Oval scoops in the purple foam interior once held the superstitious Granaglia's lucky balls; now they cradled Trang's vintage collectibles.

A yellow tack cloth was folded lengthwise and rested on a Paris art-deco globe. I pulled out one of the prettiest ones—a pre-fire Cocoanut Grove, circa 1941—and inspected it closely, turning it under the light. I shook it, flipped it upside down. The more I looked at it, the better I understood. Sure, there was something appealing about it. I understood why he loved it so.

I smashed it on the kitchen floor. The glass shattered beautifully. Water dribbled out. Silently I stared down at this mess at my feet. I felt a momentary stab of guilt. Then I pulled out each of the remaining seven globes and repeated the process again and again. Giggling, I lifted my arm over my head and heaved them down on the peeling linoleum. "Oops," I said. I chucked them into the sink and against the wall. I destroyed two and three at a time, behind my head, through my legs. I felt exalted. It was an orgy of demolition. God must have felt like this every day, striking down innocent people and animals, destroying entire villages.

A few of the spheres—Plexiglas ones—would not break. They bounced and skidded into the baseboards. No matter how many times I struck them down they remained intact. So I had to pulverize them with a rolling pin.

When the case was empty, I shoved it off the table. It clattered on the floor. My face was damp with sweat. I walked over to the window and stopped the CD. No more Slowhand. "Trang," I called out, standing serenely by the crime scene. "I think I dropped something of yours. Better come and look."

The screen door banged open. I heard the drumbeat of approaching footsteps. "Oh my God," Karen said, staring wide-eyed at the floor. "Bobby, what have you done?"

Trang followed her into the kitchen. He gawked, openmouthed. Slowly his hands curled into fists.

"Oh my God." Karen looked up at me with pity and tenderness. "Bobby," she said, low. "Are you crazy, honey?" She took a step toward me. "This is so bad."

Grinning, I leaned back against the counter, and waited. Goose bumps pebbled my forearms.

Something had to happen soon. Everyone in the house could feel it.

Dear Ray Charles

Let Us Stop Eating Meat Meat Is Very Very
Unhealthy Meat Is The Cause Of Heart Disease
And Cancer Meat Is The Cause Of Almost Every
Disease And Virus Meat Includes All Land
Animals All Sea Animals And All Fresh Water
Animals God Created All Animals And God Loves
All Good Animals Very Very Deeply God Never
Wanted Us To Eat Meat God Does Not Kill Good
Animals And God Does Not Support Those Who
Kill Good Animals In Heaven No One Eats Meat
Some Day The Earth Will Be In Heaven And No
Body Will Eat Meat We Might As Well Prepare
For Heaven —————————

"VERY VERY UNHEALTHY"

Matt Rota

SERENADE

by KEVIN MOFFETT

OLD WOMEN, NEW WOMEN, old new women, new old women. Women jogging in place at intersections until the light changes, maintaining their heart rate, trying so hard, aspiring, succeeding. How clearly they are succeeding. Tiny headphones plug their ears. What is the secret? When the light changes so do they. There is no secret.

Sometimes I follow them. Often I do. Always I do.

I stop at the supermarket where, in the rude light of the produce aisle, I see all the women I ever danced with. With whom I ever danced. Their membership is large and not one of them is acquainted with the others. They are satellites, smelling pineapples, telling me stories with their groceries. Eggs, cube steak, diet soda, baggies. Diapers, instant noodle mix, tampons, calamine lotion. Ground chuck, parsley, merlot.

We talk about the rain, how there's been no rain.

I am frustrated by how prominently the dances hang in memory. I remember each step, how the fabric of each woman's dress felt on my fingers, where their hands rested. The dances have a sharpness that other moments of intimacy cannot approach. I can replay the dances from memory, I can still be towed into desolation by them. Where do people dance anymore? Why are we still talking about how there's been no rain?

I hear music in the supermarket, a happy pineapple-sniffing song. I ask each of the women to reenact our dance. Here? they say. There's a lane between these olive bins, I say. I am desperate enough to convince them, but they are taught to find propositions like this off-putting, or to pretend to, so they do, or pretend to.

I remember one young woman years ago who rested her chin on my shoulder. We were in the early awkward part of a slow dance, still tuning ourselves to each other, pecking out a tight circle. This woman, she's a stepmother now, leaned forward as if to whisper something. Gossip? A filthy proposition? No. She lifted her chin and mounted it on my shoulder where it remained for the rest of the song. She was shoeless in a gauzy yellow dress and her hair smelled like secret berries. She couldn't know how excited her chin-move made me; if she had, I doubt (I very much doubt) she would have done it.

The other dancers were having similar episodes, I should think. A dance is an ideal vehicle for an episode, much better than a poem or a boat ride to Valparaiso. Everyone stirred by the same music, wandering within their partners, cocooned. If the other dancers were like me, they felt so good when the song ended that they wanted to mark the occasion by scarring their arms or cutting off a finger. When she lifted her chin, I looked at my shoulder, expecting to see insects writhing in wet soil like the earth beneath a rotted log. Instead there was a sweat mark, a transient souvenir.

Today I see this woman in the supermarket with her stepson, Bruce. They look alike although they're not related, same murky eyes and scattered bearing. Bruce is very interested in the fat content of the foods his stepmother is buying. His stepmother is interested in clearing a path past me once I ask her to reenact our dance. Women who do not want to be bothered should not be bothered. I have always understood this, always. I let them pass.

Cocoa Krispies, mouthwash, canned fruit, rice.

Bruce does not glance back at me sympathetically. I whisper: I know. I know your stepmother doesn't have time for my outdated reveries. I know I probably look desperate, Bruce, talk desperate, act desperate, am desperate. But... but...

If I had cut off a finger after the original dance, instead of wishing I had, now is when I would show Bruce my severed nub and say, But *this*.

I forget what I have come to the supermarket to buy, then I remember: rabbit meat.

Some women jog with their dogs, who are linked to the women by leashes and appear to be leading the women, especially those wearing waist-leashes. The dogs are learning to jog in place at intersections until the light changes. Dogs are predisposed to please, so they try their best, but they do not understand what is happening. They suspect they are on the lam, pursued by sputtering lawnmowers and the lunatic dachshunds next door.

I worry that women with dogs do not need me. I worry that women with children do not need me. Smiling women, women with talent, women with any talent whatsoever. I worry that women have a No Vacancy light they can switch on and off whenever they want. Lately all the women I meet sound like my ex-wife. This may not be uncommon, except: I don't have an ex-wife.

Before I leave the house I smear meat all over my boots. I place a saddle of rabbit meat inside each boot as an arch support and wait at busy intersections. The dogs arrive first and stop and sit and sniff my boots. Hounds and certain schnauzers will actually lick the smeared leather, which is ideal, because the women have to unplug their headphones and apologize. The apologies are stiff kisses, but kisses nevertheless. I check the dogs' bone-shaped name tags, hoping to discover valuable information. The dogs share the women's last names. Petting the dogs, who begin nipping at my boots, trying to get at the rabbit meat inside, I feel an unspoken repartee with them. As the women pull them off toward respiratory nirvana, the dogs glance back at me sympathetically, thanking me for my fragrance, and I sympathize with their sympathy for me.

Women are the only authentic fortune-tellers. The best ones, it is said, will garner all they need to know from a man's boots. They study patterns of wear on the soles and toes to predict past, present, and future. The fortune-tellers have charts and manuals they can refer to. If the boots look brand new, the laces stiff in their eyelets, he worries about women. If the boots are meat-smeared and the left sole is worn down counterclockwise, he worries about women. If the leather is gouged and ripped to expose a steel toe like a robot's cruel inner parts, he worries about women.

Along the promenade a fortune-teller sits on a stool in front of her shop. I ask her to tell my fortune. She says her heart isn't into it today. She looks tired, unhappy, perhaps hungover, but the refusal still seems like a condemnation. It won't take long,

I assure her. I'll pay you double. I hold out my money. She looks at the money, looks at my boots, and she tells me my fortune.

Women bag up certain memories like puppies and drive them to the quarry. They abandon them like snagged kites. They cancel them like dentist appointments. They do this biannually, in the morning before anyone else is awake. Finished, they look younger, healthier, happier, because they are. Their posture improves, things smell better.

More and more, I think, my hopes lie with the women jogging in place at intersections. I do not know these women, we have shared only interludes. Even so, when they unplug their tiny headphones to apologize for their dogs, it feels like a victory. I have been given access to the kingdom, to the gardens beyond the gates. What is the secret? I ask them while leaning down to pet the dogs.

They respond with benign indifference, sweet disregard, a bramble of alien flora.

The whites of their eyes are so terribly white. Their running wear is made of breathable colorful man-made fabric.

Probably they think I am talking to their dogs who, after cleaning the smeared meat off my boots, applaud me with panting smiles. The women are having a difficult time teaching them to jog in place. When the light changes, the headphones are reinserted, their stride returns. The world presents its machinery for the women to defuse and they defuse it. Finished, they hold two fingers to the carotid arteries fluttering in their necks, and stretch to its rhythm.

I have begun walking around town with a boat oar. It is a small, commemorative oar, *not intended for use* stamped on the paddle. The effect I'm going for... I want to look... unsolved.

If somebody decides to photograph me for the newspaper or for a photo-essay about handsome eccentrics, that's okay with me. If women think I'm a master yachtsman because of the oar and because on the back of my windbreaker it says Master Yachtsman, I am not going to protest.

One night, after a few weeks of no one asking about the oar or if I'm a master yachtsman, I drop the oar into a river. It has gotten scuffed and dirty and plus there's some graffiti on it. No one has taken my picture. Enough! It feels good to drop an oar into a river, even a sickly streamlike creek where the oar snags on a cement block and refuses to budge. Feels conclusive.

I turn around and see a half-dozen women with cameras waiting to take my picture with the oar. It's way down there, I tell them. Go get it, they say. And reluctantly I do, but when I return, windbreaker dripping, they are gone. Again I drop the oar into the river and again it snags on the cement block and again the women appear and want to take my picture. With the oar. I'm not going back into that river, I say. Of course you are, they tell me.

Of course I am.

I'm already wet, I reason; I'm not going to get any *wetter*. The next time I drop the oar and retrieve it I show some resistance, but after a few more trips to the river I'm just happy the women continue to return.

After the oar, I begin walking around with a banjo in a gig bag, and then, because the banjo is so heavy, just the gig bag. A banjo is the sort of thing you buy when you are between women. One day you wake up alone and realize that you probably possess several rare and unexploited talents, and probably one of them is playing the banjo. The man at the music store convinced me to buy a more expensive American banjo because I did not, he assured me, want an Indonesian banjo. While he rang me up he said, A quality banjo deserves a quality gig bag. He showed me a selection of gig bags, which are for bringing banjos from gig to gig.

The empty gig bag is less cumbersome than the oar, more open to interpretation. I can wear it on my shoulders like a backpack. People ask about it. Sometimes I run with the bag to make it look like I am late for a crucial gig. Tonight, while doing this, I trip on the sidewalk and tumble hard to the ground, where I lie for a few minutes while deciding what to do. Finally I stand up to see that a half-dozen women have gathered around me. The same women from the river, minus their cameras. Facing the sun, their faces are chiaroscuros of concern. I shudder. Everything all right? they ask.

I think I'm fine, I tell them. A few scrapes.

With the banjo, they say. We meant the banjo.

I reach around and feel the gig bag, which collapses to the touch. Seems fine, too, I say.

Then why not play us a song. Any song will do.

The women are not speaking all together, in unison. But it is clear that when each speaks, she is speaking for the group, that what is said has been agreed upon long ago.

I am *not* going to run away from the women. I will jog. I will canter. They say, Probably forgot his finger picks.

My empty gig bag is not symbolic, I should've told them. The banjo was crafted from the best American birch, which is heavy. It, the banjo, was also tedious to learn. Finger roll after finger roll—miss a note, start again, miss a note—a steady buildup to nothing. One day I wake up alone and realize that my talents lie elsewhere, much elsewhere, in memory reclamation, in reenactments of painstakingly minor events.

I know I should move on, loosen my orbit. It's time I got to work on a family and began steeping in someone else's neediness for a change. Children, and I quote, are the living messages we send to a time we will not see. I should quit sending messages to a time I have already seen. It was only a dance. A crystalline, scar-etched dance, but a dance. The young woman in the yellow dress has become Bruce's stepmother, and I am a memory miser looking backward while I walk, a fiddler crab pretending to make courtship music with my pretend fiddle, serenading.

I sell the banjo and the gig bag back to the man who sold it to me. It is one of those transactions where someone owes someone an apology but neither of us can figure out who, or whom. He gives me six twenty-dollar bills and a small gift-wrapped box.

Don't be so decipherable, he says. Nobody's going to break into a house when the lights are on and the door's wide open.

The box contains a pair of tiny headphones, which I plug into my ears when I'm outside the store. The music starts slowly in the slick folds of my bile duct and then onward into my pancreas, drifting from organ to organ, sightseeing.

I am running. Down the sidewalk, onto the promenade and past the fortune-teller on her stool, past the sickly creek, through intersections, over fire hydrants, up stairs and down. Everything is an obstacle now. I feel my body as an expanse of pores and openings, and myself as a censor voiding all that is unsavory and unpleasant and unhealthy and unmanageable and unctuous and uneasy and unavailing and unforeseen.

I stop by the supermarket, not for rabbit meat, but to run past all the women I ever danced with, my little rogue satellites. No time to reminisce! I say. I run down the aisles, past bins of discounted goods, past the seafood section, the gelded lobsters, the saddles of meat. The women move to the left, right, left, trying to get out of my way, and I mirror their movement, right, left, right. We, each of us, are too obliging. I am too fond of the me in them.

In the supermarket, my headphones make the most nause-ating music. Splenetic tangos. Bilious ballads. It is good for me. It rescues me from sentiment.

I see Bruce and his stepmother stalled behind a pallet of water-softener salt. I approach her from behind, reach around her waist to grip the handle of her cart, and steer it around the pallet. Her velour blouse scuffs along my forearm, but I'm not going to dwell on it. By the time she turns around to see who has helped her, I've already run past.

Sometimes the women who jog in place at intersections until the light changes and I will stop together at an intersection and jog in place together until the light changes. Side by side. It is an act both communal and private, not unlike dancing.

I jog in my boots. I race them all over town.

They are ahead of me, behind me.

I am losing. I am winning.

Now And Give Up Eating Meat It Is Not Hard
When You Know What Foods Are Good To Eat
Fresh Squeezed Orange Is The Highest Food Fresh
Squeezed Orange Is Extremely Healthy I Advise
You To Drink Ten Fresh Squeezed Oranges Daily
The Second Highest Food Is Hass Avocados I
Advise You To Eat Four Hass Avocados Daily
The Third Highest Food Is Bananas I Advise
You To Eat Five Bananas Daily The Fourth
Highest Food Is Apples I Advise You To Eat
Five Apples Daily The Fifth Highest Food Is
Grapes I Advise You To Eat Thirty Grapes
Daily

Love

"VERY VERY UNHEALTHY," CONT.

The Orange Man

The Anointed King Of Orange

Nate Beaty

PAMPKIN'S LAMENT

by PETER ORNER

TWO-TERM GOVERNOR Cheeky Al Thorstenson was so popular that year that his Democratic challenger could have been, my father said, Ricardo Montalban in his prime and it wouldn't have made a five-percent difference. Even so, somebody had to run, somebody always has to run, and so Mike Pampkin put his sacrificial head into the race, and my father, equally for no good reason other than somebody must always prepare the lamb for the slaughter, got himself hired campaign manager. Nobody understood it all better than Pampkin himself. He wore his defeat right there on his body, like one of his unflattering V-neck sweaters that made his breasts mound outward like a couple of sad little hills. When he forced himself to smile for photographers, Pampkin always looked constipated. And he was so endearingly down-homely honest about his chances that people loved him. Of course not enough to vote for him. Still, for such an ungraceful man he had long, elegant hands, Jackie O hands, my father said, only Pampkin's weren't gloved. Mike Pampkin's hands were unsheathed, out in the open for the world to see. He was the loneliest-seeming man ever to run for statewide office in Illinois.

It was 1980. I was a mostly ignored thirteen-year-old and I had already developed great disdain for politics. It bored me to hatred. But if I could have voted, I must say I would have voted for Cheeky Al also. His commercials were very good and I liked his belt buckles. Everybody liked Cheeky Al's belt buckles.

Probably what is most remembered, if anything, about Mike Pampkin during that campaign was an incident that happened in Waukegan during the Fourth of July parade. Pampkin got run over by a fez-wearing Shriner on a motorized flying carpet. The Shriner swore it was an accident, but this didn't stop the *Waukegan News Sun* from running the headline: PAMPKIN SWEPT UNDER RUG.

My memory of that time is of less public humiliation.

One night, it must have been a few weeks before Election Day, there was a knock on our back door. It was after two in the morning. The knock was mousy but insistent. I first heard it in my restless dreams, like someone was tapping on my skull with a pencil. Eventually, my father answered the door. I got out of bed and went downstairs. I found them facing each other at the kitchen table. If either Pampkin or my father noticed me, they didn't let on. I crouched on the floor and leaned against the cold stove. My father was going on as only my father could go on. To him, at this late stage, the election had become, if not an actual race, not a total farce either. The flying-carpet incident had caused a small sympathy bump in the polls, and the bump had held.

Yet it was more than this. Politics drugged my father. He loved nothing more than to hear his own voice holding forth, and he'd work himself up into a hallucinatory frenzy of absolute certainty when it came to anything electoral. My mother left him during the '72 primaries. My father had ordained that Scoop Jackson was the party's savior, the only one who could save the Democrats from satanic George Wallace. My mother, treasonably, was for Edmund Muskie, that pantywaist. The marriage couldn't last, and it didn't. After the New Hampshire primary, my mother moved to Santa Barbara.

My father in the kitchen in October of 1980, rattling off to Pampkin what my father called, "issue conflagrations," by which he meant those issues that divided city voters from downstaters. To my father, anybody who didn't live in Chicago or the suburbs was a downstater, even if they lived upstate, across state, or on an island in the Kankakee River. He told Pampkin that his position on the Zion nuclear power plant was too wishy-washy, that the anti-nuke loons were getting ready to fry him in vegetable oil.

"Listen, Mike, it doesn't matter that Cheeky Al's all for plutonium in our cheeseburgers. The only meat those cannibals eat is their own kind."

Pampkin wasn't listening. He was staring out the kitchen window, at his own face in the glass. He didn't seem tired or weary or anything like that. If anything, he was too awake. In fact, his eyes were so huge they looked torn open. Of course he knew everything my father was saying. Pampkin wasn't a neophyte. He'd grown up in the bosom of the machine, in the 24th Ward. Izzy Horowitz and Jake Arvey were his mentors. He'd worked his way up, made a life in politics, nothing flashy, steady. Daley himself was a personal friend. And when the Mayor asks you to take a fall to Cheeky Al, you take a fall to Cheeky Al. That Daley was dead and buried now didn't make a difference. A promise to the Mayor is a promise to the Mayor and there is only one Mayor. Pampkin didn't need my father's issue conflagrations. He was a man who filled a suit. Didn't a man have to fill something? At the time he ran, I think Pampkin was state comptroller, whatever that means.

So the candidate sat mute as my father began to soar, his pen conducting the air.

"So we go strong against nuclear power in the city on local TV here. But when you're down in Rantoul on Thursday make like you didn't hear the question. Stick your finger in your ear. Kiss a baby, anything— "

"Raymond."

Pampkin seemed almost shocked by his own voice. He was calm, but I noticed his cheeks loosen as if he'd been holding my father's name in his mouth. Then he said, "My wife's leaving me. It's not official. She says she won't make it official until after the election. She's in love, she says."

My father dropped his pen. It rolled off the table and onto the floor, where it came to rest against my bare toes. I didn't pick it up. On the table between the two men were precinct maps, charts, phone lists, mailing labels, buttons, and those olive Pampkin bumper stickers so much more common around our house than on cars.

"Can I get you a cup of coffee, Mike?"

I watched my father. He was gazing at Pampkin with an expression I'd never seen before. Drained of his talk, he looked suddenly kinder. Here is a man across this table, a fellow sojourner. What I am trying to say is that it was a strange time—1980. A terrible time in many ways, and yet my father became at that moment infused with a little grace. Maybe the possibility of being trounced not only by Cheeky Al but also by the big feet of Reagan himself had opened my father's eyes to the existence of other people. Here was a man in pain.

They sat and drank coffee, and didn't talk about Mrs. Pampkin. At least not with their mouths. With their eyes they talked about her, with their fingers gripping their mugs they talked about her.

Mrs. Pampkin?

My inclination before that night would have been to say that she was as forgettable as her husband. More so. Though I had seen her many times, I couldn't conjure up her face. I remembered she wore earth tones. I remembered she once smelled like bland soap. She wasn't pudgy; she wasn't lanky. She wasn't stiff, nor was she jiggly. Early on in the campaign, my father had suggested to Pampkin that maybe his wife could wear a flower in her hair at garden events, or at the very least lipstick for television. Nothing came of these suggestions, and as far as I knew the issue of Pampkin's wife hadn't come up again until that night in the kitchen, when, for me, she went from drab to blazing. She'd done something unexpected. If Mrs. Pampkin was capable of it, what did this mean for the rest of us? I remembered—then—that I had watched her after Mike got hit by the carpet. She hadn't become hysterical. She'd merely walked over to him lying there on the pavement (the Shriner apologizing over and over) and the expression in her eyes was of such motionless calm that Mike and everybody else around knew it was going to be all right, that this was only another humiliation in the long line that life hands us, nothing more, nothing less. She'd knelt to him.

Pampkin's hand crept across the table toward my father's. Gently he clutched my father's wrist.

"Do you know what she said? She said, 'You have no idea how this feels.' I said, 'Maureen, I thought I did.'"

"More coffee, Mike?"

"Please."

But he didn't let go of my father's wrist, and my father didn't try to pull it away. Pampkin kept talking.

"You get to a point you think you can't be surprised. I remember a lady once, a blind lady. Lived on Archer. Every day she went to the same store up the block. Every day for thirty-five years. She knows this stretch of block as if she laid the cement for the sidewalk herself. It's her universe. One day they're doing some sewage work and some clown forgets to replace the manhole cover and vamoose. She drops. Crazy that she lived. Broke both legs. It cost the city four hundred thousand on the tort claim to settle it. I'm talking about this kind of out-of-nowhere."

My father sat there and watched him.

"Or let's say you're on Delta. Sipping a Bloody Mary. Seatbelt sign's off. There's a jolt. Unanticipated turbulence, they call it. It happened to a cousin of Vito Marzullo. All he was trying to do was go to Philadelphia. Broke his neck on the overhead bin."

When I woke up on the kitchen floor, the room looked different, darker, smaller, in the feeble light of the sun just peeping over the bottom edge of the kitchen window. Pampkin was still sitting there, gripping his mug of cold coffee and talking across the table to my father's shaggy head, which was face-down and drooling on the bumper stickers. My father was young then. He's always looked young; even to this day, his gray sideburns seem more like an affectation than a sign of age, but that morning he really was young, and Pampkin was still telling my father's head what it was like to be surprised. And he didn't look any more rumpled than usual. Now when I remember all this, I think of Fidel Castro, who still gives those eighteen-hour speeches to the party faithful. There on the table, my father's loyal head.

I was thirteen years old and I woke up on the floor with a hard-on over Mrs. Pampkin. One long night on the linoleum had proved that lust, if not love, had a smell and that smell was of bland soap. I thought of ditching school and following her to some apartment or a Red Roof Inn. I wanted to watch them. I wanted to see something that wasn't lonely. Tossed-around sheets, a belt lying on the floor. I wanted to know what they said, how they left each other, who watched the retreating back of the other. How do you part? Why would you ever? Even for an hour? Even when you know that the next day, at some appointed hour, you will have it again?

Got to go. My husband's running for governor.

Pampkin droned on. He had his shoes off and was sitting there in his mismatched socks, his toes quietly wrestling each other.

"Or put it this way. An old tree. Its roots are dried up. But you can't know this. You're not a botanist, a tree surgeon, or Smokey the Bear. One day, a whiff of breeze comes and topples it. Why that whiff?"

I couldn't hold back a loud yawn, and Pampkin looked down at me on the floor. He wasn't startled by the rise in my shorts. He wasn't startled by anything anymore.

He asked me directly, "You. Little fella. You're as old as Methuselah and still you don't know squat?"

I shrugged.

Pampkin took a gulp of old coffee. "Exactly," he said. "Exactly."

Either I stopped listening, or he stopped talking, because after a while his voice got faint and the morning rose for good.

Pampkin died twelve years later, in the winter of '92. The sub-headline in the *Chicago Sun-Times* ran: AMIABLE POLITICIAN LOST GOVERNOR'S RACE BY RECORD MARGIN.)

I went with my father to the funeral. The Pampkins had never divorced. We met Mrs. Pampkin on the steps of the funeral home in Skokie. All it took was the way they looked at each other. I won't try to describe it, except to say that it lasted too long and had nothing to do with anybody dead. They didn't touch. They didn't need to. They watched each other's smoky breath in the chill air. Facing her in her grief and her wide-brimmed black hat, my father looked haggard and puny. It only ended when more people came up to her to offer condolences. I don't know how long it went on between them. I'm not even sure it matters. I now know it's easier to walk away from what you thought you couldn't live without than I once imagined.

She was taller than I remembered, and her face was red with sadness and January.

"Don't look so pale, Ray," she whispered to my father before she moved on to the other mourners, her hand hovering for a moment near his ear. "Mike always thought you were a good egg."

Dear Ray,

Hi,

My name is Brendan, and along with my brother Tim, we have been totally wacked since we started to collect autographs. We don't drink, take drugs or smoke, so this hobby is such a trip. No celebrities live around here, so we need to get all our autographs through the mail. Could you please be kind enough to send us each an autographed photo for our collection? It would be awesome!   Thanks!

Brendan   Tim

"TOTALLY WACKED"

Matt Rota

ROUGH CUT

by CHRISTIAN WINN

THE MORMON HAS fought before. Tompkins sees this right off and it scares him, his belly clenching at the ribs as he watches Bean absorb gut shots and jabs from the Mormon, a man they have never seen. Tompkins leans against the concrete wall abutting the vacant lot and stagnant summer creek, the thin hair on his arms lying sun-bright over tightening skin. The Mormon is putting it to Bean, tearing his uniform shirt, biting at his shoulder, landing three blows to Bean's one as they tumble across the oil-mottled corner of the parking lot behind Lowry's Discount Tire out Fairview, in Boise, where Tompkins and Bean work the back yard full-time.

This man has fought in crooked alleyways, Tompkins thinks, in vacant lots, in woeful heat or rampant cold. He's fought where baited air hangs like rot. The Mormon is smooth, direct, a dirty fighter. Feet shuffling like a rough-cut boxer, scratching at the pavement, he spits, purses his thin lips, and takes what he needs from Bean without recognizing doubt or disgust. A man fueled by instinct, Tompkins believes, a man born with desires he has tried to outrun.

Tompkins listens to the grunts and tussle, listens to the heavy traffic up Fairview where men and women roll and lurch in autos, in trucks, air-conditioned and unaware of his watching, his inept leaning. Bean is bleeding, and Tompkins stands still.

"You go in," Bean has told Tompkins. "Go right the hell into a fight. Strike. Shock the man, take something, before he hurts you."

"Right," Tompkins said. "Yes."

It was the second day they met, Bean explaining yellow bruises across his neck, Tompkins listening, feeling his insides flutter, whir.

"That's how I whip ass," Bean said. "Alone. Believe it. I do it alone."

Now it's turned upside down, and Tompkins, afraid for Bean, thinks, I am a statue while my only friend is being beaten. Tompkins aches to step in, but has never fought. He's heard all about it from Bean, but has never drawn a fist, let it fly toward another man, doesn't know if he could. Tompkins would love to be like Bean—fearless, bent—but he is shorter, pale and small, so drawn to the fight, but unable, he believes, to carry out the intrigue.

The Mormon looks like the others Tompkins has seen all summer—the smooth-skinned boys in white shirts and plain ties, missionaries, half-smiling, peaceful as they walk Fairview up beyond the Big and Tall, down past the Food Warehouse. The Mormon boys want someone to talk with, to impart what they know, and they seek them out, strolling over the rubble— cigarette butts and spent condoms, single shoes, underwear, half-eaten cheeseburgers—the chaff Tompkins himself sees each day. These weeks since he and his mother moved, Tompkins has intently watched the Mormons—pairs of boys looking so much younger than he who is eighteen, or Bean who now is twenty.

Bean moves in, casting a white fist that glances the Mormon's neck. The Mormon dodges, ducks, and he counters, connects, a shot to Bean's chest that sounds like a deep drumbeat.

Tompkins leers at the swaying men—Bean bleeding above his left eye, the Mormon circling, stalking. Breath whorling, weighty, their clenched fists try to outdo gravity—rise high, drop hard. Bean says "fucker," "pissant," "lemming." The Mormon says nothing, just pants, wrenches at his tie, throws it aside in a weightless arc, and again charges Bean fast with a low shoulder and quickening eyes, eyes believing in nothing but this sharp blue moment.

Tompkins and his mother came from Seattle in June. She picked him up the last day of senior classes, and they drove east in the Skylark his father left them when he moved south and away four years ago. Tompkins only had one peripheral friend—a junior who called herself Frank, a mousy girl who after school played gin rummy and walked the neighborhoods nearby with Tompkins, talking about her plans to work and travel and expertly know the world. He didn't get to say good-bye to Frank, didn't in fact know he and his mother were leaving that day until they were down I-5 and ramping east onto I-90. It was a long ride to Boise for Tompkins, who sat sullen and angry beside his mother as she smoked her long brown cigarettes and explained that it was an emergency, that they were three months late on rent, that his father and his support money were nowhere to be found. She had a plan, she said. They were going to Boise, moving in with a man she knew, a friend named Mikey. She reached across the console to squeeze Tompkins's wrist. "He's a decent man," she said, smiling wide, showing the fine wrinkles around her eyes and mouth. "People like him. We call him Thin Mikey. He's real tall, honey. You can call him that, too." She let go of his wrist, whispering, "This will all work out fine. Absolutely fine."

Tompkins felt adrift, meaningless, watching the yellow evening sky darken above the open land east of Yakima. If only he could have said good-bye, given Frank a handshake or a kiss.

Thin Mikey, his skin deeply tanned from time spent greenskeeping at the city golf course, was taciturn and almost kind. He stood over Tompkins as he ate breakfast in the cramped, blue-painted kitchen that first morning, and told him he drank with a businessman named Lowry, that he would pull strings, help get him a job.

"You better start holdin' your own now, buddy," Thin Mikey said. "You live in my house, you work. Got it, champ?"

"Sure," Tompkins said, "I guess so," captured, looking into the charming, wry smile of Thin Mikey, held by the surety of his presence. Tompkins hated Thin Mikey hard because he saw why his mother had changed into her red leather skirt before they pulled into Boise, why her voice rose and trilled when Thin Mikey said, "Look at you, Terri," then hugged her as she stepped from the Skylark and into his arms.

Tompkins was trained for the grunt job of tire stacker and gofer by Bean, who has worked at Lowry's for two years, and who took to Tompkins, telling him so many things he hadn't known. Bean has eyes like Tompkins has never seen, eyes like wishing stars. Bean is tall and lithe with sugar-blond hair, and his words have a presence. Stories fall from Bean. This man has lived.

Tompkins knew it right off, listening to Bean retell his seducing of three girls in one night at a party in the orchards. Bean has told Tompkins how he stood up to his own father, kicked his ass real good when he was only fifteen, how his daddy moved out because he was afraid of Bean. Tompkins has sat quietly as Bean's whispered tales of drinking at the High Low Bar down Fairview, where they've been letting him shoot tequila, play pool, and jukebox dance since his senior year at Capitol High. He has watched Bean's long fingers wrap up old tires with gallant strength, with grace.

"You'll see them," Bean has said. "Mormons trooping down Fairview. They like to think we need saving."

"Mormonville," Tompkins said. "That's what Mom calls it."

"They'll come to your house," Bean said. But Tompkins has only seen them walking Fairview looking feckless, so weak, peeking into windows of Confucius Chinese Buffet and Wendy's.

Now Bean and the Mormon circle, and Tompkins balances on one foot, whispering, "Punch, Bean. Swing. Act what you know." Tompkins wants so badly to step in, wants to save Bean from disgrace and pain, but his feet are leaden, hot anchors in the broken afternoon. Tompkins watches closely, listens, solving pieces of the fast-spinning world. Bean is wincing. A plane traces a contrail across the brightest sky. Bean is a staggering wayward idol. Men on that plane are going to London or Sri Lanka, to places Thompkins has never been. The smell of diesel is creeping in from the rumbling trucks up Fairview. The Mormon is so quiet, so strong. Where did he learn this?

He is base and hateful, not weak. A troubled vessel, Tompkins thinks, though he couldn't see it when the Mormon approached him and Bean, alone, straight-faced, grasping a Bible, wearing a backpack. Bean hates them, has always hated them. Bean has wanted to fuck one up, and he taunted this man with talk of sacrilege and polygamy as he has with others who have wandered through the lot to find him and Tompkins stacking used tires in the disposal truck. Bean was telling a story about Sally Beecher, his long-legged summer girl, a woman who has touched places, he said to Tompkins, he hadn't even known existed.

"Porno horny, Tompkins," Bean said. "She wraps me up and breathes the crazy shit in my ears."

"Damn," Tompkins said, and he saw the Mormon ease across the lot. "Here comes a white shirt."

"It's *Bean yes, Bean do me, Bean Bean Bean*."

"Hello," the Mormon said. "Can I talk with you, about something important?"

"Go find your own place in hell," Bean said, stepping to the Morman. "This is ours." He gave him the finger, knocked the Bible from his hands, turned and walked, winking at Tompkins. Bean expected him to walk, to just go as they have all summer, heads held up, hands in the pockets of rumpled trousers. Tompkins saw rage gather in the Mormon as his eyes landed on Bean's.

"I've had Mormon girls," Bean said, hip-thrusting, giddy. "A planet of 'em."

The Mormon set his backpack down and charged Bean hard. Bean never expected it, and now the rap of fist landing on skin levels in Tompkins's ears.

Sometimes Tompkins is curious, wishes Bean would lay off, let the boys give their pitch, let them draw him and Bean into their calm, neatly folded way. It may be easier, may hold the curious numbness Tompkins desires as he walks the avenue, watching, listening with exactitude and purpose each morning, each evening—five quiet and dirty blocks between Lowry's and Thin Mikey's place.

* * *

"Jackass," Bean says, tiptoe backpedaling, nodding, grinning at Tompkins to say, *Okay. I'm okay.* "You think you hurt me?"

The Mormon stands in the middle of Bean's showy pugilist's circle, stands smiling at Bean, a wicked smile, frigid and brave. Tompkins digs into his pockets, finds a matchbook, and lights a cigarette from Bean's pack, smokes deeply, so anxious for Bean. He hears men laughing, coughing in the bay of the Discount Tire. He hears the hum of the hydraulic lift as Bean and the Mormon for one moment stand still. A car honks in the bay, its shallow echo loud, exact. Tompkins swallows hard. His eyes water.

He's seen Bean take on all comers this summer, egg on more, and Tompkins loves him for this. Bean has long muscles tight across the six-foot-two of him, and he is strong, so much stronger than he looks. Tompkins only knows him to belt vital men to the pavement. Yet today he looks misshapen.

"Watch that Bean," Thin Mikey's told Tompkins. "He's loose with his words. I've seen him at the High Low. He comes at things too hard."

"He's tough as shit," Tompkins said. "He's a lion."

"You just watch him," Thin Mikey said. "The boy's not all you think he is. No boy is. Your daddy wouldn't let Bean in the house. Your daddy would smack your head just for thinking Bean's the type of man you wanna be."

"Dad ain't around here though, is he? Besides, I thought you hated my daddy. Besides, Bean'd whip my daddy," Tompkins said. And Thin Mikey walked, shaking his long slow head.

Today, Tompkins thinks, look at Bean fall, watch the Mormon make him look like a wrong thing.

The Mormon—rounded and shorter, his hair coarse and straw-blond—keeps fighting in a steep, rugged fashion and Bean has no chance. "Go get married again," Bean shouts, and the Mormon lunges, reaches with thick hands and ranging

forearms, broad muscles arcing elbow to wrist. He wraps
Bean up, holding him to the shaded concrete beside the
dumpster. Bean can't move, the Mormon has him pinned,
right cheek to the asphalt. Bean is winded, heaving breath for
what seems minutes as resignation creeps in and he appears
sad, quickly unfamiliar, looking to Tompkins for help.
Tompkins remains still, hoping it's over, hoping that the man
will let Bean up, let Bean curse him, send him back into the
hot concrete landscape.

The Mormon, though, is not finished. He pushes Bean's
head, twisting his cheek into the grit. Enraged, he begins
head-butting, spit spraying from his clenched teeth. A low
grunt comes louder with each thrust.

"Enough," Tompkins says, but the Mormon keeps it up,
and Bean begins to scream.

"Jesus Christ." Tompkins runs at the Mormon. "Shit
Jesus!" He lurches forward, knocking the Mormon free of Bean
with a leap, a tackle, feeling a distant weight dart in close,
merge with his own, and bound away. Bean rolls out of the
Mormon's reach, presses a palm to his forehead, pulling it away
to see a sticky bright patch of red. Bean sucks air through his
teeth as he stands, looks at the Mormon above Tompkins now,
shaking his head, still silent. The Mormon is dirty, smudged
with gray oil and dusty blood, but unhurt—maybe one scrape,
two, but nothing like Bean. It will take Bean weeks to look
right again. Tompkins sees the Mormon above him, and in his
eyes the trouble is retreating. He's folding it up, Tompkins
thinks, tucking the anger back inside.

"Don't," Tompkins says, as the Mormon crouches, shoves
his chest lightly, turning to let the fight sit behind him while
he picks up his tie, his bag, his Bible. Holding them, he walks
away, turning once to wave his wide middle finger as Bean
shouts, "God? Fuck God! You think you know anything about
heaven's high reward? Fuck you."

Tompkins stands, tight-chested, unsure, feeling a fragmented sympathy for Bean, who looks weak, twisted up. I have helped him, he thinks, Bean needed me.

Behind the vined cyclone fence, the summer creek runs slow and murky. Tompkins helps Bean creep over the low concrete wall and through a cut hole in the fence to sit beside the creek. They say nothing, though Tompkins wants to ask: "What will Sally Beecher say? What will Thin Mikey tell me about fucking with the unknown? Did you really whip your father?" But these aren't the right questions, and Tompkins waits for Bean to speak. Respect for the defeated, he thinks, plus, he may not be the same Bean. "A sound beating will shrink a man," Thin Mikey's told him. "Separate him from his true self."

The afternoon is so silent. Tompkins can just feel Bean tremble beside him as they sit and dangle their legs above the creek. The water looks rigid, unmovable. Tompkins sets his hand on Bean's left knee. Round, warbling music, bass-driven and primal, slips through the air coming off Fairview, air smelling of hot engines, stale rubber. Tompkins feels Bean breathe, and he lets his hand linger, waiting for Bean to say something bright and wise, waiting for Bean to pull his leg away.

In the creek are two pizza boxes, half-submerged. There are minnows darting, and sun-faded cola cans, water skippers, a computer keyboard, the brown-green reflection of an empty sky and crooked tree branches reaching, reflections of the boot soles of Bean and Tompkins. Bean puts his hand on Tompkins's, taps a finger, and a measured half-smile creases Bean's face.

"Buddy, he fucked me up good," Bean says.

Tompkins pulls back his hand, looks up at Bean, smiling and swollen. "Yeah," he says. "Yeah, he did." And he holds

Bean's stare. "Guess no more work today."

"Thanks for waiting," Bean says. "Before saving my ass." He spits blood and white saliva into the creek, and minnows rise through the quick ripple to peck the oblong spot.

"I'm sorry."

"No," Bean says. "Serious."

"You're not," Tompkins pauses. "I don't know, I couldn't move. I didn't want to embarrass you. I'm sorry."

"You moved. Besides, that fucker was tough."

"Yeah," Tompkins says. He turns, sees that the back lot of Lowry's is still and empty. "Is he the toughest guy you ever fought?"

"Fucking Mormon," Bean says. "Of all the goddamned things. Am I still bleeding?"

Tompkins raises his hand to Bean's head, touches a raw spot above his ear, gently lets blood collect on his thumb and pulls it away to show Bean. "Some," he says. Tompkins points to black bugs skittering the surface over clouds of algae. "Can you believe anything lives in there?"

Bean nods. "Water-walkin' Jesus bugs."

Tompkins nods back, surprise lighting in his chest as he eyes the bright contrast of Bean's red blood on his own gray, dirt-smudged skin.

"There was a guy I fought in school," Bean says. "A guy named Douglass Birr, before you and your mom moved here. Douglass Birr, I fought him because he was a liar and I thought I hated liars. He lied all the time—about girls, money, a stamp collection he never owned, a trip to Japan his family never made. He was a liar, everybody'd known it since the first grade. People hated him for the lies, but they were nice to him 'cause they wanted to hear what would come out next. They liked making fun of him so much that they talked to him, let him pull as much shit out of his ass as he could, just so they could pass it along.

"I always felt a little sorry for him. He was a nice enough dude. But one day he started telling people that he saw me stealing baseball cards from K-Mart, stuffing 'em down my pants and walking out. I knew I had to fight him. Had to."

"You beat his ass, Bean?" Tompkins feels Bean's blood dry on the contour of his thumb. As Bean talks, looking across the creek and the dry weed field, over the cinder-block wall to the black-shingled rooftops that lie beyond, Tompkins brings his thumb to his mouth and tastes Bean's blood. Salt and sweat. The red rumble of Bean. He tastes it, tastes it, wants the red rumble of Bean. It dissolves across his palate—lingers, pulses—and Tompkins remembers Thin Mikey's breath, his sullen words coming in close, slow and angry words stacking up, and he wishes he had it in him to stand and face a man like Thin Mikey, curse him, shove him, no matter.

"Douglass Birr kicked my ass sideways," Bean says. "We fought in the park, all alone, and he kicked the tar out of me."

"I thought you never lost," Tompkins says, biting his thumb, thinking to pierce it, mix in his own blood.

"That's what I always say because shit, Birr never told anyone. You know, that next day at school I told people I fell off my dirt bike, and Birr went along with it. I think he liked the lie of it. He never bragged up a real thing when he finally had a good reason to."

"You're still bleeding," Tompkins says, reaching for Bean, touching more blood to his thumb.

"Mormon," Bean says, grinning, tossing an empty beer bottle into the creek where it bubbles and drops, settles into the silt. "Birr moved to Ontario, and a year out of high school I heard he'd died of a brain tumor. Everybody said he had it coming, that that's what lying fools get. That's what my mom said—*That's what lying fools get.*"

As the new blood dries Tompkins feels it tighten. He wants to taste it again, but Bean is watching, and he wraps his hand up in a fist, taps it softly on Bean's thigh.

"I thought Birr was okay," Bean says. "Liars don't deserve brain tumors. And shit, I really *did* used to steal baseball cards, but not at K-Mart. It was at Ford's downtown. I'd stuff 'em in my underwear, just like Birr said. He knew. He just put a spin on it."

"Shit," Tompkins says, looking high into the western sky at a slowly widening pattern of round white clouds, thinking now of the mornings this summer when he will wake before dawn after lying through short hours of shallow sleep.

These mornings Tompkins will wake thinking of Bean. He will wake hearing Thin Mikey's snore through the wall and know that his mother is lying peacefully next to this man. These mornings Tompkins wants to sit beside Bean, like this now, hear Bean tell him one true thing, no matter if it's a lie. Tompkins will dress quickly in the pre-dawn, a purple light draping his room. Tompkins will lace and tie up his boots, walk the block up to Fairview, point himself toward Bean's apartment, and begin the two miles. On the corner the 7–11 will be bright, empty but for the clerk and one older man who drags a small white dog on a dirty leash. Tompkins will step into the 7–11's yellow light, becoming a part of the snapshot he thinks the truckers and cops can just make out as they speed Fairview. Tompkins pours himself a soda, pays, and sets off for Bean's.

These mornings traffic is sparse, and while walking he will regard the low hills to the east—a deep brown silhouette cast against a brightening ripe-plum sky. The traffic is one car, two—up, up, down—Fairview looking so long, so heavy and wide, as the taillights diminish and wink away, the boulevard rising then dropping toward downtown.

He will sit cross-legged on the sidewalk, tilting his neck

to see the Big Dipper, Mars, Cassiopeia, before he rises to walk past Tuxedo Inc. and The Fabric Depot, walk beyond Big Sir Waterbeds and Canned Food Outlet and the Salvation Army, where furniture and bags of clothing lie mounded in the empty parking lot.

Soon he will be standing outside Bean's apartment, staring at the red diamonds painted on the black front door, wondering what he himself is doing, wondering why, and his heart rushes as he sits on the hood of Bean's car. He imagines Bean inside, tangled up with Sally Beecher, both deep in sleep, enfolded in the trance of skin on soft skin. There are never lights on, and Tompkins always hopes he can find it in him to try the front door, realize it is unlocked, then tiptoe into Bean's kitchen, his living room, his bedroom, crouch down, so close to Bean, listen to him draw and press breath, the same air Tompkins has breathed.

But these mornings Tompkins never checks the door, and he is ashamed of this fear, lost somehow within it. Yet now, sitting creekside next to Bean in the heated summer two p.m., listening to him tell a new story, watching him smile through fast-coming swelling the Mormon has delivered, Tompkins thinks Yes, tomorrow morning I will walk into Bean's, walk through the front door. Tomorrow morning, or the day after. Yes. Soon. I will check the door and it will be open. I will walk in and find Bean, sit beside him, and Bean will not wake. He will not wake, and I will take Bean's hand hanging low above the carpet, and I will hold it close, smell on it the turn of Sally Beecher's hip and her inside, smell the blackening fight scabs and the speeding red blood beneath. I will trace the veins on the back of Bean's hand, and they will point me places that one day I might go.

Creek-side, looking pleased and fearless, Bean says, "Let's just sit here a while. Fuck this day."

"Sure," Tompkins says. And he thinks Yes, Bean, let's sit.

Yes, Bean, I will see you one morning soon, well before work, well before that Fairview fills up with its hot murmur, well before we really know what new fight lies before us.

April 22, 1999

█████████████

Ironwood, MI 49938

Mr. Ray Charles

█████████████

Los Angeles, CA 90018

Dear Mr. Charles:

Hello! My name is ████████ and I am a career counselor at Gogebic Community College in Ironwood, Michigan. I also write career-related material for the University of Wisconsin's Center on Education and Work. I am deeply interested in the area of career development among enormously successful individuals like you. In fact, this letter is part of my research for a book on the subject.

I believe that all individuals have one or more experiences from which they gain clear insight into their future career path. You may have heard people say, "From that moment, I knew what I wanted to do with my life." It is **"that moment"** that I am interested in hearing about. Bruce Springsteen once said, that the first time he strapped on a guitar was the first time he looked in a mirror and liked what he saw. For me, it happened when I was six years old. My mother and I used to watch "The Waltons" (TV show) together. As I watched, I developed a great interest in the character "John-Boy." I'd watch him write near his window and publish his newspaper. From that moment, I knew I wanted to become a writer. That Christmas I asked Santa to bring me some Big Chief writing paper (the same kind John-Boy used).

I'm finding that successful individuals are at least partially driven by an experience(s) like the one above. Please tell me about your "great moment of insight." Did it have to do with singing/music? I'm very interested in finding out how it affected your career development.

If you like, I have enclosed is a sheet of paper and a S.A.S.E. I look forward to hearing about your "moment."

Thank you for taking the time to help me out. I'll send you a copy of the book after it's published.

Sincerely,

[signature]

█████████████

" "THAT MOMENT" "

Robert Goodin

GRANDPA CLEMENS
& ANGELFISH 1906

by JOYCE CAROL OATES

LITTLE GIRL? Aren't you going to say hello to me?

He collected them: "pets." Girls between the ages of ten and sixteen. Not a day younger than ten and not a day older than fifteen. It was an era of private clubs and he was Admiral Sam Clemens of the Aquarium Club, its sole adult. Initiates of the exclusive Aquarium Club were known as Angelfish. Ah, to be an Angelfish in Admiral Clemens's club! No homely girls need apply. No gawky-gangly-goose girls. No fidgety-sulky girls. No smirking girls. No fat girls. No clumsy girls. No pushy girls. No mopey girls. No shrill girls, but girls with voices soft as goose-feather down. Girls who loved reading and being read to. Girls whose favorite books were *The Prince and the Pauper, The Adventures of Tom Sawyer,* and *The Adventures of Huckleberry Finn*. Girls who loved to play games: hearts, charades, Chinese checkers. Girls who delighted in being given billiards lessons—"By a master." Girls who were thrilled to ride in open carriages in Central Park, or in the country; girls who were thrilled to tramp out of doors, to be pulled in sleds on snowy paths in winter. Girls who were the most perfect, poised little ladies, taken to high tea at the Plaza Hotel, or the Waldorf, or the St. Regis. Girls who were very quick—sharp— bright—but not overly bright; girls who might be teased, and might even tease in return, but would never turn mean, or ironic; girls who never rolled their eyes in disgust or dismay; girls who were never, not ever, sarcastic. Girls who had spirit— spunk—but were not headstrong. Girls who thought for themselves but were not willful. Girls who were pretty—often very pretty—but never vain. Girls who were sweet and inno- cent and trusting. Girls who were *dear young creatures to whom life is a perfect joy and to whom it has brought no wounds, no bitter- ness, and few tears.* Girls who were the dearest "pets"— "gems"—"angelfish." Girls who would adore Grandpa Clemens as their Admiral. Girls whose mothers, flattered by the famous author's interest in their daughters, would adore Mr. Clemens themselves, without question. Girls whose fathers would not interfere, or were in fact absent. (Or dead.) Girls in schoolgirl uniforms, their hair in pigtails. Girls who dressed for special occasions in frilly white, lacy white, with white satin bows in their hair, to match Grandpa Clemens's legendary white clothes. Girls whose photographs, with Grandpa Clemens, adorned the walls of his billiards room. Girls who wore with pride the small enamel-and-gold angelfish pins Grandpa Clemens bestowed upon them, as ini- tiates into the Aquarium Club. Girls who were grateful. Girls who wrote thank-you notes promptly, signing *Love.* Girls who would hug good-bye but never cling. Girls whose kisses were swift and light as the peck of a darting hummingbird. Girls who would recall their Grandpa-Admiral tenderly—*Why, Mr. Clemens was the great love of my life because his love for me was wholly pure and innocent and not carnal and if there is a Heaven, Mr. Clemens is there.*

Girls who would not die young.

Girls who would not cry.

"Little girl? Aren't you going to say hello to me?"

It was April 1906. He was seventy years old. He was in a buoyant mood, signing books after a sold-out "Evening with Mark Twain" at the Lotos Club. Upstairs in the opulent paneled library he'd had his well-heeled audience convulsed with laughter, for these gents and powdered upholstered ladies came to be entertained by Mark Twain and not to be enlightened. Very well, then: he'd entertain them. And seated now in a throne-like carved mahogany chair at a desk in the opulent domed foyer he was signing copies of the reissued *The Innocents Abroad.* Hundreds of admirers and each eager to shake the author's hand and receive one of his scrawled, illegible autographs to treasure. And among the admirers waiting to have a book or books signed was this shy girl of about thirteen with her momma, possibly her grandma, one of the upholstered females whose admiration for Mr. Clemens so wearied him, for you did have to be courteous, couldn't cut them off rudely in mid-sentence or yawn in their powdered faces. For this is the damned book buying public and you had to be grateful of course. But exercising his power to behave capriciously as a snowy-haired patriarch of seventy he signaled the girl to come forward to the head of the line, yes and her momma or grandma too, and have their books inscribed and signed with the famous signature.

"And what is your name, dear?"

"Madelyn..."

"Madelyn is a lovely name. And what is your last name, dear?"

"Avery."

"Ah! Madelyn Avery. D'you know, I thought that was you: 'Madelyn Avery, than whom there is no one more savory.'" With a showy flourish, Mr. Clemens scribbled this bit of dog-gerel onto the title page of the girl's copy of *The Innocents Abroad,* and signed it with Mark Twain's signature scrawl that resembled a swirl of razor wire. Close up, the girl was prettier than he'd thought. Her face was delicately boned and heart-shaped and her skin was smooth and flushed with excitement; how like his own daughters when they'd been young, Susy especially, his favorite who had died so many years ago, it had left him stunned and confused that he'd outlived her, it was perverse for the elderly to outlive the young. And this boastful white-haired grandpa life! Madelyn wore her dark brown hair in schoolgirl plaits that fell over her shoulders and bangs that covered her forehead nearly to her eyebrows. Her jumper was burgundy velvet, her blouse had a white lace collar and cuffs; she wore white stockings with a crocheted pattern, and shiny black patent leather shoes on her small feet. Her luscious little mouth was pursed in the effort not to give way to wild laugh-ter. The way her beautiful eyes blinked, he guessed that she was slightly nearsighted; he felt such a pang of affection for her, he could only stare as he gripped the gold-and-ebony foun-tain pen an admirer had given him, in shaky fingers.

Was this a dream? Had to be a dream. Seventy years old and not seventeen. And every girl he'd loved, rotted and gone. *Nothing exists but you. And you are but a thought.*

With exasperating indifference to his other, adult admirers waiting in the foyer to shake his hand and acquire his autograph, Mr. Clemens persisted in engaging the girl and her mother (in fact, the beaming upholstered woman was the girl's mother) in playful conversation, quickly learning that they lived at Park Avenue and Eighty-eighth Street, which was not far away; that Mr. Avery was "in the fur trade"; that Madelyn attended the Riverside Girls' Academy and took piano and flute lessons and hoped to be a "poet"; that she was just slightly older than she appeared, fifteen: but a young fifteen, for she loved ice-skating, and sledding, and kittens; and her favorite of Mr. Twain's books was *The Prince and the Pauper*. Kindly Mr. Clemens said, "But you should have brought your copy along, my dear. I would have signed it for you." Reluctantly Mr. Clemens let Madelyn and Mrs. Avery go, for he had more to say to sparkly-eyed Madelyn, and hoped that she had more to say to him; having slyly slipped into her copy of *The Innocents Abroad* one of his business cards engraved with SAMUEL LANGHORNE CLEMENS and his Fifth Avenue address, and scribbled with the raw appeal—

LONELY! SECRET PEN-PAL WANTED!

Then came stiff-backed Clara, Mr. Clemens's spinster daughter who accompanied him on such occasions and had often to wait, with an air of scarcely concealed impatience, as the vain old man lingered in the dazzle of public acclaim like one besotted. Signing books, shaking hands, receiving compliments. Signing books, shaking hands, receiving compliments. In his tailored white serge suit, his hair a bushy cloud of snowy white, and his bristly downturned mustache a darker white, Mr. Clemens exerted his usual kingly, imperial air, but sharp-eyed Clara saw that he was exhausted: performing the old Missouri buffoon "Mark Twain" was wearing him out at last. He'd never recovered from the death of his favorite daughter Susy, years ago; he'd never recovered from the death of his long-suffering wife Livy, three years before; he'd never recovered from the blow to his pride, that he'd lost a small fortune in poor investments and had not had a runaway bestseller in decades, since *The Innocents Abroad* and *Roughing It*. As he was gracious, crinkly eyed with merriment, and unfailingly seductive in public, so he was sour, spiteful, childish, and impossible in private. His health was failing: his "smoker's heart," his lungs, poisoned from fifty years of cheap, foul cigars—Clara saw in her father's eyes, that had once a greeny-blue glimmer, the look of forlorn desolation of one lost.

During this evening's performance he'd forgotten several times what he was saying, the broad Missouri drawl trailing off into awkward silence and his left eyelid quivering and drooping as in a lewd wink; and during this lengthy book signing, he'd several times dropped his showy fountain pen that had to be picked up and given back to him by one of the Lotos Club minions. Clara cringed to think that his breath smelled sourly of whiskey: he'd slipped his sliver flask into a coat pocket to bring with him, that he might duck into the gents' room to sip from it, she knew as surely as if she'd seen with her own eyes. Now with a daughterly forced smile she leaned over her father holding court in his mahogany-carved throne to whisper in his ear: "Papa, what did you say to that girl?"

She could not bear it, Mr. Clemens's weakness. The most scandalous of Mr. Clemens's numerous weaknesses.

Mr. Clemens shrugged her off. He was his lofty public self, indifferent to any criticism. The crowd adored him, "Mark Twain" was so very funny, a mere wriggling of his grizzled eyebrows, a twitch of his mustache beneath his bulbous, capillary-red nose, the stiff-backed daughter Clara was no match and dared not provoke him, his good humor could turn mean in an instant, crushing her. And so for the better part of an hour Mr. Clemens remained in the Lotos Club foyer warmly shaking hands with admirers, receiving the most fulsome compliments as a starving dog laps gruel, signing for any and all who requested it in the famous "Mark Twain" scrawl that, with the passage of time, and the lateness of the hour, grew ever more grandiloquent and illegible.

Machines propagating machines! As Samuel Langhorne Clemens is a piece of machinery, so Mark Twain is machinery created by machinery. The most delicious irony and yet: who is the ironist? Who is it, who sports with and laughs at humankind? In his notebook, in his lunging scrawl, the page sprinkled with cigar ash.

Yet, waking in the night, taking up his pen, hurriedly lighting a cigar, amid the tangle of damp and tormented bed-clothes he tried to capture the remnant of a dream and its aftermath—*The most exquisitely colored angelfish, pale aqua-blue threaded with gold, delicate fins, enormous eyes, swimming innocently into my fine-meshed net, ah! The dreamer cannot sleep so roused with hard-beating heart declaring I am still alive—am I?—still alive— I am!* As the air of his bedchamber turned blue with smoke like the Caribbean undersea off the coast of Bermuda.

With the next morning's post, in a small, square, cream-colored envelope addressed in an unmistakable schoolgirl hand, it arrived! In secret, where neither the harpy-daughter nor his housekeeper could observe, Mr. Clemens tore the envelope open.

> 1088 Park Avenue
> April 17, 1906

Dear Mr. Clemens,

    May I be your Secret Pen-Pal? I am very lonely, too.

    But I am the happiest little girl in all of New York City today, Mr. Clemens. Thanking you SO VERY MUCH for your kindness in inscribing my treasured copy of <u>The Innocents Abroad</u> which I will show to everyone at school for I am so proud. Thank you for seeing in my face how I wished to speak with you. I hope that you will be my Secret Pen-Pal and no one will know that I am the little girl who thinks of Mr. Clemens every hour of the day and even in the night in my most secret dreams.

    Your New Friend,

    Madelyn Avery

And hurriedly, he replied.

21 Fifth Avenue
April 18, 1906

Dear Madelyn,

Aren't you the sweetest little girl, to write to me, as I had been hoping you would. You have no idea how d—d tedious it is to be surrounded by Grown-Ups all day long & to look into the d—d mirror & see a Grown-Up looking out at you!

Now I have my Secret Pen-Pal, I will not be lonely.

Accordingly, I am including here these two excellent box tickets to next Sunday's matinee of <u>Swan Lake</u> at Carnegie Hall, in the hope that you will join your Pen-Pal Mr. Clemens for the performance. (You will recognize "Grandpa" Clemens by his peg leg, glass eye, & walrus mustache.) After the matinee, we will have "high tea" at the Plaza Hotel, where the liveried help have learned to indulge Mr. Clemens & will treat us just fine. What do you say, dear Madelyn?

Angel-dearest, I am the happiest old grandpa in all of New York to hear that such a sweet young lady is thinking of me "every hour of the day and even in the night in my dreams"— I will place your dear letter beneath my pillow, in fact.

This from your oldest & latest conquest—

"Grandpa" Clemens

And again, as if by magic, the cream-colored little envelope addressed in a prim-pretty schoolgirl hand.

1088 Park Avenue
April 19, 1906

Dear Mr. Clemens,

Thank you for your kind and generous invitation, Momma and I are honored to say YES. We are both so very delighted, dear Mr. Clemens. Thanking you for the kindness that has stolen away my heart, I am your most devoted Pen-Pal. I am the little girl you saw amid your audience and knew, that

I would love you.

> Your "Granddaughter" Madelyn

In the heady aftermath of *Swan Lake,* and the Plaza Hotel,

> 1088 Park Avenue
> April 25, 1906

Dear, dearest Mr. Clemens,

Since Sunday I have scarcely slept a wink! Such beautiful music—and such dancers! THANK YOU dear Mr. Clemens, I will kiss this letter as I would kiss your cheek if you were here. (Oh but your mustache would tickle!) What a delightful surprise it was, when the waiters came to our table at the Plaza with the ice cream cake and "sizzle" candle and sang "Happy Birthday, Madelyn"—the most wonderful surprise of my life. As you said, dear Mr. Clemens, it is never too late to celebrate a birthday, and you had missed mine—all fourteen of them! (But I am not fourteen, in fact I am fifteen. My sixteenth birthday is scarcely two months away: June 30.)

Thanking you again, dear Mr. Clemens; hoping with all my heart to see you soon, I am

> Your Devoted "Granddaughter" Maddy

Ah! With trembling fingers Mr. Clemens took up his pen, forced himself to write as legibly as he could even as hot cigar ash sprinkled the stationery upon which he wrote, and the untidy, somewhat-smelly bedclothes amid which he wrote propped up against the headboard of the grand old Venetian carved-oak canopy bed.

> 21 Fifth Avenue
> April 26, 1906

Dearest Angel-Maddy,

What a proud grandpa here, to receive your sweet letter

covered in kisses! (Indeed, I could discern each kiss quite distinctly, where the ink is wavery and blotted.)

Grandpa is very pleased, too, that our little excursion of last Sunday was so successful; & so we must embark upon another again, dear Maddy, soon. It would be VERY SPECIAL if the SECRET PEN-PALS might meet IN SECRET in Central Park, for instance; but this is not possible, I believe, at least not immediately.

Instead, Mr. Clemens invites you and Mrs. Avery to a benefit evening at the Emporium Theatre where your Pen-Pal will impersonate that notorious Missouri sage "Mark Twain" on May 11, 7 p.m. Tickets are already scarce. (As "hen's teeth"—we may be sure.) A few ladies are admitted to these Emporium evenings—very few—but box seats would be reserved for you and your mother, as guests of the aforesaid Mr. Twain.

Let me know, dear, if this date is possible for you and your mother. Anxiously awaiting your reply, I send kisses in such profusion, there will be none left for anyone else,

Your Loving Grandpa Clemens

Swiftly there came the cream-colored, lightly scented envelope in return:

1088 Park Avenue
April 27, 1906

Dearest "Grandpa" Clemens,

I cannot think how I deserve such kindness! Dear Mr. Clemens, both Momma and I are delighted to say YES to this wonderful invitation. Both of us revere the "notorious" Missouri sage. He is the only gentleman as remarkable as you, dear Mr. Clemens!

If there are blots on this page, it is because tears are fallen from my eyes; I hope my handwriting is not shameful! On this letter, and on the envelope that contains it, I bestow

SECRET KISSES for my SECRET PEN-PAL who has so entered my heart.

Your Devoted "Granddaughter" Maddy

And, in the aftermath of the sold-out, standing-room-only, giddy triumph of Mr. Mark Twain at the Emporium Theatre,

1088 Park Avenue

May 12, 1906

Dearest "Grandpa" Clemens,

For both Momma and me, I am writing to THANK YOU so very much for our unforgettable evening with Mr. Twain. My hands are still smarting for having CLAPPED SO HARD, and my throat is quite hoarse, for having LAUGHED SO HARD amid Mr. Twain's audience of admirers. Momma says, this is a memory I will cherish through my life, and I know that this is so. I was awake and restless through the night, dearest "Grandpa," regretting that, at the theater, I could not see you after Mr. Twain's many curtain calls, to THANK YOU in person; and to KISS YOUR CHEEK in gratitude for I am the little girl who loves you.

Maddy

P.S. Now it is Spring, I am allowed to go out alone to the Park each day after school. There I have found the most secret place, on a little hill above a small pond, where there is a stone bench. To get to this secret place, you have only to follow the foot path behind the most beautiful pink tulip trees visible from the Avenue, at about 86th St. It is so very special, dear Mr. Clemens, I would share it with no one but "Grandpa."

We are all insane, each in our own way, but he could not recall which of them, Clemens or Twain, had made this pithy observation.

* * *

"Papa, is it that girl? The girl you'd met at the Lotos Club? You must not, Papa. You know how, last time—your intentions were misunderstood—Papa!"

Mr. Clemens ignored his harpy-daughter. Would not dignify her rude inquiries with a reply. His elegant cedar cane was in his hand, he was on his way out of the house, he dared not linger in her presence for fear of losing his temper and striking her with the cane.

"Papa, please! I've seen the letters she's been writing you— the envelopes, I mean. Papa *no*."

With an imperial toss of his head, the floating white hair, Mr. Clemens careened past his daughter and outside, into the glittering May sunshine, headed north on Fifth Avenue. His heart thudded in the flush of victory, all of his senses were sharp and alive! How relieved he was, to have escaped the mausoleum-mansion he'd leased for $8,000 a year, a showcase of a kind for Samuel Clemens's wealth, dignity, reputation, he had come terribly to hate. His dear wife Livy had not died in that house, nor had dear, beloved Susy died there, yet the granite mansion was so dark, dour, joyless, it seemed to him that they had; and that, in one of his fits of nighttime coughing, he would die there himself.

Now Mr. Clemens had no wife—and no wish for a wife—his daughter Clara had assumed that role. Clara could not bear it that, at an age beyond thirty, she was yet unmarried; in an era in which a well-born virginal female beyond twenty was beginning to be "old." She had come to resent, if not to actively dislike, the Missouri sage "Mark Twain" to whom she owed her financial security, yet she was keenly aware of others' interest in "Mark Twain" and fiercely protective of him. In her angry eyes was the plea *Papa why aren't I enough for you?*

That most melancholy of questions, asked of us, as we ask it of others! And what possible reply?

Some years before, while Livy was still alive, poor Clara in a sudden fit of frustration, misery, the rawest and most shocking of female emotion, had lost all composure and restraint, began sobbing, screaming, overturned furniture, tore at her hair, at her face, to Mr. Clemens's astonishment crying how she hated Papa, yes and she hated Momma, she hated her life, hated herself. Though the stormy fit had passed, Mr. Clemens had never entirely forgiven Clara; did not trust her; and did not, in the secrecy of his heart, much like her.

Ah, how very different: little Madelyn Avery.

The little girl who loves you.

God damn, that morning Mr. Clemens had *worked.* No one comprehends how a writer, even an acclaimed and bestselling writer, must *work.* Seated at his writing desk, a frayed and badly stained cushion beneath his old-man buttocks that had lost flesh in recent years, squinting through damned ill-fitting bifocals that slipped down his nose despite his nose being somewhat swollen, goitrous with broken capillaries, ah! Mr. Clemens had gripped his pen in his arthritic fingers, covering sheets of aptly named foolscap in his scrawl of a hand, composing his dark satire set in Austria, in the sixteenth century, in which Satan was to be a character; more eloquent than Milton's Lucifer, and far more canny. Except Mr. Clemens was repeatedly expelled from his narrative for he knew nothing of the sixteenth century, in Austria or anywhere, he knew nothing of the physical setting of his tale, as he knew nothing of Satan. (If you refuse to believe in God, can you plausibly believe in Satan?) His curse was to compulsively reread what he'd written, a succession of empty, pompous words, a mockery of the passion in his heart, and so in dismay and disgust he crumpled pages that had to be afterward smoothed out and recopied; for he could not bear to involve a stenographer in this mawkish literary activity just yet. He supposed that, finally, he would publish the tale as one by "Mark Twain"; and, as usual, readers would be confused. What was most upsetting to him was that, now he'd become a wise old man, a patriarch-prophet like Jeremiah, he had so much more of urgency to say than when he'd been a younger man, when words had streamed from "Mark Twain" with the jaunty ease of a horse pissing; when words came with some fluency now, they were likely to be flat, dull, banal; and when words came with difficulty, they were not much better. *A man's sexual capacity ebbs at age fifty. All the rest, that remains, limps on for a little while longer.*

Yet: when Mr. Clemens wrote to little Madelyn Avery, he wrote with ease, and great pleasure. Smiling as he wrote! *Happiest old grandpa in all of New York City.*

He had no grandchildren of his own. Doubted he ever would. His dearest daughter had died. The daughters who remained were not very dear to him.

In a pocket of his white coat, an exquisite little surprise for little Maddy.

How good Mr. Clemens felt! That old stubborn fist of a heart rousing him from bed at an earlier hour than usual that morning, hard-beating *I am still alive—am I?—still alive—I am!* In his legendary dazzling-white suit, in his white vest, white cotton shirt, white cravat, white calfskin shoes, all of his attire custom-made; with his still reasonably thick snowy-white hair (primped by a barber each morning in Mr. Clemens's bedchamber, a custom of decades) stirring majestically in the breeze: a familiar Manhattan sight, drawing admiring eyes and smiles from strangers. If only his damned gout didn't make using a cane necessary! For certainly Mr. Clemens was not *old,* retaining his youthful figure, to a degree. Yet by Tenth Street he'd begun to be winded, and was leaning heavily on his cane; a powerful craving came over him to light up one of his stogies, Mr. Clemens's cheap foul-smelling cigars that were elixir to him.

Suffocating females, you learn to ignore. Mr. Clemens's strategy was to refrain from looking at them any more than was absolutely necessary as his own father, long ago, in the wisdom of fatherly indifference, had rarely looked at him, the flamey-haired son, sickly as a small child, perhaps perceived as doomed, negligible. So the adult Sam would ignore the clinging yet shrill woman his daughter had grown into, an adult daughter now and nothing in the slightest charming about her any longer; in fact there was something distinctly repellent about Clara he could not bear contemplating.

Papa you must not. Papa you are killing Mother.

But a man must smoke! It is a principle of Nature, more basic to the species than the species' alleged Maker, a man must smoke or how is life to be borne?

"Excuse me, sir? Are you—Mark Twain?"

Smiles of startled pleasure. Childlike excitement, awe. How extraordinary it is to see, in another's face, such quick-kindled *feeling!* When one is quite dead oneself, *a dead person speaking from the grave,* to see how, in another's eyes, one is yet alive! Of course it was no trouble for the dazzling-white-clad Mr. Clemens to pause on the sidewalk, to receive the fulsome compliments of strangers, to shake hands, even to oblige with an autograph or two, if the admiring stranger has paper and pen. (In fact, Mr. Clemens never goes out without several pens in his lapel pocket.) Clara would laugh cruelly, *Papa you are a vain old man, you make yourself ridiculous,* but fortunately Clara was not here to observe.

"—so kind of you, Mr. Twain! *Thank you.*"

Strolling on, making an effort not to lean too conspicuously on his cane, Mr. Clemens could all but hear the murmured exclamations in his wake. *Such a generous man, Mark Twain! So good-hearted, so kindly! Such a gentleman.* Balm to his nettled soul after the shrill staccato of his daughter's words.

By Twelfth Street, quite winded and limping from the

damned gout-knee, Mr. Clemens irritably signaled for a hackney cab.

At once the handsome sorrel's hooves clattered on the cobblestone avenue. At once, the risky journey began.

Seated in the breezy open rear of the cab, Mr. Clemens tossed away the sodden stump of his cigar, which had become disgusting to him, and unwrapped and lighted up another. From his well-to-do friends he'd acquired a taste for expensive Havana cigars, but indulged himself in such luxuries only in company. When he was alone, the cheapest cigars sufficed. The pungent smoke made his heart kick oddly and yet, if he refrained from smoking for more than an hour, the damned heart kicked yet more oddly.

How your intentions were misunderstood. Last time.

Papa no!

The hackney cab jolted, Mr. Clemens's jaws clenched. He was thinking not of little Maddy waiting for him in her "secret place" but, so strangely, of himself as a child: the lost child-Sam, whose father had not loved him. Flamey-red-haired, sickly, a bright, restless child, his mother had adored him but not his gaunt-faced father, a circuit court justice in dismal, rural Missouri, a failed and embittered lawyer who had not once—not once!—smiled upon Sam. (It was true, John Clemens had not much smiled upon any of his children.) So strange to be recalling, at age seventy, with amusement, as with the old hurt, and rage, how his father's eyes narrowed and his face stiffened when little Sam blundered too near him, as if John Clemens found himself in the presence of a mysterious bad odor. *Yet I loved the cold-hearted bastard. Why didn't the cold-hearted bastard love me!*

Always there are those in the audience you cannot woo and you cannot win.

Yet: you must!

Work, work! All that you can do, to climb out of debt: to make yourself a rich man, to save yourself from debt, and from death.

And even then, you will never save yourself.

His Angelfish would be spared such maudlin tales. Not a word of his joyless early life would Mr. Clemens relate to his young friends. Not a word of such shame that "celebrity" could never quite extinguish, to his dear granddaughters.

And now here was—was the name Madelyn? Maddy?—a slender, very pretty girl of perhaps fourteen—though possibly thirteen—waiting for Grandpa Clemens as she'd promised, in her "secret place" on a stone bench above a pond partly hidden by flaming azaleas, a short walk from Fifth Avenue at Eighty-sixth Street. Ah, Grandpa's old heart quickened its beat! His fingers twitched in his pocket, gripping the small gift package. The girl was wearing the most exquisitely charming navy blue school jumper with a pleated skirt, beneath the jumper a long-sleeved white cotton blouse; her stockings were fine-mesh, and white; on her small feet were polished, lace-up shoes. Her dark-gleaming hair fell in two plaits over her shoulders and her heart-shaped face was rosy with expectation. *His* childhood had ended in barbarous Hannibal, Missouri in 1857; *her* childhood, in the most civilized quarters of Manhattan, would not end any time soon.

He was certain! He would see to it.

"Mr. Clemens!"—the girl leapt up from the bench where she'd been sitting in a pose of reading, or scribbling into a notebook, and in an instant was upon him, excited, giddy, hugging him around the neck with thin, frantic arms, "—I knew it had to be you, coming along the path all in white, there is no one but *you*"—brushing her warm lips against Grandpa's weatherworn cheek, flushed now with emotion as awkwardly he stooped to receive the hug, refraining from hugging her in turn, smoldering cigar in one hand, cedar cane in the other, "—may I call you 'Grandpa'?—dear 'Grandpa Clemens'—I've told Momma I am visiting a school friend—I have never deceived Momma before, I swear!—I was so very lonely waiting here for *you*—" a kick of his heart, sudden stab of gout-pain giving Mr. Clemens a moment's sobriety as he managed to say in utter sincerity and with no vestige of the stage-Missouri drawl, "Dear Maddy, I was very lonely waiting for *you*."

Can't bear to put on black clothes ever again—odious black—black the hue of mourning, & of death—

Wish I might wear colors, shimmering rainbow hues such as the females I have monopolized—a Garden of Eden!

But I will wear white—the whitest white!—purest most pristine white!—through the dark, terrible days of winter—as no man of our time will ever dare.

1088 Park Avenue
May 14, 1906

Dearest "Grandpa" Clemens,

I am so nervous, so filled with love for my dearest Grandpa, I am afraid you will not be able to read my handwriting with so many blots (tears & kisses) on the page, how can I THANK YOU for this beautiful Angel-fish pin, it is like magic enamel & gold & sapphire eyes oh dearest Grandpa THANK YOU.

At all times now, I think of my dear Grandpa. There is no one else, how could there be I am the little girl who loves you dear Grandpa,

Your Loving "Granddaughter" Maddy

*   *   *

Damned human race! Like syphilis it is. A virulent contagion that must be erased.

For I am Satan, and I know.

Into the Admiral's fine-meshed net they swam, the most exquisite of Bermudian angelfish: aquamarine, big-eyed, with translucent, glimmering fins. And small enough to fit in the size of a man's opened hand.

The youngest Angelfish in Admiral Clemens's Aquarium at this time was dear, funny, sweet little Jenny Anne, the Carlisles' eleven-year-old daughter whom Mr. Clemens would surely see again this summer, when the Carlisles came to stay with him in the country; a more recent addition to the club was Violet Blankenship who was somewhere beyond fourteen but not, Mr. Clemens dearly hoped, yet sixteen, the fickle, flighty, so very "electric" daughter of Dr. Morris Blankenship, a Park Avenue physician entrusted with Mr. Clemens's gout, arthritic, digestive, respiratory, and cardiac ailments; and there was ravishing little Geraldine Hirshfeld, youngest daughter of Mr. Clemens's editor at *Harper's* whom Mr. Clemens had known, and adored, since the child was born, now—could it be?—at least a dozen years ago. And there was the fairy-rascal Fanny O'Brien, whom Mr. Clemens claimed laughingly he could not trust, for Fanny was always teasing; and there was dear gravely sweet Helena Wallace, and there was Molly Pope whose mother could surely be prevailed, with the promise of a small monetary reward, to bring the lanky thirteen-year-old to visit Admiral Clemens in the summer, as the previous summer. Quite openly these charter members of the Aquarium Club wore their Angelfish pins, for their parents saw no harm in it; indeed their parents, well acquainted with the elderly Mr. Clemens's eccentric and generous ways, were flattered at the attention showered on their daughters. *I am seventy & grandchildless & so one might expect the whole left-hand compartment of my heart to be empty & cavernous & desolate; but it isn't because I fill it up with the most angelic schoolgirls.*

"Papa, you make yourself ridiculous. At your age! Papa, I am your daughter: why aren't I enough for you?"

Clara's voice was hoarse and raw, her eyes wild with hurt. Mr. Clemens shielded his eyes from her. He felt a moment's stab of guilt: in Clara's appeal he heard his own. "It might be, dear Clara, that I am a cold-hearted sonofabitch." Mr. Clemens laughed, and turned away.

But, ah!—the Angelfish. No matter the strain in the Clemens's household, no matter Mr. Clemens's disappointment with Clara and Jean, simply to think of his schoolgirl-granddaughters was to feel his ailing heart expand.

Of current Angelfish, all of them members in good standing of the Aquarium Club under the auspices of Admiral Clemens, it was little Madelyn Avery who seemed to Mr. Clemens perhaps the most exquisite, not only for her fine-boned Botticelli features but for her very American spirit: for little Maddy was determined, she vowed, to be a "poet"—"to make the world take notice of *me*."

Admiral's Headquarters
21 Fifth Avenue
June 5, 1906

Dearest Angelfish Maddy,

Aren't you the most beguiling little witch!—I mean, that you have so bewitched your Admiral Grandpa.

Dear girl, will you promise me you will stay as you are? Not change an inch, an ounce? Now is your golden time. Admiral Grandpa commands.

Tuesday next at the Secret Place? After 4 p.m.? The garrulous Missouri cardshark Mr. Twain continues to be so very popular, there is a Century Club luncheon in his honor, with every sort of Dignitary to offer toasts; following which, as your Admiral Grandpa will be freed for the remainder of the afternoon, he invites you to join him in the greenery of the Park; & perchance afterward to high tea at the Plaza. Ah, if my dearest Angelfish can placate Momma, with a tale of a music lesson, or a visit to a girl friend's home! For we must not arouse suspicion, you know.

Ah, I hate it! For it seems to matter not how innocent we are in our hearts, the world of d——d Grown-Ups will judge crudely & harshly & so we must take care.

Love & kisses from the Doting One,

SLC

The utmost caution was required at 21 Fifth Avenue that the harpy-daughter Clara did not waylay Mr. Clemens's innocent missives: he dared not place them on the front table in the foyer for a servant to post, nor even inside the mailbox beside the front door, but made it a point to walk out, to post these tender letters himself.

21 Fifth Avenue
June 8, 1906

Dear Miss Avery,

WANTED FOR LEASE OR PURCHASE: 1 VERY BRIGHT & VERY PRETTY LITTLE BROWN-EYED GIRL-POET STANDING TO THE HEIGHT OF A MAN'S SHOULDER & WEIGHING BUT A FEATHER TO BE LIFTED IN THE PALM OF HIS HAND. ALL RESPONSES DIRECTED TO ADMIRAL SAMUEL CLEMENS, ADDRESS ABOVE.

Very sincerely,

SLC

At the stone mansion at Fifth Avenue and Ninth Street, Mr. Clemens had to be particularly cautious about incoming mail on those mornings when, it seemed likely, he would be receiving an

Angelfish letter: throwing on his dressing gown, kicking his swollen feet into slippers, limping down the massive staircase and with his cane making his way out to the front walk, or up to the street, eagerly greeting the startled postman before Clara could intercede.

1088 Park Avenue

June 20, 1906

Dearest Mr. Clemens,

It is very late—stealthy-late!—at night & the Park Avenue Episcopal Church bell has tolled the lonely hour of 2 a.m. I feel such love for you, dear Grandpa, & my dearest Pen-Pal, Momma believes me to be asleep & has scolded me for "fevered" behavior but how am I to be blamed for it is out of such fevers that poems come to me, that so strangely "scan"—

For My <u>Admiral</u>

No Secret

Is Sacred

Except Shared

'Twixt Thee & Me

For Eternity

Your Devoted "Granddaughter" Maddy

This enigmatic little poem Mr. Clemens immediately committed to heart: the most charming female verse, that quite captivated him.

"'Eternity'! A very long time."

Several of Mr. Clemens's other Angelfish spoke of literary aspirations, and scribbled the sweetest little doggerel-verse, but it did truly seem that Madelyn Avery was in a category of her own. In the Secret Place, Maddy had shared with her elderly admirer some of her pastel sketches she had done for an art class; and he had no doubt, judging from the fervor with which she spoke of her music lessons, that she had some musical talent, as well. He would send the girl prettily bound books of verse by Elizabeth Barrett Browning, and Tennyson; and the newly published *A Garden of Verse Petals,* a gathering of work by American women poets. (He had glimpsed, and been quite shocked by, the rough, rowdy, coarse-minded, and yet strangely thrilling poetry of Walt Whitman, unsuitable for the eyes of any girl or woman.) Mr. Clemens had already given Madelyn a special edition, in fine white-leather binding, of Mr. Twain's *Personal Recollections of Joan of Arc,* which the dear child had accepted with tears of gratitude.

Thirteen was the age Susy had been, when undertaking an ambitious project: a "biography" of her father, of whose worldly fame and reputation she was beginning to have a faint notion. Of course, Susy's father offered her some assistance with the project. Canny Mr. Clemens hoped to publish *Papa: An Intimate Biography of Mark Twain By His 13-Year-Old Daughter Susy* with great fanfare, hoping for sales in the hundreds of thousands of copies; but dear Susy, in the way of growing girls, suddenly lost interest in the project and abandoned it in mid-sentence:

We arrived in Keokuk after a very pleasant

Papa encouraged Susy to continue, perhaps Papa harangued Susy a bit, yet Susy seemed never to have time; and so the "biography" existed in several notebooks, in schoolgirl handwriting, and was too slight and incomplete even to be doctored-up by Mr. Clemens. In later years, he could hardly bring himself to look through the notebooks, which he kept with his most precious documents and manuscripts, to see again the darling girl's large wobbly handwriting with its many charming misspellings and grammatical errors; he felt almost a stab of physical pain, to hear again Susy's voice.

How young Sam Clemens had been in 1886, how young his

beautiful family, and how idyllic the world had seemed! It must have been the case that Satan prowled the larger world and that humankind was as mendacious, wicked, and generally worthless as at all times in history; and yet it had not seemed so, to Sam Clemens. His wife Livy, his daughters Susy, Clara, and Jean, had adored him. And he had adored *them*. Sam Clemens had wanted for nothing then. (Except money. Except fame. Except prestige.) He could not quite comprehend how, not many years later, his world had changed so horribly, in August 1896, when Susy died, it seemed overnight, of spinal meningitis.

After this, life was a cruel cosmic joke. How could it be otherwise! Years, decades, moved swiftly: dashing Sam Clemens became an old man, the flamey-red hair turned snowy-white, his carriage became hesitant, as one walks who anticipates sudden pain; his Missouri drawl, the trademark of his doppelgänger Twain, struck his ears as vulgar and demeaning, yet he dared not abandon it for such buffoonery was Mr. Clemens's bread and butter on the lecture circuit, where money was to be made, far easier than the effort of writing in solitary confinement. (Writing! The activity for which the only adequate bribe is the possibility of suicide, one day.) Mr. Clemens's love for his surviving daughters was a grim duty: they could not manage without him, especially the invalid Jean. He could not bear their company, and understood that they resented him. Clara had quite broken his heart on an anniversary of Susy's death when her Papa had been drunkenly maudlin at their dinner table, in reminiscing of the old, idyllic days at Quarry Farm (east of Elmira, New York), by telling him bluntly that she and her sisters had always been frightened of him; they had loved him, yes, but they had dreaded him more, for his sharp tongue, unpredictable temper, "mercurial moods" and his habit of teasing that was in fact "tormenting." And the damned cigars! The perpetual stale bluish smoke cloud, a stink to be associated with any habitation in which Papa Clemens dwelled.

Of that, these terrible harpy-words, Mr. Clemens would not think.

Instead, he re-read little Madelyn Avery's letters, in the schoolgirl hand he treasured; and re-read the quite astonishing little poem, which, while it did not "scan," did seem to him true poetry, at least of the kind a female sensibility might yield. "The dear child is an inspiration to me. My Angelfish-Muse." And yet: his own words came very slowly, quite literally his old, arthritic right hand moved with crabbed slowness, and his thoughts were so disjointed, he did not wish to squander money on a stenographer. He was having a damned difficult time writing a commissioned piece for *Harper's*, and a yet more wretched time, that was driving him to his favorite Scotch whiskey at ever earlier hours of the day, with his gnarled allegory of Satan in sixteenth-century Austria. Vivid as a hallucination he'd seen Satan as an elegantly attired, monocled and mustached Viennese gentleman, with a seductive smile. Satan as the Mysterious Stranger who inhabits us, in our deepest, most secret beings. *The Mysterious Stranger*—for that was the inspired title—would be quite the finest tale Mark Twain had ever written, the great work of his life, that would catapult Twain finally to the height which his more fervid admirers had long since claimed for him, as the greatest of all American writers; as *The Mysterious Stranger* would compare favorably with the strongest of Tolstoy's moral fables.

Gaunt-faced old John Clemens, in cold storage these many decades in his dour Presbyterian heaven, would look down with abashed admiration at his red-haired son's achievement, would he?

Mr. Clemens laughed to think so. "Revenge is a dish best served cold."

Following *The Mysterious Stranger,* Mr. Twain would embark upon a project to arouse enormous excitement at his publisher's, and among readers in America: a revisit of Huckleberry Finn and Tom Sawyer and Becky, an energetic, heartwarming *New Adventures of.* "This, a runaway bestseller. Perhaps I will publish it myself, and not be content with 'royalties.'"

These leaping, vaulting thoughts, these hopes were to be attributed to little Maddy Avery. Yet actual words, on sheets of foolscap, came with crabbed slowness. Though Grandpa was inspired by his prettiest Angelfish, he was also distracted by her, obsessive thoughts of her. For perhaps he could not entirely trust her not to share the secret—sacred—place with someone else; a "boy friend," as the vulgar slang would have it. Nor did he like it that the girl's mother so politely declined his reiterated invitations to visit him at 21 Fifth Avenue, where he might instruct her daughter in the innocent art of billiards; and seemed to have declined his invitation to be his houseguests at Monadnock, Mass. where he and Clara would be renting a summer place. Other guests would keep the elderly, restless Mr. Clemens preoccupied, of course!—and among them, several very charming Angelfish—but he would miss little Maddy, and he quite resented it.

21 Fifth Avenue

June 26, 1906

Dearest Angelfish,

Are you quite certain, my dear, that your Momma will not consent to bring you to Monadnock, for a week in July? Your doting Grandpa will pay rail fare, & other expenses, happily!

Little Maddy & Grandpa might tramp about the hills, & hunt butterflies with nets; while your Momma, who does not look like the type to "tramp," could sit relaxed upon the terrace overlooking the hills, & be quite content, I am sure.

Ah! Do ask, my dear; I am quite vexed otherwise.

Love & blots (many blots!) from your Grandpa,

SLC

21 Fifth Avenue
June 29, 1906

Dear, dearest Maddy,

I have been troubled, not to have heard from you, dear. My daughter Clara is very annoyed, I have put off our removal to Monadnock for a week, with the excuse that my commissioned piece for <u>Harper's</u> must be completed before we leave.

Our last meeting at the Secret Place was precious to me, tho' seeming very long ago now. Dearest Madelyn, recall

No Secret

Is Sacred

Except Shared

'Twixt Thee & Me

For Eternity!

Your loving Grandpa SLC

21 Fifth Avenue
June 30, 1906

Dearest of all Angelfish—

Forgive me! Your doting Grandpa realized only this morning, dear Maddy, that today is a Very Special Day for you: your birthday. And so I have directed that fourteen "ivory white" roses, one for each year of your precious life, will be sent to you at once with a greeting of HAPPY BIRTH-DAY DEAR MADDY.

Grandpa has been vexed not to see his favorite granddaughter in some time. Please do come to the Special Place tomorrow at 4 p.m.? More gifts shall come to you, I promise.

Do not break my heart, dear one. It is a hoary old "smoker's heart" & quite the worse for wear.

I will seal this letter with blots (kisses!) & hurry to post it, that, if I am very lucky, it will reach my Birthday Girl before her birthday is quite ended.

Your loving Grandpa SLC

21 Fifth Avenue
June 30, 1906
Afternoon

Dear Birthday-Granddaughter,

Tomorrow when we meet (as I dearly hope we will!), I will bring several of Admiral Clemens's special cakes, with magical properties: for my beloved Angelfish to nibble, to keep her always young & so very dear; & always mine; that she might fit into the crook of Grandpa's arm, better yet, so very secretly & cuddly, in Grandpa's very armpit with the grizzled gray hairs that are so ticklish. (For there my Susy pretended to hide, when she was a wee girl.)

Your loving Grandpa has not slept these several nights in the fear that his most tender dreams will vanish & his airy castles topple to the earth, yet again!

Your loving Grandpa SLC

We are all insane, each in our own way. After some deliberation Mr. Clemens decided not to include his gnomic utterance in a postscript but to mail the scrawled letter at once.

Two days later, Mr. Clemens interceded the postman on the front walk at 21 Fifth Avenue, taking from him a number of letters of which but one was of interest to him.

"Papa?"—there stood Clara close behind him, observing him sternly. "You've gone out into the street in your dressing gown and slippers. Really, Papa!"

So distracted did the elderly Mr. Clemens appear, Clara had to wonder if he recognized her.

Upstairs in his bedchamber, Mr. Clemens hastily opened the envelope. His practiced eye leapt to the signature, *Your loving Granddaughter Maddy*, which was consoling, but the letter was a disagreeable shock.

1088 Park Avenue
July 3, 1906

Dearest Grandpa Clemens,

You are SO KIND to send such beautiful roses. Thank you THANK YOU, dear Grandpa! (Not one of my other presents meant nearly so much to me.) I am so sorry that I have missed seeing you in our Secret Place, and I regret that Momma declines your gracious invitations. (There is some unhappiness in the Avery family, dear Mr. Clemens, I will not burden you with, at this time.) Dearest Grandpa, I will be in our Secret Place on Friday, and will hope very hard to see you then. Grandpa's magical cakes will be a treat, I know!

Except I am sixteen, dear Grandpa; and not fourteen as you have been thinking. Already it is a bit late for "nibbling" Grandpa's magical cakes, I'm afraid. But sixteen is a good age, I think. I will be much freer, Momma must concede!

Hastily I must seal this with MANY BLOTS, for Momma is lurking outside my room; and is very jealous, you know. (As my school friends are jealous of my beautiful Angelfish pin, indeed! For I have boasted, Admiral Clemens gave it to me.)

Dear Grandpa, I am anxious to see you on Friday, if that is possible, for my dear Grandpa is quite the most precious being in all the world to me, and no one's opinion means a straw except yours, whether I am a "budding poetess" or not, for my secret identity is, I am the little girl who loves you more than all of the world.

Your loving Granddaughter Maddy

In his state of shock, Mr. Clemens stumbled to his writing table, where for some dazed minutes he sat without moving, as if paralyzed; then fumbled to take up his pen, to write in a rapid, haphazard scrawl,

Dear Miss Avery,

Friday is not possible, unfortunately. My daughter Clara insists we must leave at once for the country, & is already badly vexed, we have lingered so long in this city quite stuporous with heat.

Your devoted friend,

SLC

This terse letter Mr. Clemens quickly sealed, and took away to be posted, for he feared opening it, and amending it; but later that day, having shut his bedchamber door against the ever-vigilant Clara, he wrote, in a more controlled hand,

21 Fifth Avenue
July 5, 1906

Dear Madelyn,

I am pleased that you found my little gift of roses so beautiful; yet must apologize, the bouquet was less plenteous than you had reason to expect. Apologies, my dear! But then S.L.C. is an old man, as we have known.

Sincerely,

SLC

Again, Mr. Clemens hurriedly sealed this letter, and limped out onto Fifth Avenue, using his cane, to post it. And in the morning, after a miserable night of sleeplessness, wracking coughs, cigars, and Scotch whiskey, in a fever he wrote,

21 Fifth Avenue
July 6, 1906

Dear Madelyn Avery—

Sixteen!—that will not do, you know. A most beguiling little witch, to give no hint of your age—

It will not be possible for us to meet again, I am very sorry. Mrs. Avery may now relax her vigilance—

I regret that I will not be able to peruse your verse any longer, dear Madelyn—as I am expected to deliver to my publisher a "major" new work, very soon.

Sixteen is something of an awkward age—is it not? You are both a schoolgirl & a "young lady"—& soon to be schooled in witchery. Your Grandpa might regret, he failed to provide you with magical cakes to nibble in time; & so the old fool must refrain from sending you a final lot, for that would not be appropriate any longer—would it?

When Sam Clemens was sixteen, a century ago, in the raw State of Missouri, he was obliged to be an adult; & to work a ten-hour day, at the least, when he was lucky. In New York City of our time, in the civilized domains of Park Avenue, et cetera, a sixteen-year-old young lady is poised on the brink of "fiancée"—"bride"—"wife"—indeed, "mother": quite beyond the old Admiral's jurisdiction.

If you wish to wear your Angelfish pin, my dear, I hope that you will not go about boasting of its origins—

Unless—there is a magic in such wishes—you might go back to fourteen—to thirteen!—for there is such innocence in your dear face, there could be no impropriety.

Auf wiedersehen, & goodnight—

SLC

So vanished my dream. So melted my wealth away. So toppled my airy castle to the earth and left me stricken and forlorn.

Ah, Sam Clemens was a revered man among men! A man with countless friends of whom many were very wealthy. Yet Mr. Clemens's closest friend was Mr. John whom he'd met long ago in 1861 in Carson City, Nevada, in a rowdy and drunken poker game.

Mr. John was a perpetual houseguest at 21 Fifth Avenue. Mr. John traveled with Mr. Clemens into the country. Mr. John listened closely to the applause erupting in Mr. Clemens's presence: how protracted, how ebullient, how punctuated by whistles and cries of *Bravo! Bravo!* Mr. John was not invariably impressed. Mr. John was by nature not very impressionable. Mr. John was a cold-hearted sonofabitch, in fact. Yet Mr. John was Mr. Clemens's dearest comfort. Mr. John nestled snug in Mr. Clemens's inside coat pocket. Mr. John was warmed by Mr. Clemens's blood. Mr. John slept beneath Mr. Clemens's goose-feather pillow. In the night, Mr. Clemens was wakened, shuddering, for his skin had turned cold, his blood-warmth drained from him by Mr. John.

In the filigree-framed mirror Mr. Clemens stood with Mr. John tremulous in his right hand.

Mr. John?

Yes, Mr. Clemens?

Are you at the ready, Mr. John?

I believe so, Mr. Clemens.

You will not flinch, Mr. John?

Sir, if you do not flinch, I will not flinch.

Is that a promise, Mr. John?

Why no, sir. It is not a promise.

What? Why not? Are you not my Mr. John?

Indeed yes, Mr. Clemens. Which is why I cannot be trusted.

Mr. John would be discovered by Clara in a locked cabinet in Mr. Clemens's bedchamber, after Mr. Clemens's death.

I am alive, still—am I? Is this life?

* * *

Mr. Clemens withdrew to Monadnock where, to fill up the hole inside him, he was determined to *write*.

In Monadnock Mr. Clemens too up again, with the fever of madness, as with muttered curses, the turgid tale of the Viennese-gentleman Satan; with Mr. John as his solace, though the cold-hearted sonofabitch could scarcely be trusted, he managed to finish, in the fever of loathing, a ranting polemic titled "The United States of Lyncherdom," which no magazine would publish during his lifetime; he exhausted himself and all who attended to him in that household on tiptoe, with his scattered imaginings of *The New Adventures of Huckleberry Finn*: "For surely there is a God-damned bestseller here. And surely, it is time." Yet in his notebook recording in a wandering and dreamlike hand, the page sprinkled with hot ash, *Huck comes back 60 years old from nobody knows where—& crazy. Thinks he is a boy again, & scans every face for Tom & Becky, etc. Tom comes, at last, 60, from wandering the world & finds Huck, & together they talk of the old times, both are desolate, life has been a failure, all that was lovable, all that was beautiful, is under the mold. They die together.*

"Well, Papa. You must be flattered, your Park Avenue pen-pal is most tenacious."

There stood Mr. Clemens's devoted daughter Clara, hands clasped in a lace handkerchief that looked as if it had been strangled.

Dear Clara, glaring-eyed and smirking. Yet, in the sprawling country place in the scenic Monadnock hills, where Mr. Clemens took care to surround himself with a succession of lively houseguests, including the Hirshfelds, the Wallaces, and canny Mrs. Pope and her daughter Molly, calmly the elderly gentleman received the letters forwarded from 21 Fifth Avenue as from another, left-behind life: cream-colored and lightly scented envelopes addressed in an eager schoolgirl hand to *Mr.*

Samuel Clemens. Too elderly, and too much the gentleman, to rise to the bait of Clara's sneering tone but calmly taking away the cream-colored envelopes with his morning's stack of mail, to open and peruse in the privacy of his bedchamber where Clara dared not venture. At least not while Mr. Clemens was on the premises.

"'Tenacious'—yes! As a blood-sucker to the carotid."

1088 Park Avenue
July 7, 1906

Dear Mr. Clemens,

I am conscious of having offended you, for your letter of the other day that had no date but seemed to have been written on July 5 was so abrupt—have read & read it with eyes dimmed by tears—I will not wear my beautiful Angelfish pin—if you do not wish—I will return it to you—if so instructed—

It may be that Momma will be taking me away to the Jersey shore—Momma's family at Bayhead, on the ocean—this year, I don't wish to go—

I wish—dear Mr. Clemens—that I could "turn the clock back"—I think you would not be angry with me then

May I send love & blots? For I am feeling so lonely, for I am the little girl who loves Mr. Clemens Who else am I

Your Devoted Friend,

Madelyn Avery

1088 Park Avenue
July 8, 1906

Dearest Mr. Clemens,

I have just now received your letter of July 6—it is horrible to me, to think that there has been a misunderstanding—Mr. Clemens, I did not think your lovely bouquet of roses was "less plenteous" than expected but wished only to inform you that I am not fourteen but sixteen. Dear Grandpa, I meant no harm!

I hope that you will forgive me? I am not sure what I have done that is wrong. I am very stupid I know. At school our teacher praises my work & there is this buzzing in my head <u>Oh but you are stupid, & you are ugly</u> & it seems that my teacher is mocking me & all the other girls know. Momma has scolded me lately, for it seems that I can do nothing right, Momma says I am "clumsy"—I am always "blundering." If I thought that my dear Admiral Clemens was unhappy with me or scorned me I would be struck to the heart & like Joan of Arc I would welcome any hurt to be done to me.

Your Devoted Friend,

Madelyn Avery

1088 Park Avenue

July 11, 1906

Dear, dearest Mr. Clemens,

Re-reading your letter, I seem to feel that you are unhappy with me because I am *sixteen.* Please don't stop loving me Mr. Clemens, you are so kindly a person, my dearest "Grandpa" who would not hurt me? May I send you love & blots? Admiral-Grandpa has teased to make me laugh, please when I wake from my sad dream, let this be so.

Your Devoted Friend,

Madelyn Avery

1088 Park Avenue

July 15, 1906

Dear Mr. Clemens,

I believe that you are away in the country—"Monadnock"—which I have not seen—where you were so kind to invite Momma & me—but we could not visit Oh I wish that I could be there now, dear Admiral Clemens! It would be so wonderful to see your kindly face, & hear your voice again dear Grandpa it is very lonely here

You promised to teach me billiards dear Grandpa have you forgot

I wish I knew why, you are angry with me. I had thought that sixteen was a hopeful age for it would allow more freedom, even Momma must concede. When you gave me books & encouraged my poems, Mr. Clemens it seemed you had hope for me, in two years I will go away to college & be a "young lady"—I had not thought that was shameful

I hope that you will write to me soon, I am feeling very sad for I am the little girl who loves you,

Your Devoted Friend,

Madelyn Avery

223 Oceanview Road
Bayhead, New Jersey
July 23, 1906

Dearest Mr. Clemens,

As no letters have been forwarded to me here, at my grandparents' summer place, I am fearful that you have not written; & that you continue to be displeased with me. I wished to say that in your letter of July 6 which I will cherish for all of my life, you are so correct, sixteen is an "awkward" age, & a very unhappy age. I am not conscious that "witchery" will come to me but other things will come, unwished for. I am ashamed, that I have become this age, that I could not help. I have cried myself to sleep many nights, I feel that my heart is raw & sore like something scraped. Dearest "Grandpa," I promise I will not be a "fiancée"—"bride"—"wife"—"mother." Not ever!

How I wish that I had been able to meet with you in the Secret Place, in June; but there was much confusion in our household at that time, as there is now.

I have kept the beautiful Angelfish pin to place beneath my pillow, & to kiss recalling your kindness & how you seemed to love me then. It is Pudd'nhead Wilson, I have been reading lately, who speaks in a strange jeering voice in my head: "How hard it is that we have to die"—a strange complaint to come from the mouths of people who have had to live.

Hoping that you will write to me soon, & we may meet again in the Secret Place when this summer is over, I am the little girl who loves you,

"Maddy"

223 Oceanview Road

July 27, 1906

Dearest Mr. Clemens,

Forgive me this page is splotched with tears & spray from the surf. I am writing to you in my Secret Place here, where nobody comes for the sand is coarse & the jutting rocks ugly & it is too far for them to hike, so they leave me alone. My dearest friend now is Pudd'nhead Wilson you once told me, so strangely dear Mr. Clemens, was but a machine: "Why is it that we rejoice at a birth and grieve at a funeral? It is because we are not the person involved."

Thinking of you, my dear, "oldest" Pen-Pal, I am the little girl who loves you,

"Maddy"

223 Oceanview Road

August 1, 1906

Dear "Grandpa" Clemens,

In a dream last night you spoke to me, & I heard your voice so clearly!—though I could not see your face, all was blurred. "I am not well, dear Maddy. I am waiting for you here." This is what I heard, & woke excited & trembling! Oh I wish Monadnock was close by here—I would walk to see my oldest & dearest friend—I would bring you bouquets of the most beautiful wild roses & marsh grasses that grow here, I believe you would like for you had many times said, you adore Beauty.

As Love is not visible
So Love is not divisible
Love is framed in Time
Yet Love is of No Time
Love twixt thee & me
Is a promise of Eternity

I promise I will not eat, dear Grandpa! To keep myself from growing. I am very disgusted with myself, to look into the mirror is a horror. Yet I would nibble the magical cakes, like Alice to become smaller. Very secretly & cuddly then to hide in Grandpa's armpit, for I am the little girl who loves you, please will you forgive me?

"Maddy"

223 Oceanview Road
August 19, 1906

Dearest Mr. Clemens,

This long time I have been waiting to receive a letter frm from you but none has come, it is a shamful thing to confess Momma did not wish anyone to know Father does not live with us now. When I was so happy with you at the Plaza Hotel, & Momma scolded me for being so excitable, this was a time of worry for us, for Father had only just left us, & there was talk of Father returning. But Momma is always saying this, & weeks & months have gone by, & no one in the family (here at Bayhead, where I am so lonely) will tell me about him. But I know that it is a shamful thing. Sometimes I believe I see Father at a distance on the beach & he is with strangers but it is never Father really. And sometimes it is you, dear Mr. Clemens. But it is never Father, and it is never you.

Still I am hoping you will forgive me. Momma says I am very childish for one reputed to be "smart" & I cry too often yet Momma does not know, my deepest tears are hidden from her.

Sending my dear "Admiral-Grandpa" love & blots from this little girl who loves him for Eternity.

"Maddy"

1088 Park Avenue

August 24, 1906

Dear Samuel Clemens,

Excuse me for writing to you! For I have become quite desperate.

I hope that you will remember me from happier times, I am Muriel Avery, Madelyn's mother. Once you were so kind to invite my daughter and me to Swan Lake, and to the Plaza Hotel afterward; and to a memorable "Evening with Mark Twain" at the Emporium Theatre.

Dear Mr. Clemens, I think that you would be concerned to know that my daughter Madelyn has become, over the past several weeks, deeply unhappy and distraught and refuses to eat so that she has become shockingly thin, like a living skeleton it was a terrible discovery I made helping her to bed, to feel her poor sharp bones through her clothing. Her skin is so pale, her wrist bones like a sparrow's bones, I have tried to seek help for Madelyn but it is very hard to force her to eat and if you become angry with her, she will turn her face to the wall as if to die. Madelyn is a shy girl, lonely and confused about her father (who has left his family and is seeking a divorce, against all reasonable decent behavior). We have returned to the city in this sweltering heat so Madelyn can receive hospital care. I am afraid her condition will worsen quickly. Mr. Clemens I am sick with worry over my daughter, she has told me you stopped writing to her. At the ocean Madelyn would walk along the beach for miles, we did not know where she was often and feared she might wade out into the surf and drown. She is so thin, Mr. Clemens, but appealing to you out of the kindness of your heart if you could simply write a brief letter to the child as you had done before, if you could explain to her that you are not "angry" with her—not "disgusted"—for Madelyn has got it into her head that this is so. You have had daughters, you said, & so you know how emotional they can be at Madelyn's age. Any kindness you could do for Madelyn, I think it would help very much.

To save my daughter's life I am writing like this to a famous man, please do not be angry with me. I am not a very good writer I know. Madelyn has said you appear in her dreams but your face is turned from her now, she is heartbroken! Please Mr. Clemens tell this poor child who adores you that you do not hate her.

Thanking you beforehand for your kindness, I am,

Sincerely yours,

(Mrs.) Muriel Avery

> 1088 Park Avenue
>
> August 28, 1906

Dear Samuel Clemens,

It has been some days and I have received no reply from you on an urgent matter regarding the well-being of my daughter Madelyn Avery.

Mr. Clemens, please know that yesterday evening Madelyn was admitted to Grace Episcopal Hospital on Lexington Avenue for her weight has dropt terribly, the doctor says she resembles an eleven-year-old more than a girl of sixteen. She is very quiet and depressed in spirit not seeming to care if she lives or dies, not any of us in her family can appeal to her. The doctor has warned that her young heart will be damaged and her kidneys will suffer a "shock" soon if she does not nourish herself with liquids at least. Oh I have prayed to God, all the family has prayed, and our minister, Madelyn's father has been to visit with her but Madelyn shuts her eyes and will not hear.

Still I think, dear Mr. Clemens, a letter or a card, still more a visit (but I would not hope to wish for this!) would make all the difference to Madelyn. If you could find it in your heart, dear Mr. Clemens, I would be so very grateful.

Thanking you beforehand for your kindness, I am,

Sincerely yours,

(Mrs.) Muriel Avery

1088 Park Avenue

August 30, 1906

Dear Samuel Clemens,

Mr. Clemens, I have discovered your numerous letters to my daughter that Madelyn had hidden in her room. I am so very upset. Such talk of "Grandpa"—"Angelfish"—the "Secret Place"—"love"—which has come to light, has made me ill. In the hospital, Madelyn will not speak of this, & nobody wishes to frighten her. Unless I hear from you by return post, Mr. Clemens, I will turn these letters over to my attorney & we will see if a "lawsuit" might not ensue!

Sincerely yours,

(Mrs.) Muriel Avery

I am saying these vain things in this frank way because I am a dead man speaking from the grave. I think we never become really & genuinely our entire & honest selves until we are dead yet waking to discover himself short of breath stumbling in the tall marsh grass at Monadnock, the girls had run ahead, Angelfish leading their Admiral on a giddy moth hunt by moonlight each of the girls with butterfly nets and handkerchiefs soaked in chloroform (the most merciful means of death, Mr. Clemens was given a small bottle of chloroform by his physician), ah! the smell was sweetly sickening yet strangely pleasant, Mr. Clemens called after the impatient girls to wait for him, please

wait for him, but the girls were hiding, were they?—laughing? *Mr. Clemens! Grandpa!* Sharp, cruel cries he felt like pain
stabbing inside the bony armor of his chest, laugher like shat-
tering glass, the great glaring white eye of the moon overhead
unblinking and pitiless in judgment as Mr. Clemens staggered, slipped to one (gout-stricken) knee in the marshy soil,
was it possible that one of the ravishing Angelfish had tripped
him?—had snatched away his cane?—another was tormenting
him with her butterfly net striking at his shoulders and bowed
head, and yet another—the beguiling little witch Molly
Pope?—swiping at his face with her chloroform-soaked handkerchief for by dusk of this long late-summer day the
Angelfish had grown bored with such childish games as
hearts, charades, Chinese checkers, only a moth hunt by
moonlight would satisfy them, wildly swinging little nets and
their moth prey trapped and quickly "put to sleep" and tossed
into a bag, running into the marsh grass, Clara had strongly
disapproved of the Angelfish's shrieking careless play but
Clara had hardly dared to pursue them, Mr. Clemens had
hardly dared to "rein them in" for fear of provoking their vex-
ation, poor Mr. Clemens in grass-stained white clothing, the
elderly man uncertain as a giant moth that has been wounded,
his white hair floating upward as you'd expect a ghost's hair to
float, no wonder the girls shrieked with laughter at the dod-
dering old Admiral who could not keep up with them, could
not turn quickly enough to defend himself against their sly
pokes and jabs and the fiercest of the attacks came from—could
it be sweet, grave little Helena Wallace?—by moonlight transformed into a demon, legs like flashing scimitars and eyes like
smoldering coals. *Mr. Clem-mens! Grand-pa! Over here!* Teasing,
or tormenting, for the elderly man had fallen behind in the
hunt, clumsily he'd swung at moths, dusky-veined moths,
moths with the most intricately imbricated wings, this long
day he'd been distracted by harmful thoughts, a succession of

telephone calls, hateful calls from Mr. Clemens's attorney in Manhattan, harried consultations about an urgent matter not to be revealed even to Clara (at least, not until there was no alternative except revealing it) for it was a very delicate matter, a matter of absolute privacy, for Mr. Clemens was a gentleman of the utmost integrity and reputation, an emblem of purity in an age of the impure, observe how Mr. Clemens never appears in public except in radiant white, the sole living American male so pure of heart and motive he might clad himself in spotless white, it must not be allowed that a conniving blackmailing female might destroy Mr. Clemens's reputation and so Mr. Clemens's attorney would see to it, cash payments would be made in secret, promises of confidentiality would be extracted, legal documents signed, a young lady's hospital and medical expenses paid in full, perhaps an extended stay in an upstate sanitarium in which Mr. Clemens's miserably unhappy invalid-daughter Jean resided. Ah, this day! this troubled day! this day when the Admiral had been feeling most vulnerable and needy of kisses, Angelfish on his knees, surprisingly long-legged and robust Angelfish, hot-skinned Angelfish, giddy, reckless, taking advantage of an old man's weakened state, winking at one another behind the old man's back, cheating at hearts and Chinese checkers and even at billiards which was Mr. Clemens's sacred game, that sly little witch Molly Pope had won five hundred copper pennies from him, he'd managed to laugh as if the loss had not irked him, had not angered him, he'd been hurt, too, by the capricious behavior of Violet Blankenship all but laughing in his face, Violet's soft young breasts poking against her white middy-blouse that was damp with perspiration, and her eyes!—Violet's eyes!—unnerving as the eyes of a giant cat. Stumbling now in the tall damp spiky-sharp marsh grasses behind the summer house, his swollen feet throbbing with pain, and pain in his chest stabbing and fierce leaving him panting, who has taken Grandpa's cane?—for Grandpa cannot walk without his cane, poor Grandpa is forced to crawl. Up at the house where a light was burning Clara called to him in a pleading voice *Papa come here! Papa this is very wrong!* Sudden as a demon-quail the girls flew up at Grandpa out of the tall grasses poking at him with their moth-nets, swiping at his nose with chloroform-soaked hankerchiefs, how pitiless their young laughter, how cruel their taunts, Grandpa Clemens has slipped and fallen flailing his arms to regain his balance managing with difficulty to right himself, despite the terrible pain in his legs, reaching out for his Angelfish, yearning to embrace his Angelfish, his heart kicking and pounding in his chest and so he knows *I am still alive—am I?—still alive?—is this life?*

NOTE: At his death in April 1910, at the age of seventy-five, Samuel Clemens was survived by his daughter Clara who eventually married and had a daughter, Clemens's sole descendent, who committed suicide in 1964.

"Grandpa Clemens & Angelfish 1906" is a work of fiction drawing, in part, upon passages from *The Singular Mark Twain* by Fred Kaplan, *Mark Twain's Aquarium: The Samuel Clemens-Angelfish Correspondence 1905-1910* edited by John Cooley, and *Papa: An Intimate Biography of Mark Twain By His Thirteen-Year-Old Daughter Susy.*

Middle Island, NY 11953-1453

Dear Ray Charles,

Man, it's been a long time.

I've written a "rap" song, that I'd like to ask you to sing or talk.

You don't have to do this. If you do, I expect a reasonable residual, And I hope I can count you amongst my friends.

"It's not, burn, baby burn.
It's not loot, baby loot.
It's not fight, baby, fight.
It's not shoot, baby, shoot.
It's learn , baby learn
So you can earn ,baby earn.

That's Ray Charles on Adam Clayton Powell
How do you expect to tell the future
if you can't learn from the past.

So let's vote, baby, vote
so we'll have hope, baby, hope

                    Please write and tell me what you think,

Notes from the underground,
Your Friend,

PS Thanks for the photo.

"SING OR TALK"

CONTRIBUTORS

GREG AMES lives and works in Brooklyn. His stories have appeared in numerous literary journals and magazines, including *Open City, Fiction International, The Sun,* and *Other Voices.* A frequent reader at the KGB Bar in Manhattan, Ames received a special mention in the 2003 Pushcart Prize anthology and in the *Best American Nonrequired Reading 2004.* To learn more, visit www.gregames.com.

ARTHUR BRADFORD's first book, *Dogwalker,* was published by Knopf in 2001 and is out in Vintage paperback now. His stories have appeared in *Esquire, Zoetrope, The O Henry Awards Anthology,* and *McSweeney's.* He is the co-director of Camp Jabberwocky, America's longest-running sleepover camp for people with disabilities, and the creator of the documentary film series "How's Your News?"

RODDY DOYLE's new novel, *Paula Spencer,* will be published in January 2007.

STEPHEN ELLIOTT is the author of the novel *Happy Baby* and the story collection *My Girlfriend Comes to the City and Beats Me Up.*

CHLOE HOOPER's first novel *A Child's Book of True Crime* (Scribner) was shortlisted for the Orange Prize. She is working on a second novel.

MIRANDA JULY is a filmmaker, performer and writer living in Los Angeles. Her first feature film, *Me and You and Everyone We Know,* was released in 2005. Her book of short stories, *No One Belongs Here More Than You,* will be published in the spring of 2007.

KEVIN MOFFETT's short story collection, *Permanent Visitors,* won the Iowa Short Fiction Award and was published in October. His stories are forthcoming in *The Best American Short Stories 2006* and the Pushcart Prize anthology.

YANNICK MURPHY writes stories and novels. Her latest book, *Here They Come,* was published in March by McSweeney's. Her next novel, a fictional account of the life of Mata Hari, will be published in 2007.

She lives with her husband Jeff and her three children, Hank, Louisa, and Kit.

JOYCE CAROL OATES is a recipient of the National Book Award and the PEN/Malamud Award for Excellence in Short Fiction. She is the Roger S. Berlind Distinguished Professor of the Humanities at Princeton University and has been a member of the Amercian Academy of Arts and Letters since 1978. She is the author of *We Were The Mulvaneys, Blonde, The Falls,* and the forthcoming *Black Girl White Girl.*

PETER ORNER is the author of *The Second Coming of Mavala Shikongo* and *Esther Stories,* a finalist for the Pen/Hemingway Award. He is the winner of a 2006 Guggenheim Fellowship. Born in Chicago, Orner currently lives in San Francisco.

RAJESH PARAMESWARAN is a writer from Missouri City, Texas.

HOLLY TAVEL is a writer and artist who was born in Florida, moved to Brooklyn, and resides, for the time being, in Providence, Rhode Island. She received her MFA from Brown University. Her project "S Returns to the Phantom City," a "story-walk" based around the 1915 Panama Pacific Exposition, was recently included in the 2006 Conflux Psychogeography Festival in New York City. She is at work on a novel.

A. NATHAN WEST lives in Philadelphia. He works at Tangerine restaurant and studies Spanish at Temple University.

CHRISTIAN WINN lives in Boise, Idaho, where he writes and teaches and bartends. His stories and poetry have appeared in *The Chatta-hoochee Review, Gulf Coast, cold-drill,* and *Faster Than Sheep.* He is a recent graduate of Boise State University's MFA program.

For more information on the Ray Charles letters, visit www.letterstoray.com.

OUR NEXT ISSUE:
ACTUALLY MAGNETIC

Issue 22 will be a three-part exercise in inspired restriction, bound together by invisible chains of force. Book One: poets like DC Berman, Mary Karr, Michael Ondaatje, and Denis Johnson pick poems of their own and poems by other poets, who then pick poems of their own and poems by other poets, who then—etc. Book Two: F. Scott Fitzgerald's unused story premises, realized by writers of today—Diane Williams, Salvador Plascencia, Sam Lipsyte, and others. Book Three: France's legendary Oulipeans offer a rare glimpse into their current experiments with linguistic constraint. All this in our biggest issue ever, out by the end of the year.

ALSO WORTH CONSIDERING:
FOUR ISSUES FOR $55

Subscribe today to guarantee a year of intermittent fulfillment and a 30ish% savings off the cover price, as well as a complimentary copy of *The Better of McSweeney's,* a collection of favorite stories from our long-gone first ten issues. We have also developed every conceivable combination of subscriptions to our other publications— the *Believer* (our monthly magazine of essays and interviews, featuring Nick Hornby, Amy Sedaris, and more), *Wholphin* (our new short-film DVD quarterly, full of movie stars and rare aquatic life), and the McSwys Book Club (our next ten books, for just $100). You'll receive deeper discounts, more mail, and a canonical knowledge of our various arcane obsessions.

SUBSCRIPTIONS MAKE SENSE FOR EVERYONE
—STORE.MCSWEENEYS.NET—

THE CHILDREN'S HOSPITAL
BY CHRIS ADRIAN

A hospital is preserved, afloat, after the Earth is flooded beneath seven miles of water. Inside, assailed by mysterious forces, doctors and patients are left to remember the world they've lost and to imagine one to come. At the center, a young medical student finds herself gifted with strange powers and a frightening destiny. Simultaneously epic and intimate, wildly imaginative and unexpectedly relevant, *The Children's Hospital* is a work of stunning scope, mesmerizing detail, and unexpected grace.

"Chris Adrian is truly brilliant."   —Nathan Englander

WHAT IS THE WHAT
BY DAVE EGGERS

Separated from his family, Valentino Achak Deng becomes a refugee in war-ravaged southern Sudan. His travels bring him in contact with enemy soldiers, with liberation rebels, with hyenas and lions, with disease and starvation, and with deadly murahaleen (militias on horseback)—the same sort who currently terrorize Darfur. Based closely on actual experiences, *What is the What* is heartrending and astonishing, filled with adventure, suspense, tragedy and, finally, triumph.

"I cannot recall the last time I was this moved by a novel."
                     —Khaled Hosseini, author of *The Kite Runner*

"I said 'Gosh this ice cream is good.' Then I said, 'Gosh, there's something hard in my ice cream," said Clarence, remembering the moments before he found the finger. Clarence said he wished he'd realized it was a finger before he tried to eat it. "I proceeded to put the object in my mouth. Got all the ice cream off of it, spit it in my hand, said 'God, this ain't no nut!" So I proceeded in here to the kitchen, rinsed it off with water, and realized it was a human finger, and I just started screaming," he said.

—*Ann McAdams and Jeremy Godwin*

Johnny O'Hara of Natick witnessed what happened from his boat. "A bunch of us came running over and sure enough, pulling the two girls from the water was Nomar," he told the newspaper. "It was crazy. Nomar was like jumping over walls to get to the girls and the other guy leaped off the balcony. It was unbelievable."

—Gayle Fee and Laura Raposa with Erin Hayes